THE SEXIEST,
MOST AUTHENTIC
POLITICAL NOVEL
OF THE YEAR . . .

"If the Godfather had ever known where real power resides he would have been a character of the size of Mr. Weissman's governor of New York!"

—Murray Kempton

"Fast-reading . . . a considerable achievement in the political drama, considering its competition from the real world these days!"

—John Callaway, CBS Radio

"Lively . . . wheeling and dealing in the corridors of power and the sexual highjinks of the high and mighty!"

—*Publishers Weekly*

LORDS OF POWER
by *Newsweek* and CBS Reporter
Paul Weissman

D0755699

LORDS OF POWER

Paul Weissman

Mentre che la speranza ha fior del verde.
—*The Divine Comedy*
Purgatorio III

BANTAM BOOKS · TORONTO · NEW YORK · LONDON

For Hillel Black, John Hawkins
and Paul Mann

*This low-priced Bantam Book
has been completely reset in a type face
designed for easy reading, and was printed
from new plates. It contains the complete
text of the original hard-cover edition.*
NOT ONE WORD HAS BEEN OMITTED.

LORDS OF POWER

*A Bantam Book / published by arrangement with
William Morrow & Company, Inc.*

PRINTING HISTORY
*Morrow edition published August 1972
Bantam edition published December 1973*

The victor belongs to the spoils.

F. SCOTT FITZGERALD

CHAPTER ONE

THE LAWYER PULLED IN next to a fire hydrant and left the engine running. He had to remove his glove to pick a coin out of his pocket, and after he did, he dialed the unlisted number, heard the metallic click that signified a connection had been made, and said:

"WGR one."

A high-pitched beeper indicated the automatic transfer of his call. He knew his client's voice well, and now he waited for the reassuring sound of the rich Brahmin tones of Alexander Christman, governor of the state of New York. Instead, he heard four electronic blips at increasing levels of pitch, like a series of rising electronic chords. A young woman's voice respectfully told him:

"The governor is not available, Mr. Roe. There are no instructions."

He was silent for a moment as he stamped his feet on the frigid floor of the metal booth.

"I am returning to my office," he told her. "Make sure he knows I called."

He banged open the door of the booth and stepped out quickly, relieved to fold himself back into the enveloping warmth of the car.

The complex switchboard system had been designed to screen the governor from a world full of people who always urgently needed to talk to him. It conserved and gave him control of his time. It guarded him from anyone audacious enough to attempt to tap his telephone. It made it impossible for anyone to know whether they were talking to Alexander Christman in Albany, in New York City, on his ranch in Arizona, or thirty

1

thousand feet above the earth in the cockpit of his private plane. And it annoyed the hell out of Arthur Roe, who could not effectively administer the $400 million empire that was the property of the governor of the state of New York, unless he could reach him on the telephone.

The lawyer was edging the car slowly into the tight lane of passing traffic when a blue Pontiac cut across his path, forcing him to push down the power brake. Roe was a short man with a mop of black hair and a face that looked as if he were in perpetual anger. When he boiled over this time, he jammed the horn hard at the vanishing blue car, and then pushed the horn again so hard there was a sudden pain in his thumb.

"Christ," he shrieked, shaking the hand up and down inside the glove to alleviate the sudden pain. He pulled off the glove with his teeth. The pain was intense, and for a moment he thought he might have dislocated his thumb. He bit into the second joint and moved the skin back and forth in his mouth. He could feel no break in the bone, and with relief, he edged into the traffic and carefully drove with one hand onto the access road that led to the six-lane highway. Slowly he calmed himself as the pain subsided, and then held the hand in front of him so that he could examine his thumb and watch the road at the same time. TMC, he told himself. I've got TMC again: Too Much Christman.

The Thomas E. Dewey Thruway ended at the New York City line, and he lifted the car phone, poked a finger at the channel button, and signaled the mobile telephone operator. He gave her the private number in his office.

"Seven-six-three-o," he heard Esther Serene respond, the volume of her voice drifting as he followed the curve of the road.

"It's Arthur," he shouted. "I'm on my way in."

"Are you there? Arthur?" her voice came back. "Arthur?"

"I'll be there in twenty-five minutes."

"Right, boss."

Twenty minutes later he left the car in the garage

under 345 Park Avenue, turned his key in the lock that brought the private elevator to the subbasement garage, and then unconsciously tensed his muscles for the rapid upward twist of the high-speed car. Being the youngest partner in the long and distinguished history of the law firm of Whitman, Gelman, he felt perfectly in control of himself, and a sense of exhilaration as he stepped onto the White House blue carpet that lined the wide hallways of the famous firm. He nodded to two young lawyers in one of the firm's seven law libraries, and walked down the wide corridor past the burnished bronze nameplates with the famous names in politics, government, and law: the counsel to the ex-president he himself had served, two federal judges, a former attorney general, and finally his own complex of offices.

Marion Cunningham, Harvard *cum laude,* caught him two steps inside the door.

"We have an informal advisory from our friend at Justice that they will prosecute if we go through with the Ontario Airline merger."

"Later," he replied.

Other staff members were out of their cubbyholes. They swarmed around him. Jack Clarity, law review at Yale Law School, his brown eyes smooth as marbles behind thick bifocal lenses, tugged the long brown hair curling over his collar. He raised his index finger and said, "When you get a chance, Mr. Roe."

They were the best in the firm and Roe knew it, as he knew it made him the envy of his partners. It amused him. For he knew that while it was his own youth combined with his ability to deal with his staff that held them, it was the magic aura of success surrounding Alexander Christman that had brought them to him in the first place.

Young lawyers crowded around him like lion cubs at feeding time. He raised his throbbing hand above his head to silence the din.

"Easy," he shouted, bringing the aching hand down in pain. "This is a law office, not a campaign headquarters."

They laughed and then separated, opening a path

for him to his private office. He closed the door behind him. Esther Serene, his secretary, was the only
girl he had ever known who at twenty-seven already
looked like an old maid. She was born street tough,
and if there was a half-ounce of sex appeal in her
hundred-and-thirty-two-pound body, he was certain no
one had found it. She was pure staff sergeant. And because she coveted her power as his secretary almost
as much as she detested the formalities of Whitman,
Gelman, he trusted her as completely as he had trusted
anyone in his thirty-nine years on earth who was not
utterly dependent upon him.

"Sit, Arthur," she said, pushing him to the chair
behind his desk. "What the hell happened to your
hand?"

The slab of flesh at the base of his thumb was swollen and turning blue.

"Forget it," he told her, avoiding her touch.

"Jesus. At least let me put some ice on it."

"Forget it," he snapped again. "Did Christman call?"

"No," she shouted back. "Will you let me put an
ice pack on that finger."

Roe slammed his hand down hard on the desk and
jumped with the pain. Esther Serene rushed instinctively toward him and grabbed the hand. He yanked it
away from her and began shaking it in the air and
waited for her to organize herself.

She handed him a two-page, single-spaced list of
telephone calls, and with a blue pencil he checked off
less than a dozen messages he wished to return.

"What did Mayor Thayer want?"

"A benefit. I told him you were going to be in
California."

Roe looked at her quizzically, knowing he had no
plans to go to California, and then he grinned.

Few outsiders in the early days identified him with
his famous client. He had been careful to stay clear of
the Executive Mansion then, as well as the Christman
campaign headquarters. The mayor of the city of New
York, an alumnus of another Wall Street law firm, had
been startled, after he was inaugurated, to learn that it

was Roe who had quietly suggested Christman not allow the state's banks to purchase the city's bonds at 4.1 percent, even after a personal appeal from the mayor to make up for a deficit in state aid. Christman was not going to be intimidated by anyone, least of all a new mayor, and so with the help of the banks he forced Thayer to resubmit the issue at a higher rate. The mayor was embarrassed; he called Roe.

"You actually work for Alexander?" the mayor asked him.

"Yes, George," Roe replied, amused at his naïveté.

"Everybody seems to work for him," Thayer said, not trying to hide the tension in his voice.

"I guess it seems that way sometimes."

"Well, I don't work for the son of a bitch, and you can tell him I said so," Thayer snapped and hung up.

Roe did. "You know what's under that veneer of righteousness?" Christman had asked him with a grin. Roe shook his head. "More righteousness," the governor said, delighted with himself.

Christman never attacked Thayer directly or openly. The worst he ever said about the mayor came during an introduction at the annual Alfred E. Smith Dinner after a particularly bitter fight between the two men. Christman lifted his glass to the 2,600 guests, grinned, and turned to the mayor. "Here's to Mayor Thayer," he saluted, "victim of a profound, constant, but ever changing sincerity."

It was the last hint the press had of the feud between the two men. Christman simply went to work behind the scenes and decimated Thayer's hand-picked staff. A year later the mayor's press secretary was more lucratively employed by Consolidated Electric, a company regulated by a commission appointed by the governor; his deputy mayor, a lifelong personal friend and campaign manager, had become president of a Dallas-based mutual fund in which Christman held substantial stock; and the city's finance administrator, another lifelong personal friend of the mayor, had won nomination to Thayer's old congressional seat, without even discussing the matter with Thayer. It had chastened Thayer, but not cured him.

Arthur Roe's blue pencil paused again.

"Who is Martin Soshin?"

Esther Serene shrugged. "Said he had to see you personally. Cunningham knows him."

"What did he want?"

"Arthur!" she responded shrilly. "Who the hell knows! I brushed him."

"Didn't you find out?"

"Jesus Christ, will you stop taking it out on me. I'll find out from Cunningham," she told him, making a note on her stenographic pad.

He held out the typewritten list and she snatched it from his hand.

"Will you try the governor again?" he asked her. "Please."

She stepped out for a minute and he began gnawing at the base of his thumb again. But he knew what was wrong. For nine years Alexander Christman had applied his considerable skills and economic resources to a single personal project: the creation of nothing less than a consortium that would control the development and sale of nuclear power in the United States. If he was successful, Christman would hold in his hand the kind of economic power over American industry that had not existed in the hundred years since John D. Rockefeller built Standard Oil of New Jersey.

The consortium was developed quietly, privately, and secretly. Without public notice its members bought in concert uranium mines, engineering companies, plant sites, and a hundred related companies. A year ago, it was Roe's brief that turned the corner on the Christman dream and persuaded the Federal Atomic Energy Commission to permit private ownership of nuclear patents. But as successful as the enormous venture seemed it had one dismaying effect: Christman seemed to be steadily losing interest in national politics.

"You've been in the White House, fella," the governor told him one day. "What's that compared to real power?"

Roe did not push him. No one pushed Alexander Christman. In New York State when Alexander Christman pushed, people got out of the way. Yet it was precisely that kind of push, less than a year ago, that might have been just a bit too hard.

Consolidated Electric, the biggest power company in the state, wanted permission to locate auxiliary power generators on barges anchored on the Hudson and East rivers. The State Power Commission turned them down and the company's chairman of the board, Whitney Parsons, demanded and got a private audience with the governor. Roe was there.

"Governor," Parsons said, cordially enough, when he walked in.

"Who the hell are all these guys?" Christman asked, waving his hand at the utility executive's entourage.

Parsons, smoothing the immaculately razored white hair at his temple, started to introduce them.

"Whit," Governor Christman told him, "I said you could have ten minutes."

Parsons did not bother to sit down.

"Alex," he said harshly, "unless you get your commission to approve these barges, we can't guarantee an adequate power supply to New York."

Christman shrugged. "That's their decision."

"I'm warning you that there could be another blackout, Governor. Don't you understand that?"

"For ten years you guys have been pushing out the juice and paying dividends. Now you want me to worry. Bullshit."

Parsons winced. "Governor, you're forcing us to go to the public—"

The governor smiled broadly. "Fella," he said, "do you really think they're going to believe you?"

Esther Serene returned and sighed unhappily. She shifted the packet of file folders and briefs on her lap. Once she leaned forward and started to speak, changed her mind, and then began awkwardly shifting and rearranging the folders. When he finally looked up, she shook her head and said, "No. He will call you when he can."

He looked at the list of telephone calls again. "Did you find out who Soshin is?"

"Of course I found out," she flared. "He's an assistant U.S. attorney. And he's still waiting to see you."

"Let him wait," he told her, massaging and squeezing his thumb again. She rapidly handed him the purchase agreement for 3,020 acres of land near Ocala, Florida, that Christman himself had bought; a brief to be submitted to the Federal Aviation Commission seeking a freight rate increase on a Christman airline; an envelope containing the two-page weekly *Research & Development* report of American Nuclear, which he put to one side of his desk with a draft of the monthly status report to Christman's partners in the consortium; and a voluminous contract with the firm of Carl Kaufman & Sons, Ltd., for construction of a forty-two-story office building on Water Street near Wall Street. The blue note on top said, "Kaufman demanded an extra half-percent in his fee or $650,000 as opposed to $600,000. No dissuading him. Instead I took commitment of 65-week completion, against penalties. Estimate we save minimum of $1½ million. What do you think? Jeff."

He dialed seven-three-one and said, "Mr. Duross," before the secretary at the other end of the line had a chance to say anything but "Yes, Mr. Roe."

"Jeff, is the long-term financing on the Water Street deal placed yet?" he asked.

"The commitment came this morning, sir. Sixty million from the Southwestern Teamsters' Pension Fund at six-and-one-quarter percent."

"You had to go to them?" he muttered. "What kind of points?" he asked, the "points" in a mortgage commitment consisting of the percentage of the total the borrower paid as a kind of "service charge" on the mortgage. To Roe, points were an under the table payoff to the officers of the lending institution, in this case the union, who never reported the additional fee as income to the fund.

"Nothing. It's straight six-and-a-quarter."

"You're kidding."

"They admire the governor. In their words, 'no one excels his credit.' "

Roe laughed softly. "Thanks, Jeff," he said. "They ought to be in jail."

"Yes, sir. Some of them are. Chase, by the way, will take the construction loan at seven-and-three-eighths, which means that our actual cash investment is the cost of the property itself. We can sell the property and lease it back, which would produce a net profit of—oh, say three point two million before we start."

"Jeff, you ought to be president of a construction company."

"If I have your permission to call it Christman Construction, it's a deal. If this was my own proposition, the Teamsters would probably wind up owning half and some Italian gentlemen the other half and I would be filing a Chapter Eleven for bankruptcy in six months. Hell, they still own the construction unions."

"Will you take a bonus?" Roe said, without waiting for a reply. "American Nuclear will go ten points this week. Buy yourself five hundred shares."

"With what?"

"Call my broker, Jeff. Tell him I'll guarantee the margin," Roe said, and hung up without waiting for the effusive thanks he knew would come. But he did not feel any better.

In the next hour, Roe rapidly dictated a dozen letters. He scribbled a brief note to an important banker that said, "Any objections? Arthur," and told Esther Serene to send it with the list of names that had just been cleared by the State Investigation Commission for appointment to important state offices by Governor Christman. He rubbed his thumb and took the blue folder containing the morning mail, amused by another try from Mayor Thayer, this one an invitation to serve on the city of New York's Board of Ethics. He dictated a three-sentence reply, declining as graciously as he could. "Send a Xerox to Christman," he said, "with a note that says, 'You still think he's bright?'"

For the rest of the letters, he either scribbled a one or two word reply across the top with a black felt tip pen or routed it to a member of his staff. When he finished, he closed the folder and handed it back and

took the black leather-jacketed binder containing weekly status reports from his staff. It had been his suggestion years ago that the chief executive officer of each
Christman enterprise report directly to one of the lawyers working under Roe. It was a suggestion that did
not sit well with most of the Christman corporate presidents, but Roe convinced the governor it would force
his executives to maintain constant contact throughout their operations.

"They aren't schoolboys," Christman complained at
the time. "Gee whiz, with options some of these guys
sit on their duffs and make a half-million bucks a
year."

By then, Arthur had learned to recognize the whine
of pain in the governor's voice that indicated he was
impishly delighted with a proposal, and he simply took
it from there, cementing his own power and status at
the pinnacle of the empire.

The system worked well, which meant it worked to
the governor's satisfaction. And despite hurt feelings,
Christman's chief executives were no more inclined to
dissent from a decision made at the top than were the
commissioners he appointed to serve the state of New
York. It also meant that each young lawyer on Roe's
staff was knowledgeable enough to serve as a potential
replacement for the corporate officer for whom he acted
as a liaison officer. Twice the governor had appointed
young members of Roe's staff as chief executive officers of Christman corporations, as twice he had made
appointments from the staff to important state posi-
tions, and each time the reverberations through the
Christman empire obliterated dissent.

It was getting darker outside the window, and Roe
looked down at the heavy traffic moving north on
Park Avenue. Where the hell was Christman? He
stopped in front of the framed portrait he cherished of
himself with the late President Kennedy. The president
was smiling and clapping his hand on the back of
Roe's neck. He thought he looked boyish and embarrassed, but the picture gave so much life to the coldly
architectural office, it was impossible for any visitor to
miss.

"Kennedy liked me because he thought I was Irish," Roe would tell them, his black eyes wide open. "After the campaign, I was on the White House staff for eight months before he found out I was a Jew, and then he thought I was the greatest." There was always a touch of modesty in Roe's laugh, like the laugh of those who are embarrassed to trade on a relationship once held in reverence. But it had been a long time before he stopped wearing the PT boat tiepin that had been the symbol of the other campaign.

Esther Serene had come into the office again, and he took the paper container of warm vegetable soup from her hand.

"Did you try him again?"

"Every hour, Arthur. Calm down."

"Try him again."

"Are you going to see Soshin?"

"Who?"

"He's still here. I get the feeling he will still be here when you leave. Whenever that is."

He ignored the signal and swiveled his chair to stare again at the blackened avenue below. "What does he look like?" he asked.

"A redhead. He looks like an Irish cop."

His thumb was swollen, but the ache was gone. He stood, took off his suit jacket, and pulled down his vest. Then he rolled up his sleeves and walked slowly toward the door.

"He's in the waiting room," she told him.

Soshin was taller than Arthur Roe thought he would be. His gray pinstripe suit was pressed and the black cordovan shoes were thick-soled and new.

"Mr. Soshin," he said warmly, his right hand extended. "You're a very persistent fellow."

"Can we talk somewhere?"

Roe held out his hands to indicate the conversation would be brief. The visitor seemed to be more than a little amused with the lawyer's method of dealing with him.

"You are Arthur Roe?" the younger man formally asked.

Roe nodded, a trifle confused.

"Martin Soshin," the young man said, reaching into his breast pocket and removing a federal grand jury subpoena. He handed it to Roe, who unfolded it quickly, assuming it was for a client. It said:

BE IT KNOWN THAT ARTHUR ROE, A PART-
NER IN THE FIRM OF WHITMAN, GELMAN,
345 PARK AVENUE, IS HEREBY COMMANDED
BY THE PEOPLE OF THE UNITED STATES OF
AMERICA TO APPEAR THURSDAY, DECEM-
BER 11TH, AT THE UNITED STATES COURT-
HOUSE, FOLEY SQUARE, AT 10 A.M. BEFORE A
FEDERAL GRAND JURY EXAMINING THE
AFFAIRS, METHODS AND FUNCTIONS OF
AMERICAN NUCLEAR ENERGY, INCLUDING
ITS USE OF FEDERAL FUNDS ALLOCATED TO
THE STATE OF NEW YORK, SAID CORPORA-
TION WAS DULY·ORGANIZED IN THE STATE
OF DELAWARE, WITH PRINCIPAL OFFICES
IN WHITE PLAINS, NEW YORK.

Roe's throat was dry. "There's been a mistake," he said, the words sounding like an anguished croak. He handed the subpoena back to Soshin, but the single sheet of paper fluttered to the blue-carpeted floor. The redhead touched it with the toe of his polished cordovan, but he did not pick it up.

"You are Arthur Roe." This time it sounded like a statement of fact, not a question.

He nodded and gritted his teeth. The jaw muscle was working hard in the side of his face. "I said there has been a mistake."

"It's no mistake, Counsellor," Soshin told him, treating the legal title as if it were an insult.

Roe stared at Soshin's pockmarked face. With a faint trace of a smile at the corner of his mouth, the redhead said, "I'm certain there is no mistake. It's my case."

Soshin turned to press the elevator button, ignoring the subpoena on the floor between them.

"Can we handle this?" Roe asked.

"How would we do that, Counsellor?"

"Say you never served it. By tomorrow I can straighten it out."

"Counsellor," Soshin said with a grin, "I told you, it's my case."

The doors of the automatic elevator opened. He reached behind his back to grasp the rubber safety guard. He took a step back into the mahogany-paneled car, but kept the door from closing in front of him. "See you in the grand jury, Counsellor," he said, letting the doors close in front of him. And then he was gone.

Roe flicked his sore thumb against his index finger and then bent over and picked up the document. He walked quickly past the empty offices, down the broad hallway, and turned into his own suite of offices. He waved his secretary back behind her desk, locked the door to his private office behind him, and then quickly dialed the governor's switchboard, ignoring the elaborate code system.

"Roe speaking," he said.

"There is a message, sir."

"I have to talk to him."

The wait was less than ten seconds. He heard Devlin's voice and knew he was using the radiotelephone in the Christman limousine.

"Tell him I've got to see him."

"What?" Devlin called back.

"I've got to see him," Roe shouted.

For a minute there was nothing but static. Devlin quickly switched channels and the line was cleared.

"I've got to see him," Roe shouted.

Devlin said, "Take it easy. He is meeting with the Polish-American Brotherhood. Then he's got a speech at the Americana."

"I said I've got to see him," Roe said again, trying to penetrate the wall he had helped build around Christman with thick, padded layers of schedules and handpicked bodyguards like Devlin.

"I'm sure you know what you're doing, sir," he said. "Hold on."

Roe sat on the edge of the desk, tapping his knee angrily with the subpoena. The bumper-to-bumper traffic below was gone and he watched the headlights of taxicabs whip toward Grand Central Station like homing pigeons. He held the telephone an inch from his ear as he waited for Alexander Christman, wondering if it was still possible to persuade him to postpone the final steps in the creation of the American Nuclear consortium.

Finally he heard the familiar voice with its broad Boston *a*'s. The tone was tolerant irritation.

"What is it, fella?" Governor Alexander Christman said.

"A problem."

"I'm scheduled up to my neck. It can wait," he complained.

"No."

The governor was silent for a moment. Any ham radio operator might pick up a radiotelephone conversation, and he knew it.

"Swing by the Americana after the speech. Say eleven-twenty," he drawled. And then the line was dead in Arthur Roe's hand.

CHAPTER TWO

At 10:15 P.M. the paneled elevator quickly dropped Arthur Roe thirty-seven floors, and he stepped out into the empty lobby of 345 Park Avenue. He started toward the Lexington Avenue escalator, stopped, realizing only the Park Avenue entrance was open at night, and walked back the length of the building. Roe signed the register, noting without surprise that all his partners had preceded him out of the building.

It was windy in the 345 Park Avenue plaza, and he decided to walk west along Fifty-second Street. Roe knew Alexander Christman well. And so he had learned long ago that Governor Alexander LeMoyne Christman's fame rested not on his money, which was only $100 million or so less than his predecessor Nelson Rockefeller, or on his charm, which was absolute, or on his political acumen, which invariably seemed without error. He was late. Always late. Forever late. Magnificently late. And one small measure of his power was the amount of time people were willing to wait for him, be they huge crowds on a rainy upstate street or men with sufficient importance to demand better treatment.

Roe had seen him communicate to his audience from his own vast resources of energy and pleasure a sense of the coming perfection of existence, a sense of joy in themselves and a oneness with each other. He knew that the individuals actually admitted to see him cherished the summons, and shone in his presence, as if the number of minutes allotted were coin of the realm. And because so many accepted it as such, accepted one's proximity to the man himself as a symbol of

15

status, his minutes in fact became coin of the political
and social realm of the state of New York.

But it was the subpoena in his pocket, not the magic
of the man he was about to see, that was in the lawyer's
thoughts as he walked briskly westward. It was a raw
December night and the smell of snow was in the chill-
ing night air. He knew that if he was formally summoned to testify before the federal grand jury, it was
unlikely that he was the target of the investigation. No
one, even a lawyer, could be forced to testify against
himself without immunity from prosecution. A grand
jury witness faced only one real danger. If it could be
proven he had not testified fully or truthfully, he
risked a charge of perjury. He knew there could be
only one target in this investigation: Governor Alexander Christman. No one before had ever seriously
challenged him. Who was now trying to obliterate the
tiger?

Roe believed that this was Christman's year, that
the governor would respond to pressure and reach for
new power, power so vast it was unimaginable to anyone who had not seen it as Roe himself had, from
inside 1600 Pennsylvania Avenue. There had been a
hundred phone calls from men who were ready to back
Alexander Christman with hard cash and their own
prestige.

"At least let us set up a 'Draft Christman' organization," Johnny Marks begged when he called from Sacra-
mento.

"Let him do it his own way," Roe told him, not
willing to admit Christman's reluctance to run.

"I can raise three million bucks right now just from
guys who want to get in at the bottom. Talk to him.
Christ, hasn't he seen the polls?"

"If he didn't know what he was doing, you'd be
treating him like those other clowns that are running."

"My guys are going to bust loose with or without
his approval," Marks threatened.

"No, they're not, Johnny," Roe told him.

Others were pleading too, and Roe dealt with them
with the same teasing reassurance. But he could not

ignore the devastating effect on the governor's political
career of any public disclosure of American Nuclear.
One line of print, one breath of the consortium Christman had put together, and all of the potential that
lay in Alexander Christman could not get him elected
town clerk of Oneonta, New York. And now a subpoena. Jesus! Even American Nuclear would not be
worth the risk. Christman had to see that.

The Americana was ringed with chauffeur-attended
limousines. Roe hated the speeches, the phony camaraderie, and, most of all, the people who bought a tiny
bit of influence by taking a hundred-dollar-a-plate table on the tough turkey circuit. Eighty percent of the
paying guests were the same people, whether it was a
Republican or a Democratic party dinner. The guests
at this dinner were so much richer, he thought it might
be different until he saw the hefty Irishman with a
face like porous concrete.

"Hiya, Artie," he heard the Irishman call, as he
walked up to him on the carpeted staircase.

"Good evening, Mr. Chairman," Roe replied to the
leader of the minority party in the state of New York.
"Very good to see you so fit."

The sixteen hundred guests, some wise enough in
the ways of politics to eat before they arrived, were
fed chilled fruit cocktail with a sticky raspberry sherbet,
chicken soup that tasted like soap, and a dry, thick
slice of overcooked roast beef. Six of the one hundred
seventy tables were filled with reporters who paid nothing to attend the dinner, accepting the free meal as
their tribute, much as a cop appropriates an apple
from a pushcart. They ate well, ignoring the preliminary
speaker, who offered a "laundry list" of statements calculated to offend no one: housing, federal aid to cities,
civil rights, education. They had heard it before. They
had come to hear Alexander Christman.

Arthur Roe followed the signs to the ballroom escalator. A dozen security guards, reporters, and members of the governor's staff, wearing formal dinner
jackets, were gathered in the lounge outside the ballroom. The lawyer quickly spotted a round, popeyed

man who was so obese he looked like a huge beach ball resting in a sandbox: Harvey Kuhn, the governor's press secretary.

Kuhn nodded secretively. "There's so much money in there; three of those guys are even richer than Mr. Alex." He had been using the line all night long. "Figure fifty billion dollars wall to wall."

Roe patted Kuhn's stomach. "At least you're getting down to fighting weight," he said.

The press secretary's pudgy right hand reached inside his dinner jacket and extracted a mimeographed copy of the governor's address. "I may not have to get down to fighting weight," he said, handing it to Roe. "The press eats up that kind of shit, but Jesus, does he really have to lay it on these guys? Minga," he said, shaking his left hand in front of him like a man who has touched a hot stove, "he sure as hell doesn't sound like he'll run."

The lawyer's eyes moved quickly across the mimeographed sheets. He shrugged mildly and handed the speech back to the press secretary. "Let him get into it any way he wants. Then we can worry about what he says."

A reporter, who had already filed a story based on the text Kuhn distributed, stopped next to him.

"Well, Harvey," he asked, "what's he up to, as if we didn't know."

"Look, Alan," Kuhn replied, without taking the dead pipe out of the corner of his mouth, "the guv is off his nut. Everybody knows that. So stop asking stupid questions."

The young man, who desperately needed a haircut, smiled and said, "Do we get a crack at him when he's done?"

"Not on your life, shmuck. Who the hell knows what he's liable to say if he gets a look at you. Jesus, that hair is enough to frighten a pregnant Ubangi."

The young reporter walked away. Roe reminded himself that part of Kuhn's extraordinary skill was his ability to say outrageous things about his boss. That in turn gave him leave to say even more outrageous things about the men who wrote about The Boss. Thus Kuhn enjoyed a level of communication that for any of his colleagues would have offended the press. Kuhn was an outrageous man, who honed his natural antipathy for almost everything into a working tool. And Alexander Christman knew how to use the tool well.

"Isn't there a press conference after the speech?" Roe whispered.

"Sure," Kuhn whispered, "they know that. I spent twenty minutes telling them 'no questions.' "

The lights were dimmed inside the vast blue and gold ballroom, but even in the dimness Roe recognized a dozen men. He nodded to the tall, forty-one-year-old new president of one of the Big Three automobile companies. He noticed his hair was a quarter-inch below the collar of his dress shirt. There was a rumor he was about to publish a novel, and one of Detroit's current games was guessing who had written it for him. Roe saw bankers, oil men, the Akron crowd, and even a table of West Coast types. He assumed his father-in-law was somewhere among the subdued guests, but he had no desire to see him.

Alex is a pro, a real pro, Roe told himself as his eyes moved from the floor to the dais. If he charms two-thirds of this room, they won't even have to hold an election.

Standing before them all, his hands clutching either side of the rostrum, the governor of the state of New York exuded an air of reasonable calm that frequently lulled audiences into accepting the fact that he, rather than what he said, was unquestionably right. He was not an exceptional public speaker, or even an outstanding one, but he was the kind of big, muscular, impressive man whose stolid physical presence gave special weight to what he said. Christman had a short neck, and his face had the leathery toughness of a Marine sergeant who has not gained an ounce in twenty years. The eyes behind the oversize gold-rimmed glasses he wore softened the edge. They were deep blue and they made him seem as easily approachable as the family doctor.

It was the kind of charisma that was unbeatable in a crowd, and Christman knew precisely how to make

the most of it. The press called him the "touchingest"
politician in America, for whomever he was with there
was a hand on an arm, a pat on the neck, a friendly
slap on the cheek, as if the only contact that was
real for him was, by necessity, a physical one.

The tables were filled with impressive-looking men.
They seemed angry and sullen. Roe edged his way toward the dais. Above him, he could see the blue eyes
magnified behind the governor's glasses, and there was
still a touch of eczema on Christman's left cheek. The
fit of his dinner jacket was less than perfect. But underneath the dark material was the kind of muscle that
could provide great strength or the cruelest kind of
punishment. He was that rare man whom women
adored and men coveted as the closest of friends.

"This country is falling behind," Christman was saying, his finger jabbing the air, warming to the hostility
he sensed in the wealthy audience. "You're leaders!
You must become the example! You must use your
power to change. But you won't use what you've got
to make a better America—only more dividends for
stockholders.

"You won't use what you've got to see to it that
the best men we have are elected to lead—only to see
to it that they serve your interest.

"You won't use what you've got to develop the human resources of this nation—only to create more con-
sumers."

They were whispering now, grumbling, angry, and
wondering whether they were really listening to Governor Alexander Christman. In the front row, the
chairman of the board of a big oil company stood,
straightened his dinner jacket, and marched out of the
room. The rest of the table followed him.

Christman used it, with a wave of his hand toward
them. "Those guys don't like facts," he said, his voice
rising.

Then he stopped and stared at them. He leaned forward, winked, and said, "I'm going to talk turkey to
the American people. To you fellas. To labor. To the
poor. To the blacks."

The applause was stronger. But the press and television reporters had no way of identifying the claque Christman knew had been planted in the ballroom.

Kuhn was right. It was hardly the standard Christman fat cat speech. What was he doing, Roe wondered, as he began to listen to the words for the first time.

Christman held up both hands. He rose on the balls of his feet and shouted, "Do you think it's time somebody told it straight?"

The applause was mild.

"Do you think it's time somebody laid it on the line?"

The noise was building slowly now.

"Do you think it's time *somebody* leveled with the American people?"

It was building to a crescendo, the handclapping louder, coming back at him so strongly he had the feeling the platform beneath him was rising before his eyes.

"Judas!" the distinguished-looking man who had been planted by a Christman aide in the third row shouted, as he waved an advance copy of the text in the air. "You're a Judas. They ought to shoot you in the back."

The boos came strong. Christman stared hard at him, as if he were making it clear he would never forget his face. But he held up his hands, palms toward the ballroom. The redfaced man who had berated the speaker opened a side door and ran quickly out of the ballroom.

"Fellas, fellas!" Christman called. "Listen to me. We have a job to do together. We have the power to get things done, right? And listen, if you think I'm against you, just wait and see what I tell the National Association of Colored People next week."

His arm went up in the Black Power salute, and the big teasing Christman grin spread across his face. It was not unlike the blessing of a Lord who has accepted those present as equals and cohorts. Roe was astonished as he saw they were smiling back. Almost to a man, the lawyer realized, the audience believed he was putting them on.

They applauded politely again, as sophisticated au-

diences will do to tell a performer he is treading on
delicate ground. The governor did not miss the cue.
He skipped three pages of his speech that had been
filmed earlier that afternoon for television news broadcasts, and then began to playfully attack his own text.

"Abolish the corporate state," he said, grinning.
"Hell, you don't want to hear that." Then he ignored
his own proposals for the reform of American business,
though he knew they were already page one news across
the nation, whether he spoke the words or not.

Roe did not know the governor had seen the early
edition of *The New York Times* in his car before ar-
riving at the Americana. The portion of the speech he
now omitted was the three-column lead story on page
one:

> Governor Alexander Christman proposed to Ameri-
> ca's leading financiers last night that major corpora-
> tions be dissolved by Act of Congress and permitted
> to form again only as businesses providing a single
> product or service.
> The proposal by the governor of the state of New
> York would, he said, "split General Motors into
> seventy-one different companies and affect virtually
> every multimillion-dollar conglomerate in the United
> States."
> "Competition has become an American myth," the
> governor told the businessmen, "and the myth is
> strangling this country."
> The proposal, which was expected to startle the
> business community by coming from the wealthy
> governor of New York, is believed to be the first step
> in Governor Christman's presidential campaign. Indi-
> cations were that the governor had written off the so-
> called Party fat cats as potential contributors and
> was prepared to spend some $50 million in his campaign
> for the White House.
> Expected to create even greater animosity among
> investors was the governor's proposal that the present
> oil depletion allowance providing special tax benefits
> be abolished, and replaced with a special tax on those
> that profit from the country's natural resources.

Christman had thrown the paper back to Harvey
Kuhn without even reading the portion of the story
continued in two full columns on page eleven.

"Those newspaper guys ought to be in the can,"
he said.

"The speech knocked off their jocks," Kuhn replied.
"It was good. Half of them will try to cream you after
dinner tonight."

"Yeah, but they didn't get the point. Seventy-one
GM's with seventy-one sets of directors is a helluva lot
healthier than four elitists calling all the shots. We got
to tell the middle-class guy he doesn't have to be a
back-seat fella all his life."

They were out of the limousine, and Kuhn, as he
always did, was becoming red-faced. He tried to keep
his stubby legs moving fast enough to propel his 270
pounds at Christman's pace.

"You ought to get a little exercise," the governor said.

"I get my exercise," Kuhn puffed, "going to the
funerals of my friends who exercise."

"Fella," Christman said, "just be glad you don't work
for Mayor Thayer down at City Hall."

Earlier Kuhn had told the three tables of reporters
the governor would hold no press conferences after his
speech. Predictably, they wedged themselves into the
wings on either side of the stage to insure access to
Christman after his speech. Many of them followed the
prepared text as he spoke, underlining those sections
the governor omitted.

Christman finally waved to the audience, winking at
someone down front he chose to recognize, turned
twice toward the wings and, with a look of mock
despair, seemed to be searching for an escape route
that evaded the press. He took a step down toward
the audience and turned to see the reporters stepping
onto the stage to follow him, so he turned, and with
his head bowed, walked toward them. They had six
microphones stuck in his face before he got off the stage.

"Hey, fellas," he said, grinning, "take it easy. You
want to knock out my bridgework?"

They laughed with him, relieved they were going to get a story.

Kuhn was trying hard to push them away from Christman.

"No press conference, come on, gang. Lay off him," he said, but as he had anticipated, it did no good. The governor stopped a dozen yards into the wings and, leaning against one of the flies, permitted the reporters to collect around him.

"Okay. Okay," he said, still grinning. "But let me breathe."

"Governor," the tall pipe-smoking reporter from *The New York Times* said, louder than the rest, "can we consider tonight's speech a tacit announcement of your presidential candidacy?"

"Gee whiz, Mickey," Christman said, his voice rising, "you keep writing that I'm a candidate and it just isn't so. The president made his choice of a successor clear. Stop trying to get me into a fight with him."

"Are you ready to make a Sherman statement?"

"I'll make a Sherman statement. Or a Johnson statement. Or even an Alf Landon statement," he said, grinning. "I am just not a candidate," Christman said, winking at the *Times* reporter. Not a man among them believed him.

"Will you make the Sherman statement for our camera, Governor?" UBS's political reporter asked.

Everyone laughed. A Christman wink never confused anyone at all.

"I'm simply not a candidate. Period," he said. "I'm not even a contender. I won't even seek the nomination. Okay?"

"Governor," someone called, "if you're not a candidate, then why do you go around making controversial speeches?"

The governor turned his head until his eyes met the reporter who had spoken.

"Next question," he said sourly.

"Do you think President Griswold has done a good job?"

"He's had two tough terms."

"I don't think you answered my question," the reporter persisted.

Christman turned away as if he had not even heard him.

"Do you think President Griswold has been a great leader?" someone else asked.

Christman's head snapped about quickly to see who asked the question. They knew he had rarely agreed with the president. The governor assumed the question had been asked by a reporter ever ready to lend a hand to the man in the White House.

"Well," he replied slowly, "he's not only the president, but the leader of my party. And I'm not prepared to publicly question his judgment. But I'm afraid I would have to say he's the followingest leader we've ever had."

Christman saw the startled double takes on the faces around him. He held back the smile. There was the real story. They knew it and he knew it: GOVERNOR BELITTLES LEADERSHIP OF GRISWOLD ADMINSTRATION. It was time to end the press conference, and he tugged at his ear to signal Kuhn. But there was one more question he knew was coming.

Roe had reached the backstage area by now. He relaxed as much as he could when he saw Kuhn smiling, but he still wondered whether Christman had gone berserk.

"Governor, why did you omit the key proposals of your speech tonight?"

They were alive again, the younger reporters envious of the man with sense enough to ask the most obvious question. Christman took a deep breath and rubbed the touch of eczema on his jaw.

"Fellas," he said, "there are a lot of things you say privately. Sometimes you think you should say them publicly. Know what happens? You get a little more candid than you really should—and everybody gets mad at you."

"You're trying to tell us you decided not to make these proposals?"

Christman shrugged and held out his hands.

"Governor, this story is page one news all over the country."

"I can't help that," he said, smiling again. "Thanks a lot."

He was pushing his way past them now, leaving them perplexed and uncertain of precisely how the story already in print could be rewritten to conform with the facts.

"Let the desk worry about it," one reporter muttered. "He's really a piece of hard cheese, ain't he?"

If political reporters agreed on anything, which they did not, a consensus might well have emerged from the Americana that Governor Alexander Christman had just done precisely what he denied doing. He had stepped forward as an "unannounced" candidate for the presidency of the United States.

Harvey Kuhn happily thought so too as he pushed his way through the crowd beside the governor. The boys had gotten their story, Kuhn thought, and now he was pleased with the notion of collecting the favor. Christman had stopped beyond the press and motioned to Arthur Roe. The Los Angeles *Times* correspondent got Kuhn's ear for a moment.

"What does he really think of the president?"

"He thinks he is a medium-hard asshole," Kuhn shot back. "But you can't print that."

"Is it safe to go hard on his becoming a candidate?"

Kuhn smiled broadly, shook his head solemnly, and muttered, "Jesus, shmuck. What do you think?"

He moved back to the governor's side and stepped behind him onto the escalator. A special security man was three steps in front of Christman. Two trailed behind Kuhn. When they reached the bottom of the stairs, Christman ambled slowly through the foyer and Kuhn easily fell in step alongside him.

"Governor, it was brilliant," Kuhn said softly. "Brilliant. No one else, I don't think anyone else," he was choking up, "no one could have pulled off a speech that was as big a loser as that one. Bang! The newspaper guys were eating out of your hand."

"The newspaper guys!" Christman said with a laugh. "Believe me. We are off and running. Bang!"

Christman usually respected Kuhn's political brains and always thoroughly enjoyed his company. But he shook his head and said very gently: "You're a great fella, Harve, but sometimes I don't think you really know anything about American politics." He was smiling. Kuhn's shoulders drooped and the governor patted the back of his neck to perk him up. "After that speech I should be as dead as the New York State legislature. And that's as dead as you can get."

They were standing in front of the governor's green Lincoln. The press secretary was baffled and hurt. Holding both his arms, Christman looked into his eyes and wondered whether he was on the verge of tears. But it was not the words that baffled Harvey Kuhn so much as the gaiety of the governor's manner.

"You want to be another nut candidate?" he asked, knowing no other man spoke that way to Alexander Christman.

The big man smiled again and gently slapped Kuhn's cheek as if they had just closed a partnership on a garment district showroom. Then he patted Kuhn's stomach.

"You're losing weight, Harve," he said. "Better go fill it with manicotti. Then get some sleep. We open the gates at four tomorrow."

Kuhn hunted around for a stray reporter he might talk to for a couple of hours over dinner, but uncharacteristically decided he preferred to be alone. It was not that he was troubled with another Sunday afternoon of work. That was routine. What troubled him was a matter of direction. Like Arthur Roe, he had plotted a road map to the White House. And Alexander Christman seemed to him to be on his way to the moon.

CHAPTER THREE

THE LAWYER MOVED quickly toward the limousine, ducked his head and flopped into the luxurious rear compartment beside Governor Alexander Christman. Devlin shut the door quickly behind them. Then the governor's bodyguard looked left, then right, and signaled to the black-jacketed traffic cop, who quickly stopped two lanes of southbound traffic. As soon as Devlin was inside, the limousine pulled away from the curb.

In the dimly lit rear compartment, Roe looked hard into the governor's brilliant blue eyes. The whites, as always, were absolutely clear, but nothing could hide the growing patchwork of crow's-feet or the weary sense of relief that was always there when the audiences were gone. Christman felt again for the eczema on his cheeks, and again touched it with his finger-tips. Then he took off the oversize glasses and rubbed the corners of his eyes.

Roe watched him carefully, knowing from past experience it was better to permit Christman to focus fully on his presence. The governor stopped rubbing his eyes, replaced his glasses, and punched the lawyer on the arm.

"Helluva speech," Roe said dourly. There was no mistaking his meaning.

The famous smile spread across the governor's face like a sunrise after a bitter, wintry night. With his huge paw, he grabbed the lawyer by the back of the neck and patted him like a collie pup. "My kid's been working me," he said defensively. "At fifteen they're pretty tough."

28

"That's no answer, Alex."

His head snapped quickly toward the lawyer. "That speech didn't change a thing." The grin turned to total pleasure. "I even told the press guys I wasn't a candidate."

"They didn't believe you."

"I meant it."

"You can win, Alex. You can run this goddamn country."

Christman was shaking his head back and forth, trying to shut out the words, or the lawyer's lack of understanding, or both. Then he was silent.

For a minute Christman's head did not turn from the window. He began slowly as if the words had been stoppered up inside him too long. "I wanted to quit after the second term," he said softly, "but sometimes in this business you have to run just to prove you can win. The last time I ran was to stop the guys who cut up the pie when they were sure I was getting out."

He turned toward Roe. The words were coming quicker, surer now. The lawyer regretted the conversation. He knew now he should have avoided the subject. He had accomplished nothing but the crystallization of what had only been vague feelings in Christman into the hard specifics of words. And he could not stop him now.

"Do you know how often in fourteen years I've actually been able to be a leader?" he asked. "As often as most of the people agreed with me. Sure, you can handle it when they are against you. You can swing them to your side. You hold the contracts. The jobs. You can use the banks and the insurance companies, cajole the publishers, and suck up to the union guys. You can squeeze the do-gooders who get their money from the state. And buy off the clergy with parochial school aid. But how often can you do that? Twice a year.

"And when you master that, it still doesn't change a thing. A politician is everybody's doormat. You're nothing but chief mediator between the special interests and all the other kinds of greed. I used to be able to tell myself 'that's politics.' But that doesn't work anymore, except for the guys who just take the money and run."

Christman was breathing hard like a swimmer coming up after a deep dive. The limousine pulled up between First and Second avenues. Devlin was out of the car quickly. He disappeared into the garage of a three-story brownstone.

"Alex," Roe said, trying to reach him and yet still not certain how he could use the subpoena in his pocket to change the governor's mind. In the light from the side panels, he appeared to the lawyer as immovable as he had ever seen him. He had known for a long time that Christman detested the ugly free-trading machinations of politics, and he had seen him wriggle away from the wheelers and dealers in his party. But Roe knew Alexander Christman never forgot how badly he needed them, and so he had accepted the fact that he could not change them any more than he could stop letting it out now.

"You can't fight them, Alex. This country is a machine. They have the boards. And the banks. And the Congress. You know that."

The grin started slowly, spreading across the creases in his face. "Maybe I can now," he said. The smile faded. His eyes were searching in the cold darkness outside the window for Devlin. Roe watched the electric door of the garage in the three-story brownstone rise slowly, and a grimy white Chevrolet Impala rolled out and stopped behind the limousine. Devlin was at the wheel. Christman craned his neck to look out the rear window and then turned back to Roe.

"Something is very wrong in this country," he said, "and nobody knows what it is. For a while we thought it was the war. It wasn't. It's so deep, nobody sitting in the White House is going to be able to do anything about it. That isn't the way you change this country. Because nothing is going to change until business is dependent on something outside the government.

"That's what American Nuclear means. In three years it will supply ninety percent of the power to this country's economy. In ten years it will virtually control the economy. We can build cities. We can regulate the price of goods. We can decide priorities. Can I do that in the White House?

"Right now, this country is going to go bust no matter who is elected president. It's going bust because there is no way to change the system. Jesus! A creative president could follow Griswold into office and start writing his depression recovery program before he took the oath of office. But if you're outside, if you're not in the middle of it, you know what happens? You're the guy who picks up the pieces. And then you shape them the way you want."

He looked gently at Roe and tapped the lawyer's thigh. "Come on, fella," he told him happily, "I got to keep going."

Christman stepped out of the car into the cold night air. Roe followed him to the Impala and moved in beside him.

A faint aroma of perfume clung to the doeskin cushions. The trunk of the car had been scooped out and the rear seats formed a V shape. Behind the driver's seat there was a console with three television sets, a radio telephone, and a hot line to the governor's office. A mahogany centerpiece decorated with a gold Florentine crest pulled down into a small bar. Roe thought he was sitting in the rear seat of an airplane.

"Some Chevy," the lawyer said.

A light came up from the floor. Looking at Christman, Roe remembered the time years ago when curiosity had led Christman to a psychiatrist's couch. He quit after the first session. "The son of a bitch didn't tell me anything," he complained. "But I fixed the bastard. I paid his bill and appointed him to the State Board of Health."

The governor closed his eyes and slumped contentedly in the seat, unaware that they had not discussed the matter that brought Roe urgently to meet him. Much as the lawyer now wished to delay dealing with his client, he knew he could not. He withdrew the folded

subpoena from his pocket and tapped Christman light-
ly on the arm with the paper. The governor did not
open his eyes.

"Alex," Roe said.

Christman took the document and reached back
and snapped on the light behind his left ear. He unfolded the paper and studied it carefully, not missing
a word. Then he turned it over and read the typewritten portion on the back with an air of untroubled
calm that indicated his only surprise was with the
degree to which it had troubled Arthur Roe. His expression slowly turned to one of amusement, and he
touched Roe's arm, as if he were wondering precisely
how long it would take the lawyer to share his understanding. Roe waited for Christman.

"When he offered me the carrot," the governor told
him gently, "I wondered what happened to the stick.
Now I know." He flipped the subpoena into Roe's lap.

"You talked to President Griswold?"

Christman grinned. "He's sending the vice-president
up to see me."

"What did he offer?"

The governor looked at Roe with amusement, but
the lawyer had not yet found a way to convince him
that this was not a joking matter.

"Secretary of state in the new administration," he
said, "if I support his candidate."

"You always wanted it, Alex," he said tentatively,
still not certain that the governor was not talking to
him from a promontory so distant that they were not
really making contact with each other at all.

"That was before," he told Roe. There was no tension in his face as they stopped for a red light. Christman snapped out the lamp, as if he were turning off
the conversation. In the glow of the street lights, Roe
saw him reach into a side pocket and withdraw a silver
pillbox. With his thumb, he flicked it open and popped
a red gelatine capsule in his mouth. The governor
closed his eyes and his facial muscles sagged. There
was a slight twitch in his temple above the left eye.
Roe realized he was waiting for the red pill to start his
system working again.

"We have a lot of problems," his lawyer said softly.

"Jesus, not now," Christman replied. He did not open his eyes.

"Alex? Do you want to go to jail?"

"Oh, come on. Hey, what's happening to you? Don't you know it's a mistake? Arnold Guyman is the U. S. attorney in the southern district, and he wouldn't go after me if I walked off with all the U. S. Treasury bonds in the Chase Manhattan vaults. That kid never earned ten thousand dollars a year before he was Queens coordinator in the first campaign. I put him on the State Investigation Commission. Then I made him a Supreme Court judge. That's thirty-eight thousand dollars a year. President Griswold appointed him on my recommendation."

Roe sensed Christman's irritation. "Do you want me to call him?"

Christman's eyes opened and he popped forward. "All right. I'll go see him."

The white Chevrolet passed Cleopatra's Needle again, cruised through the hairpin curves between upper Fifth Avenue and 125th Street, and came down slowly along the west side of the park. When they reached the rowboat lake, Alex Christman was rubbing his eyes and smacking his palms together, as if he were collecting the enormous energy that almost always was apparent in his muscular frame.

The lawyer tried to tell him gently of the burdens of American Nuclear, but he seemed not to be listening at all. There was a look on Christman's face that Roe had rarely seen, except when he was dealing with another politician, a labor union, or anyone else who believed his hand was strong enough to defy Alexander Christman. It said the matter was not negotiable. You could have anything you wanted except what you came for.

Christman slumped in the thick cushions and shut his eyes. The powerful muscles in his face had gone slack like a balloon that has run out of air. The creases were deeper.

Roe knew he had to do it. He had to try again. Christman stopped him with a wave of his hand.

"Arthur," he said, "I'm not a Rockefeller. Nobody left me anything. The money I have came out of these two hands. And with all of this, who else can dream of what I can do? Sure, I knew about politics when I ran for governor. But I thought I could change things in this state. And I thought I could change the system. I didn't. A politician is nothing but an ass on which everyone has sat except a man. And it doesn't matter whether he puts his ass down in the Executive Mansion in Albany or Sixteen hundred Pennsylvania Avenue. Now do you understand what American Nuclear means?"

Roe nodded.

"When we are finished, nobody will be able to touch me. Nobody will be able to tell me what to do. Not the Griswolds, not the bankers, not the corporation guys, no one."

"Did you really have to make that speech tonight, Alex?"

Alexander Christman's eyes opened quickly as the car pulled up in front of Roe's East Sixty-third Street brownstone.

"Well, fella," he said, "no matter how you look at it, somebody did." With his huge paw, he grabbed the lawyer again by the back of the neck. Then Christman released him and let his own body slide back into the cushions. His eyes were closed again. Roe stepped out of the car. The lawyer was certain that "Gramercy Park" were the two words the governor muttered to Devlin, as the fragrance of eau de Calandre struck him again. He slammed the door behind him and began to walk away from the car.

As he unlocked the wrought iron gate of the brownstone, Roe was uncertain that his own dream for Alexander Christman had really come to an end. He had failed to persuade him to move slowly on American Nuclear, but the presidential thing was not dead.

For the first time in the years since he had known him, he understood that Alexander Christman had somehow ceased to compare himself to other men. He had come to a point in his life when he compared himself only with himself; and so, he thought, he loved the man now, as he had not ever cared for anyone else. And so he envied him, as he had never envied anyone else. He told himself he would pray that God would protect the big man from foolish dreams that come from wanting to save with futility instead of serve with honor. In the long run, it might even make him one of the six or seven men who had functioned competently enough to lead the people of the United States.

CHAPTER FOUR

HE HAD SLEPT no more than three hours, but he had slept deeply, and so he felt like a boy again. In appreciation the governor leaned across the immense round bed and softly stroked the back of Athena De-Witt Thompson Woodward Courtland, as if it were rare satin. Then his lips followed his fingertips, leaving a trail of moisture that ended at the swell of her breast. She stirred. But she did not waken. And for a moment, he did not wish to leave the intoxicating aroma of eau de Calandre or the moist warmth of her perfect body.

Alexander Christman rose reluctantly and picked up the three-inch-thick television shooting script from the night table marked "CONFIDENTIAL UBS NEWS —The Power Crisis." As he often did, he searched for the telephone before he brushed his teeth, and found it on the Louis XVI desk in the massive living room. He opened the thermopane doors and carried it to the terrace overlooking the East River. The metal chair was cold. The governor dialed twelve digits, permitted the phone to ring a single time, and then hung up. In less than ten seconds, the instrument rang. He lifted it quickly and a voice said cheerfully:

"Good morning, Governor."

He recognized the voice and said, happily, "Good morning, Mary Todd. I didn't know you worked on Saturday."

"It's Sunday, Governor. And this is Aileen Rosen."

"Gee," he complained, "I guess I did it again."

Long ago he had realized the importance of dedicated personnel to man the massive switchboard and robot telephone system installed in the basement of the Windy Meadow Mansion. Every call he made, whether it was from New York, the ranch in Arizona, one of the three Christman airplanes, or a telephone booth in South America, first went through the private switchboard.

The telephone operator, a young, dark-haired girl, knew his routine well and quickly pushed a button that would record his instructions. On a busy day, it might take five girls to make the telephone calls to carry them out. In the early days, everyone had very much wanted to talk to Christman personally and take their instructions only from him. He had put a stop to that, and by now they had accepted his habits, whether they liked them or not.

On this Sunday morning, he summoned the New York County party leader to that afternoon's regular weekend meeting at Windy Meadow. He also wanted to see a major contractor; the senate majority leader, for whom he would send his own plane to Hornell, New York; the budget director; and the state's new commissioner of natural resources. He debated calling Arnold Guyman, the U. S. attorney, and then decided that since he had told Roe to handle the subpoena problem, he should permit him to handle it unimpeded. Finally he spoke a code number into the instrument and Aileen Rosen was back on the line. He knew she was reading from the printout in front of her that catalogued all calls and messages. Those of lesser importance were given to Christman's executive assistants. The rest went directly to him.

"The White House has been trying to reach you, Governor," Aileen Rosen said. "President Griswold wishes to speak to you."

"Again? What time did he call?"

"Twelve-seventeen."

The speech, he thought, smiling. "He'll call again."

"The press. Seven calls."

"Kuhn," he said.

"Mr. Roger Courtland."

"Where did he call from, Elly?"

"Miami Beach. He will be in New York at lunch time."

"Add him to this afternoon's list. Four o'clock." He grinned and craned his neck toward the bedroom. He wondered if Athena Courtland would be amused when her husband arrived home in time to bring her to Windy Meadow. He needed Roger Courtland.

"Mr. Foreman called from Philadelphia, Mr. Mc-Cloud from Houston, and Mr. Siemanowski from Los Angeles."

Eighty percent of the consortium. It was not unexpected. What was wrong with Gutstein in Chicago?

"Get me the fella in Los Angeles," he said.

"It's three-ten A.M. out there, Governor."

"Good."

With immense physical pleasure, he watched the orange-white sun come up across the East River, as if it had been manufactured in a plant on Long Island. He stood, and turned to watch the sun glistening on the buildings to the west. I carried the son of a bitch by 640,000 votes, he thought, and then told himself: I can really win. They are not kidding at all. But for what?

He heard the call go through quickly as a computer card automatically dialed the private Los Angeles number of the executive vice-president of the Northern Hemisphere Bank. The system worked well. There was no need for anyone in communications to have access to telephone numbers.

Siemanowski answered as if he was sure the caller had a wrong number. If it had been a voice other than his, the governor would not have spoken.

"Dick? Alex."

"Hey," he said loudly, before his wakening mind focussed on why he had called Christman in the first place. Then he said, "You are a real mother."

Siemanowski's language always mildly surprised Christman. The banker held a Ph.D. in physics from Cal Tech, he was a noted scholar of Sanskrit, and he personally owned most of the land that was slowly being condemned by the governor of California he helped elect. The mortgages, oil interests, and mineral rights (including uranium) the banker personally held were only a small part of the fortune his father left him that had grown to $400 million. I always wondered whether it's good to be that lucky, Christman thought.

"Alex," he said again, "you are a real mother."

"What did I do?" the governor complained happily.

"For chrissake," he said, "every radio station in the state says you have opened your campaign for the presidency. Your buddy, His Honor the Mayor, announced formation of your first volunteer group. What are you trying to do?"

"I should be dead after that speech, fella."

Siemanowski didn't bother to answer him.

"Everybody called but Gutstein," the governor said. "He's convinced you're running."

"I made three commitments to you guys. One: We bought the engineering company. Two: I'll sell nuclear power my own way. Three: I won't run."

Siemanowski caught the tone this time and reassured the governor.

"You call the others and tell them I'm doing it my way."

"You'll have trouble. McCloud thinks you're going to blow it and get the government on our ass. Foreman thinks—well, I take that back. Who the hell knows what Foreman thinks. Take my advice: call them yourself."

The banker heard the deep sigh which he had learned might mean resentment, encroachment, pressure giving way to anger.

"Fella," the governor said, "there are other things."

"Sure," the banker said. But Christman knew he would make the calls, however reluctantly, and handle it well. "We're coming to the payoff, Alex," he warned. "That means you may be in for a real crunch."

"When the going gets tough," Christman said, "the tough get going."

"Alex," the banker said, "do me a favor? Fire your speech writer. He's jerking off on your time."

Christman put down the telephone and it rang quickly.

"Governor?" Aileen Rosen said.

"Tell my wife I'll be home at three."

"Yes, sir."

He felt tense in the muscles of his legs, his chest, and arms. It was as if he were walking a guy wire between two unfinished buildings and as he neared the opposite side a brisk wind came up unexpectedly and began to sway the wire.

It was not unusual for him to think of his wife when he had been with another woman, even though it had been years since their sexual relations had ceased to exist. And when he did not quickly distract himself, he could not at those times blot out those early days when he first emerged from obscurity.

He did not start rich. His father owned a successful Syracuse printing business, which made it no real hardship to ship him off to Dartmouth for four years, even at a time when colleges and universities and the Ivy League schools, in particular, were havens solely for the sons of wealthy men. Alex Christman took his law degree at Yale, but to everyone's surprise he did not settle into the comfortable life of the upstate city. He moved to New York City, turned down three good offers from Wall Street law firms, and started looking for his own clients so that he could prove what he could do.

He found that a lawyer without clients is worse than a professional ballplayer without a team. He cannot even practice throwing at a barrel. And Christman, like other young lawyers, found the one place he could scrounge an occasional case was in the local party clubhouse. His skill brought him to the attention of local ward bosses in general and Miles Wiggens, the party's county chairman, in particular. There came a time when Wiggens was promised the state contract for construction of a $4½ million housing complex outside Newburgh, New York. The only problem was that he did not own a construction company. It did not stop Wiggens.

Christman could still remember the day he stood in the back room of the Empire Chess Parlor that Wiggens used for an office, and he could hear the old man bellow:

"Alex, my boy, you're going in the contractor business. Go out and hire some people."

"I appreciate it," he replied, "but all I really want is the legal work."

"I think your hearin' aid needs a little booster," Miles Wiggens bellowed. "I tole you once and I don't think I want to say it again. Take out the papers and call it the Christman Construction Corporation."

Wiggens threw him an oversize manila envelope that bore the return address of the state's Department of Audit and Control. He had not expected it to be so heavy and he dropped it and had to stoop awkwardly to pick it up.

"Judas priest," Wiggens shouted. "That's the company's first bid and make sure it's mailed by the tenth."

"Yes, sir," he could still remember saying. Because by then the magnitude of what he held in his hand already had come into focus. He turned to leave, which was the best way to mask the degree to which he was overwhelmed.

"Oh, by the way, Christman," Wiggens had called after him, "I'm your senior partner, but for chrissake don't put *that* in the incorporation papers. When you get set up, just issue a call on the stock in the name of Timothy Xavier Cooney."

"Who's that?" he asked.

"A bloody dummy, just like you."

A lesser man would have hardly appreciated the fact that the creation of the myth that Alex Christman was a man who could do anything was of immensely greater value than cash in the bank. He became the incessant confidant of men with power who understood the essence of politics was financial profit. And he was always ready to tell them how to turn public funds to their own welfare without fear of jeopardy.

There was also the Christman luck. Wiggens died just four days after the state of New York awarded the Christman Construction Corporation its first contract. Whoever Timothy Xavier Cooney might be, he had been issued no Christman stock. Newburgh became solely Alex Christman's property. Four decades later, when the outstanding stock in the company, with its vast real estate holdings, was worth $200 million, he was still convinced the $73,411.91 he had given to Wiggens' widow not only symbolized his honesty but was ample payment.

In those days, Christman sensed, and rightly, that the visibility of public office could easily expose and destroy him. He knew the picture of a man as a manipulator, no matter how clever, was equally dangerous. As his investments began to leapfrog into mail contracts, commercial airlines, a chain of hotels and movie theatres, and a dozen other enterprises, some said Christman's actual working capital was thin. The fact was that he was $2½ million in debt, a fact he seemed to take lightly. After all, was not the appearance of vast success as much coin of the realm as a profitable balance sheet?

Not quite. Christman had never moved from the tiny law office over the bank on West Seventy-second Street. If his rent was past due, nobody had ever cared before. And so he was startled one day when a city marshal politely knocked on his door and handed him an eviction notice. He was, after all, a winner. And how could a winner be gratuitously kicked in the shins for three months' rent? Absurd? Jesus! He'd go downstairs and straighten the goddamned thing out in the morning.

It was a sweltering July day in 1946 when he marched straight into the office of the bank's president, V. K. Morgan. He still remembered the banker's immaculate blue suit. And he also remembered how he thought the extension would come as a matter of course. Morgan did not even offer him a cigar.

"No, we can't extend two weeks. There are certain rules we are bound by. You know that."

"Hey," he remembered saying, "we are friends. Isn't that so?"

The banker's answer was firm. And before he left his office, Alexander Christman could not resist leaning across the desk, his face less than an inch from the old man, and hissing in as even a tone as he could manage:

"Now I know you, fella."

He walked three steps at a time up the stairs to his own office, still not believing anything could topple his growing empire, even though actual eviction could precipitate a call on every note he had outstanding.

He called four other banks and was turned down. Then he called the four county leaders that controlled the banks. They were polite but, they said, unable to help him. He worked through a list of more than thirty banks across the state in which he had personal friends, because now he knew it was more than rent, but roughly a half million dollars' worth of refinancing he needed. It was well after five o'clock before he fully comprehended what was happening. He had worked his way down the list until he reached Jess Bowman, executive vice-president of the First National Bank of Canandaigua. Few cities in New York were more backward than the capital of Ontario County, but Jess was close to the party's power center in Rochester. At first Jess was simply polite. He followed the script. Perhaps it was the lack of anxiety in Christman's voice that changed that. He did not whimper. He did not rail. He sounded like a lawyer dealing with someone else's problem.

"You're a friend," Christman said. "Then level."

And so Jess Bowman, who owed him no more than a hello and a handshake, told him what no one else would tell him. The boys in Albany simply decided Alex Christman was ready to be plucked.

"It's their game," Bowman said. "That's the way they play it."

"Thanks," Christman said.

"Too bad, Alex. You know the old one, 'If you lie down with dogs . . .' "

"Don't believe it, fella," he said softly, "I'm not dead yet."

Strangely, Christman did not blame the politicians. He had always understood and accepted the crude concept of profit and loss that controlled their game. But V. K. Morgan was something else. He was a gentleman, and Christman had learned a lot about gentlemen. Whatever strange quirk was in him, it was to the

Morgan mansion he went that night. And once again there was the Christman luck. The banker was not home. But V. K.'s daughter Morganna was home, and though they had met casually before, he had shown no real interest in her.

When he walked into the chintz-lined library on the second floor of the house at 57 East Eighty-second Street, she was reading *The Man in the Iron Mask*.

He told her the story. Without a word, she wrote a check for $1,500 to cover his rent.

Christman sighed, shrewd enough to realize that with thirty years of anger out of his system, now he would remember only the best things.

He had taken the check and kissed her cheek. She was perplexed by his laughter, so he told her the rest of the story: he needed $500,000 to save the business he had created.

"Oh," she had said, as if he had asked to borrow no more than a pencil. "Let me help."

Christman had never taken her seriously, though he had agreed to meet her for tea the next afternoon at Delmonico's. She was wearing a long white lace dress when she arrived, flushed and excited, with a large white embroidered beaded bag. He barely had time to pull out her chair when she struggled to bring the manila envelope from her bag. He opened it and saw the thick sheaf of stock certificates—thirty thousand shares of Lehigh Valley Railroad.

"I can't take them," he told her.

"Oh," she said in her birdlike voice, "I'm just glad they can finally be put to use. Please," she begged him.

"I never even gave her a receipt," he murmured to himself. "I married her instead."

The debt was paid, he told himself, as he told himself each time he could not keep from remembering the story. She had rescued him from disaster, out of which he was determined to overwhelm the political forces that had tried to do him in. It had taken a good part of his lifetime to defeat them, but he had not changed them. And all he had given Morganna Morgan Christman in return was one son and an even better name than she had had before.

The marriage had worked well as his businesses solidified with her new capital, and for ten years she had been an active partner. Even when he became more active in politics, she had stayed with him, gamely lending her intellect and support in everything he did.

But for all her help in his first campaign for governor, it was his victory that was as responsible as anything else for pushing them apart. Christman had found in himself a sympathy for the poor, and he was determined that his state would be wrested from the control of the insurance companies and the banks and returned to the hands of the people. He was fascinated with programs for the redistribution of wealth, which began with sizable increases in inheritance taxes. Morganna balked. She believed that men were born to rule, born to wealth, born to the realization of the responsibilities conferred by inherited money.

"Alex," she told him, "you're a fool. Even if all the money in this country were divided equally, it would be back in the same hands in less than a generation."

Christman stepped into the study, removed the borrowed red silk robe, and peeled off the pajama top she had given him. Standing in the center of Roger Courtland's elegant living room facing a bank of three television sets, Christman did twenty perfect deep knee bends. Then he stood up and touched his left hand to his right foot ten times and his right hand to his left toe. He was barely sweating. He walked to the bar and poured a champagne glass three-quarters full of LaIna sherry. In the kitchen, he filled a water tumbler with ice and orange juice. Then the governor of the state of New York took both glasses in his big fists and walked back to the terrace.

He sipped the sherry and then the orange juice as the sun rose over the city, and found his thoughts would not leave the extraordinary woman in the bedroom, Athena Courtland. He succumbed, toying with himself, and momentarily forestalled the impulse to return to her bed.

Three years ago, *Vogue* called her one of the most beautiful women at forty that had ever been made. They were right. But Christman knew that before she divorced the scion of a famous racing stable because he tried to kill her, she had never thought of herself as particularly pretty. The divorce changed that. Or the men who flocked to her after the divorce changed it. Out of the heap she had selected Roger Courtland, because for her he seemed more powerful than any of the other men of her class who pursued her. He remembered the wedding. And he remembered that he had not been mistaken about the look that had passed between them. The day after she returned from her honeymoon, he had called her himself to offer the co-chairmanship of the state's Environmental Protection Council.

"It will please Roger," he told her.

Her voice was slow and hot. "Right now, I'd like to please you, Governor," she said.

It had taken him twenty minutes to work out the rescheduling of his afternoon appointments. And ten more minutes to get to her apartment. It made him feel like a teenager again.

Shutting his eyes, he saw her clearly as she had been a half-dozen hours ago, her huge brown eyes shining as she stared down at him, with hands on her smooth hips, in absolute control of the situation.

"I never knew a woman who shaved there before," he remembered saying. "It's really beautiful."

"It's also better," she told him, as he touched her, caressed her, wondering how she had removed all trace of a stubble from her shaven body. She was moist and hot, and she had told him to taste her and he did.

Christman opened his eyes and shook himself. The first time he had tried to rise from the bed, she pushed him flat on his back. When he thought he was about to burst, Athena Courtland spread her marvelous golden thighs and straddled his body. She moved forward until the clean-shaven lips were above his face, and then caressed his nose, his forehead, and his lips. Perfume mixed with her woman smell, and he writhed beneath her on the bed, as if she were subjecting him to a form of exquisite torture.

Then she released him and moved back until she sat on his stomach. With her soft, slim hand she reached behind her buttocks and grasped the base of his penis, pulling it gently. He groaned a warning. She released him. Her hands went to his face and with one fingernail she caressed his lips and finally covered them with the clear viscous substance she had taken from him.

The governor remembered how she had slowly leaned forward, her long blond hair caressing the sides of his face, and kissed his mouth teasingly, gently, delicately, as exquisitely as any woman had ever done. She rested on her elbows and slowly raised her buttocks. Then she plunged herself down upon his penis, riding him, pounding against him in full attack. When she finally raised her head, she was sitting firmly upon him, smiling. The muscles inside her body toyed with him, squeezed him, made him feel as though he was larger than he had ever been before.

And then she rode him, plunging her body up and down upon him, pounding him into the huge bed. She rode him as if she were a wild animal, demanding he extend himself for her, insisting he move against her, fight her, meet her. They were defeated together.

She straightened on top of him, smiling broadly, and he would never forget the way she had said: "God. You're marvelous!" Her body was glistening with sweat, and he ran his hands down her arms, across her stomach and her groin and finally touched her nipples gently.

Christman opened his eyes and stared at his erection. The air on the terrace was chilly now. I'm fifty-three years old, and I came four times last night. Four goddamn times! And here I am with the pistol loaded again. Jesus! The society columnists may think she's one of the ten most beautiful women in the world at forty. But they don't know the half of it.

Each time their lovemaking cooled, Athena Courtland lay herself down in the crook of his arm, her lips touching his ear. She would tell him stories. Erotic stories. Sexual stories. Lascivious stories. Fantastic stories. Stories in which he made love to a hundred women. Stories in which women tantalized and teased his body. Caressed his legs. His arms. His genitals. And each time he became aroused, she would touch the tip of his penis in search of a drop of moisture. When she found it, her finger would touch his lips, the story would end, and she would find some new way to satisfy him again.

He tried to rouse himself now, refocus his thoughts, not wanting to return to the bedroom yet, and at the same moment, annoyed that the fantasies so occupied his attention.

The last time she had aroused him, when after three orgasms he was sure he was finished for the night, she told him he had become headmaster of a European girls' finishing school. One of his duties was to examine each applicant. He was to determine her development as a female. As headmaster, he "tested" the physical reactions of each girl: breast sensitivity, development of her vaginal muscles.

Christman stood up, stretched, and focussed his attention on the play of sunlight on the Fifty-ninth Street Bridge. There was almost no traffic at all. In a moment, his erection subsided, and he stepped into the living room to pick up the television script marked "Confidential."

"The Power Crisis," he muttered to himself. Where could you find a friend with a body that might have been designed by a Greek artisan, who was also married to the most powerful broadcast executive in the world? But it was Christman's special genius that had seen to it that she was elected cochairman of the state's Environmental Protection Council. Her help was invaluable, and he knew he would have to find a very careful way to tell her about the American Nuclear

consortium. He did not think she would be upset.
People who were born rich, he discovered, only became angry when you used them to promote something
to make money. And American Nuclear had gone far
beyond that.

He flipped through the pages absently. UBS News
fully accepted Christman's Commissioner of Natural
Resources as their expert. He had her to thank for
that, too. It was the governor's promise to his partners
that he would shape in the American mind a new
image of the crisis toward a single end: private development of nuclear energy. The commissioner, a
fomer dean at Berkeley, was an outstanding expert.
And he was also expert enough to know that if he
disagreed with the boss at all, he did it privately.

He read the narration on the left side of each page,
ignoring the visual summaries of film that would appear with it on the screen.

"THE UNITED STATES, WITH SIX PERCENT
OF THE WORLD'S POPULATION, CONSUMES
THIRTY-FIVE PERCENT OF THE ENERGY
OUTPUT OF THE EARTH." Good. "BY THE
YEAR 2000, THOUGH, THIS COUNTRY WILL
NEED FOUR TIMES OUR PRESENT POWER
SUPPLY.

"THIS IS THE DIMENSION OF THE POWER
CRISIS AT A TIME WHEN WE ARE LEARNING
OUR PLANET IS FACED WITH A SCARCITY
OF ENVIRONMENT." Perfect. "WE ARE BURN-
ING EARTH'S CAPITAL INDISCRIMINATELY
IN A SITUATION WHERE PRESENT UTILITIES
HAVE ONLY ONE OBJECTIVE: 'PUSH THE
JUICE OUT AND PRAY.' " God bless, Christman
murmured.

The script carefully showed how nuclear energy not
only was America's salvation but how new "breeder"
generators actually produced more fuel than they
consumed, creating an ever-growing stockpile of re-
source.

It touched all the bases, showing how both the
do-gooders and the profiteers were wrong. Environ-
mentalists fought progress. Power companies were

making too much money to either consider the environment or the welfare of their customers. President Griswold had done no more than support "continuing study of the problem."

The script touched on the twenty-one nuclear generators in operation (without mentioning the common bond between the men who owned them), the leadership provided in New York State, and even a film clip of Christman throwing the switch on the first atomic-powered generator in the nation. It was five years old, but even now he remembered what he had said:

"That's real power to the people!"

He smiled. The blacks had been madder than hell. But when they found he really meant what he said, and the state's newest office building, complete with a 23,000-seat arena, actually *was* going into central Harlem right on 125th Street, they calmed down.

He was pleased with himself, and he knew the three-part prime time series would ease tension within the consortium. Then he read Part Three of the script.

"SINCE THE FIRST DETONATION AT ALAMAGORDO IN 1945, MAN HAS DISCOVERED SOME OBVIOUS FLAWS TO NUCLEAR POWER. FIGURES COMPILED BY UBS INDICATE THERE HAVE BEEN 640 DEATHS FROM RADIATION POISONING IN THE UNITED STATES IN THE LAST TWO DECADES, 40,000 HEAD OF CATTLE DESTROYED."

He stopped. The TV sons of bitches always play both sides, he remembered. Christman threw the script across the room, stood and stared down at it. Roger Courtland, he wondered? A conservationist producer? Or just the news guy's usual idea of balance? Roe or somebody else in the law firm could handle it. And the "other side," he also knew, could not make seven cents worth of difference to the listeners after three hours of heavy pro-atom message.

She was lying still. Not a muscle in her extraordinary body seemed to move, except in unison with her breathing. He did not consciously want to waken her, and so he dropped the borrowed pajama bottoms and slid into the big bed beside her, his nose underneath her armpit, his body grateful for the warmth of her closeness. She did not smell as other women did at morning, and partly in gratitude he blew gently at the tip of her breast, wishing he was offering something special of his own to whatever she might be dreaming.

He absorbed himself wholly in the exquisite shape of her nipple and the faint pink color of the aureole surrounding it. She was so soft.

"What happened, Alex?" she murmured, then rolled over, half smiled, and touched him to see if he was hard. She moved her body, still partly asleep, and then stroked the nipple on his chest with the soft pad of her index finger. He groaned with delight, a plea not to discontinue the perfect sensation.

"Next time, I'll shave your chest," she murmured.

"The hell you will," he said, but he did not think she heard him.

Her hand lay flat on his breast. He shut his eyes and felt engulfed in the delicious warmth of her closeness. She did not move and he did not wish to waken her. And so he permitted himself to slide slowly into sleep. If he dreamed at all, he did not recall having done so. It was, he thought, a few moments and no more before he realized consciousness again. And then he was at the last meeting of the consortium, remembering it rather than dreaming it, knowing he had sensed trouble then. But he still had not found the facts that gave rise to the instinct.

His eyes were still closed. His hand moved slowly across the bed, seeking the touch of her flesh. He found nothing and slumped back on the bed. When he opened his eyes, she was fully dressed, standing beside the bed smiling, staring down at him. Her make-up was as precise as if it had been painted on by Botticelli, and her caramel-colored hair gently brushed her shoulders. She was wearing a white satin blouse that creased perfectly at the points of her breasts. She could not be wearing a brassiere, and he wondered how quickly the material sensitized her nipples.

A red, white, and blue belt held in the waist of her full white jersey skirt, cut three inches above her tanned knees. He knew her well. And so he leaned over the edge of the bed and saw the white patent high-heeled boots that rose to just below the knee.

"Hey, you're dressed."

She lifted her boot to the edge of the bed beside his face. He kissed the gleaming leather.

"Do you really think I'm dressed?" she asked, lifting her skirt slowly.

The skirt passed her full thighs, exposing the hairless crotch that so excited him. It was glistening as if she had massaged herself with mineral oil. Christman moved his arms toward her, but she took a small step backward, still teasing him. Then she turned and bent over straddle-legged, her white buttocks near his face.

"Kiss me," she said.

He bit each cheek and moved his hands to her hips to drag her backward toward him. But she stood up.

"Can we do this in the White House?" she asked.

He let go of her and rolled over on his back. "Why? Do you think it's better?"

Her warm hand gently grasped his testicles. "Much better."

"Crap," he said, as she fell on top of him and straddled his neck. Her hands went to the top of his head, gently forcing his face toward her crotch. He kissed the bare skin tentatively, again breathing deeply her woman's odor mixed with perfume.

"I love you, Alex. I love you very much."

The loud, grinding sound of the door buzzer made them both jump.

"It can't be Roger," Christman said.

She brushed her hair back with her hands and tucked the satin blouse into her skirt. She looked at the clock. It was 9:15 A.M.

"Who else could get past the doorman? In this building, they announce everybody." She was frightened. "Will you get dressed? Please."

"Why?" He was grinning. Amused at her agitation. She stamped her boot.

"Get dressed."

Christman shrugged. "Don't answer it." He reached for her husband's red silk robe, still grinning, and watched her turn on her high heels and walk through the living room to the front door. He watched her open the one-way peephole.

"Goddamnsonofabitch, Alex!" she shouted, turning to stare at him, hands on her hips. Still facing him, she pulled the bolt without even looking at it and turned the brass head of King Rex that opened the door.

Devlin had a sheepish smile on his face, and he nervously brushed back his white hair with his hand. He walked right past her when he saw Christman and then closed the bedroom door behind him.

"Guv, I'm sorry," he said. "They didn't want to call you."

Christman shrugged. He was still smiling, relaxed, and, Devlin thought, satisfied.

"Siemanowski called back. He said it was important. Mr. Roe said to get to you, wherever you were."

Christman moved quickly to the white princess telephone on the vanity table.

"Stupid bastard," he muttered to himself, as he punched the twelve-digit code that would identify him at the Windy Meadow switchboard. He sat down on the quilted hassock, idly scratching himself. Athena Courtland opened the bedroom door and started to walk toward him. Her brown eyes were filled with anger.

"Not now," he said flatly, waving his hand.

Devlin caught her by the elbow and turned her gently back out of the room. He closed the door. Christman's eyes went back to the telephone.

"Get me the California call," he ordered.

The governor waited patiently as he heard the electronic noise in his ears. Siemanowski was there before the second ring.

"Where the hell have you been, Alex?" He was agitated, but it was well under control.

Christman was still scratching himself. He looked over at Devlin, who was standing with his back square against the door.

"I'm here now, fella," he said.

"Gutstein seems to have gone over to the utility guys. I think he's selling us out. My people report he met with a dozen of them Friday night from all over the country."

"How much do you think he told them?" Christman asked Siemanowski.

"The raw tapes of their meeting at the Palmer House should be here by noon, my time. You and I can meet with him in Chicago tonight." Siemanowski stopped for a minute. "I'll take a baseball bat and break both his goddamn legs myself, Alex."

"Spilt milk," the governor said.

"You have got to make it tonight, Alex."

"Calm down," he said. Even if he did not want to see Vice-President Whitmore, there was no way to cancel that appointment.

"Christ, you know what's at stake."

"Calm down."

"Jesus, Alex."

The governor looked at his watch.

"Call the other fellas," he said. "We will meet at the ranch tomorrow. That should give them enough time. I don't want to scare them. Then call Gutstein. Get him there, too."

"Don't you want to hear the tapes?"

"No," he said.

"Alex. Christ only knows how you survive."

"See you, fella."

He stood, grinned at Devlin, and walked to the closet. He dressed quickly, firmly knotted his tie, and looked at Devlin for approval.

"What are you going to do about the broad?" the sergeant said, not expecting an answer, but merely reminding the governor, as he might after a speech in a packed auditorium, that the route back to the privacy of his car was not yet clear.

Christman shrugged happily, delighted to deal with a problem immediately within his grasp. "Gently," he said. "That's all thirty-six flavors."

Athena Courtland stretched. Her harlequin glasses

were perched on the tip of her nose, and she was reading the Sunday *New York Times*.

"You're page one, fella," she said, mocking his nasal voice.

He bent over the chair and kissed her neck, but she did not stand up.

Devlin already had the door open and was looking up and down the long carpeted hallway.

"Hey," Christman called, "I'll see you at dinner."

"Roger is coming home, Alex. It's Sunday."

"Sure," he told her with a grin, "my office called him in Miami and invited you both to dinner tonight at Windy Meadow."

And then before she could get angry with him, he was gone.

CHAPTER FIVE

IT WAS not yet 9 A.M. and it had already been an unpleasant morning for U. S. Attorney Arnold Guyman. When his chauffeur dropped him off at 7:45, Arthur Roe was already in the waiting room of the office. He had controlled his startled anger in the presence of the man he knew was closest to Alexander Christman. It was embarrassing to tell him he knew nothing of the case. And even more difficult to maintain the kind, sober, judicial posture that would augment Roe's respect for him. But he finally reassured the angry lawyer that the last individual on the planet Earth he wished to offend was the governor of the state of New York, Alexander Christman. It had not been a pleasant visit.

Arnold Guyman was not the kind of man who lived with the self-assurance of a Wall Street background. When he was fearful or uncertain, his staff learned he was prone to extreme rage. Some reasoned that he was simply an incompetent lawyer, which was partly true. A handful of assistants, who knew how important it was to leave the office with Guyman's recommendation, told themselves and each other his outraged anger was a sign of personal affection.

Federal Bureau of Investigation agents assigned to Guyman's office simply considered him a sick man and accepted the irrational behavior. The agents had friends at Internal Revenue Service. They had seen Guyman's old tax returns and were amused that their bellicose boss never had earned ten thousand dollars a year in private practice. And so they filed their weekly reports that included a summary of the activities and behavior of the chief prosecutor in the Second Department. At the proper time, they believed, the director would decide to bring the matter to the attention of the president.

There was no one in the U. S. attorney's private office, and so when his anger was released, it produced even less than its usual response. Guyman punched the red button that summoned his confidential secretary, and he waited for her, still not attempting to control his anger.

"What is this?" he screamed when Mary O'Leary entered his office.

She walked to the side of the desk and squinted through her steel-rimmed glasses.

"It looks like a subpoena," she said, recognizing the carbon copy in his hand.

"I know it's a subpoena, Miss O'Leary," he told her, rubbing his forehead as if he no longer could maintain the patience to deal with a congenital imbecile. "Whose subpoena is it?"

"It's Soshin's case, sir," she said.

Guyman shook his head in dismay. "Well then, get him, Miss O'Leary," he screeched, trying to keep the high, feminine quality out of his voice. "Go and get him."

"Yes, sir," she said dully. "Right away, sir."

"And get me a new blotter," he called after her.

"Another one, sir?" she replied, turning her head so that he could not see the smile on her face.

Guyman stared at the 7 by 4 foot oil portrait his wife had given him of Miss Jane Morrell, a turn of the century lady tennis star. He had come into this office with that portrait and 1,740 pending cases. No one gave a damn about his problems except the party leaders who sent him job applicants. So his staff was cluttered with amateurs, young publicity-seeking hot shot assistants like Martin A. Soshin who could only make trouble. Jesus! He should have had sense to stand up to the politicians. Morgenthau did. Dewey did. But how the hell are you supposed to know that when a county chairman tells you his man is one helluva lawyer.

Soshin knocked twice before he walked into the office. He sat down in the green leather chair in front of the desk and waited for Guyman to acknowledge his presence. When he did not, the young lawyer said, "Good morning, sir."

"Soshin," the U. S. attorney said quietly, the explosive anger held in check for a moment, as he lifted the piece of paper, "what is this?"

"It's a subpoena, sir."

"Soshin," he repeated, beginning to lose control, "I know it's a subpoena. I've seen a subpoena before. Is it your subpoena?"

The young attorney leaned across the desk and read Arthur Roe's name upside down in the space where the name of the recipient is typed.

"Yes, sir," he said, "that's mine."

Guyman slammed down the piece of paper. "Soshin, you can't do this," he roared.

"I served it myself."

"You what?"

Guyman was walking briskly back and forth across the room. His face was bright red.

"Arnie, will you look at the case?"

Guyman shut him up with a single wave of his hand. When he reached the desk, he picked up the piece of paper between his thumb and forefinger.

"Is this thing registered with the clerk?" he asked, holding it distastefully in front of him.

"Yes, sir. That's one of the rules you set for the office."

Guyman took a deep breath. "Go down to his office right now and cancel it."

"Sir," Soshin said, fully aware that Guyman had not yet even looked at him. "You'll have to give me a memorandum for my files to that effect."

The U. S. attorney was quickly at his chair and he leaned over, his mouth inches from the assistant's ear, and shouted, "I'm not giving you any memorandum! I'm giving you an order!"

Soshin stared straight ahead, holding his head erect. A minute later Guyman walked away from the chair. Soshin said again, "Will you just look at the

case? We have reason to believe the man has violated
federal law. We have a right to ask him to testify before
a grand jury." He hesitated, gauging the effect of a
calculated threat. "The grand jury," he said, "certainly
might request his appearance on their own initiative."

Guyman calmed himself and slowly the apoplectic
color in his face subsided. He sat down behind his desk
and finally looked at the young man.

"Marty," he said softly, "the president appointed
me on Governor Christman's personal recommendation. I appointed you. Do you understand that?"

"You're talking about politics. This is a matter of
law."

Guyman did not reply when Soshin stood up to
leave. He knew the only way to persuade the young
man was to dismantle the case now, before it went
any further. Jesus! he thought. This kid really wants to
go after Alexander Christman. And he remembered
the sense of awe he had felt the last time he and his
wife dined at the governor's mansion in Irvington.
Even if he were not Christman's nominee, that was
enough to make anyone think twice.

A few minutes later, the young man returned carrying two 36 by 48 inch white cardboard charts. He
propped them on the conference table in front of the
portrait of the tennis player, and Guyman got up and
seated himself in the armchair facing Soshin.

"Go ahead," he said, one hand covering his face.
"Show me what you call a case."

Soshin talked for twenty minutes, uninterrupted
by his superior. On one chart he had listed eleven
sites in New York State that had been condemned
and purchased by the State Mental Hygiene Fund with
federal monies, ostensibly as locations for nursing
homes, narcotics in-patient facilities, and hospitals. The
chart showed that eight of the sites were subsequently
sold by the state to American Nuclear, at prices
ranging from $100,000 to $650,000 less than the state
had paid for them.

"So what?" Guyman said.

"Sir, the chairman of the fund is prepared to testify
that those sites were sold on direct orders from the

governor. I believe he recorded several of the telephone conversations when he became really frightened. That was his insurance policy. At least, he's hinted that he did. And I'm sure he won't admit it before we give him full immunity from prosecution."

"How the hell can you prove the governor owns that company?"

"He owns it, Arnie." Then he added slyly, "We can always get his testimony."

Guyman turned red again.

Soshin held up his hand to calm him and then lifted the second chart. It was covered with lists of names and a complex series of arrows in colored ink. At the top it said: STATE CONSULTANTS. The second column was headed: AMERICAN NUCLEAR CONSULTANTS.

After Soshin explained the chart, warming now to the attention he was getting from Guyman, he said, "Sir, none of these men are paid by American Nuclear. He's using state funds to pay men working for his private company. Look. Christopher Bodeen, $72,000. Ralph Dean, $187,000. Those men are important scientists. We've subpoenaed their bank accounts, their deposits. None of these men received a dollar from American Nuclear. But look," he said excitedly, picking up the top copy of a stack of the company's annual reports, "every one of them is listed as an employee or consultant to the company."

Guyman sat back in the armchair.

"Are you sure there is a federal jurisdiction here?"

"We got lucky. Really lucky. Every dollar in the state's Science and Space Foundation comes from federal appropriations. Actually, we have the clearest jurisdiction."

Guyman rubbed his face with his hands, as Soshin held the subpoena out to him. He ignored it.

"Did the FBI guys work on this with you?"

"Nope"—the young man grinned—"just our own staff. Smith, Hurowitz and Sand."

The U. S. attorney still did not look at the piece of paper. He stood up and stretched his arms, yawning as he did. "Sorry," he said, "I jogged an extra mile around the reservoir this morning. Too much."

"Well?" Soshin prodded.

Guyman waited a moment, seemingly studying the charts he now held in his hand.

"Let me study these, all right, Marty?"

After Soshin left, the U. S. attorney called the chief clerk and told him the practical joke had worked. "You guys have some sense of humor," he said. "But don't let me catch you messing up the registry with those kind of subpoenas. Redo the page at the end of the month."

Arnold Guyman got up and unlocked the small safe he had ordered installed in his closet, and inside he carefully placed the subpoena requiring Arthur Roe of 345 Park Avenue to appear before a federal grand jury. He had kept his promise to Arthur Roe and corrected the mistake.

Two floors below in the federal courthouse, the chief clerk turned to his chief assistant and said, "Wowee, something's really going on upstairs. I've never heard him so calm." Then he decided he could never willfully alter federal records for anyone. And he quickly entered the subpoena on his log and ordered the chief assistant to file the copy in the office's record room. Bosses come and go, but the civil service lasts forever. He told himself that if anything was good for the country, it was the goddamn civil service.

It was well into December and the rolling lawns of Irvington were no longer the color of new money. Athena Courtland sat cheerfully in the rear of the big blue limousine marked NYP-1, the car owned by United Broadcasting and assigned by her husband, the chairman of the board, to himself.

She sat holding his hand as they watched a commercial for a product called Ty-D-Bowl that showed a man in yachting costume driving a motorboat inside a bathroom fixture.

"Gawd," Athena Courtland groaned. "Do you really watch that kind of thing all day long?"

"If I didn't," the chairman replied, "you would have married a man with nothing but his father's fabric business."

"Do you really think so, Roger?" Athena Courtland said, turning her head slowly toward him, careful that the question was taken as a tribute to his eminence rather than a gibe at her affection for him as a man.

On the screen, the impish host, publicized widely as a Harvard Ph.D., was stretching the show's closing theme song, "A Pretty Girl Is Like a Melody."

"Is he a fag?" Athena Courtland asked, drawing out the word to make it sound as if she were referring to an exotic nationality.

"Quit it, will you, Babe," he said gently.

"I'm just curious, Roger. Is he a fag?"

"What difference does it make?"

The limousine was moving at no more than twenty miles per hour through the winding roads that lead from the thruway to the cliffs overlooking the Hudson River.

Athena Courtland lifted one green velvet pump and tapped the button that turned off the small television set. She stretched her legs above her, pointing her toes to accentuate the bone in her ankle. The Swiss embroidered skirt rode high above her thighs.

"Why don't you have someone invent a nylon that doesn't make my legs sweat," she said softly.

Courtland leaned forward and gently took her ankle, turning her in the seat, so that her feet rested in his lap.

"Careful, husband," she said, as she began to grind the heel of the sling-back into his crotch. Roger massaged the calves of her legs. She lifted one foot from his lap, and he slipped off the sling-back and lifted her foot to his face. His lips touched her big toe, as he felt the other heel hard in his crotch.

"Nylon does make your feet sweat," Roger said. He had never known any woman who perfumed her feet before. It had taken him so long to find this woman. And now, for all he had, nothing meant so much in his world as Athena DeWitt Thompson Woodward, now Courtland.

He sighed. His manicured finger touched the button that lowered the window to the driver's compartment. "How far away are we, Martin?" he asked.

"The Christman grounds are just ahead, sir. We have at least ten minutes."

"Let me take off your stockings," Courtland said.

"Take off one, darling."

The winding road cut a diagonal path through Windy Meadow, past a three-foot illuminated sign that said:

PRIVATE PROPERTY:
PERMISSION TO PASS OVER
CAN BE REVOKED AT ANY TIME

"Well, what do you know." She whistled, feeling his uncovered warmth beneath her foot. Roger Courtland took a handkerchief from his back pocket as she began caressing him between the naked foot and the nylon-covered one.

"Isn't this a public road, Roger?" she said, tensing her toes to scratch him with the tip of her nail.

"Please," he said, his body tightening in the seat.

"And he owns it, Roger?"

Roger Courtland's eyes were closed. "Please, Babe."

He sighed deeply. She still could not tell whether the sound was an expression of physical pleasure or mental irritation.

"Will you take the job?" she asked.

"Christman is going to be president," he said. "He is also the major shareholder in three of the companies that are our seven largest advertisers in the New York market."

"That means yes," she said, squeezing him hard.

He groaned again, undulating his body in the soft cushion.

"Well now," she said, feeling the moisture he was wiping off her feet with his handkerchief, "I guess I had better take off my other stocking."

Babe and Roger Courtland were too late to see the pink California clay tennis courts off to the left of the road or the Christmans' shimmering blue, heated outdoor pool set into the forest like a woodland lake. Nor did they see the private guards or the state police barracks tucked into a corner of the estate. Christman would have it appear he had no enemies and was hardly in need of protection. But for all the openness of Windy Meadow, it was a fortress, carefully guarded by the pick of a Florida detective firm owned by former agents of the Federal Bureau of Investigation. With them came a sophisticated system of television surveillance, electronic traps, and even long-range parabolic microphones. They could record every sound uttered within seven miles of the main house. At times, it amused the state's First Lady to listen as guests drove away from the estate, but the governor considered it obscene, and said as much.

She took particular pleasure in the juvenile delight the men found in devising new investigative techniques, much as a child is fascinated by a bedroom keyhole. In the second year of the governor's first term, it was Morganna Christman who dealt with the rivalry between the private detectives and the state police bodyguards assigned to the governor. She simply created a status system based on merit. Those at the top were permitted to use the athletic club, the courts, the pool, and the estate's pistol range. She even appointed a code committee that devised names each month for the family and important figures in the Christman administration who had frequent contact with the governor. It delighted her when the code was used as an expression of opinion. Somewhere in her study she had framed a red-striped laminated card that was the first code system used to identify key personnel:

> The Governor: *Lincoln*
> Mrs. Christman: *Alice in Wonderland*
> Josh Christman: *Little Boy Blue*
> The Press: *The Cong*
> TV Press: *Ant Cong*
> Attorney Arthur Roe: *Hitler*
> General Carmody: *Cub Scout Leader* (the private guards were referred to as *Cubs;* the state police, *scouts,* a permanent designation)

The Christman Mansion: *Base*
The Governor's Albany Office: *North Pole*

The 324 policemen, personal staff, butlers, and Windy Meadow aides were each involved in preparations for the governor's small dinner party inaugurating the Environmental Activist Association of America. The guard headquarters had been given the names of each of the 126 guests who received engraved invitations, individually printed by Everett Gebhardt Singer, Christman's seventy-six-year-old engraver. Dinner preparations began three days before with the first air shipment of Gulf Stream shrimp. The preparations would involve five chefs and forty-five assistant chefs, butlers, and bakers, before dinner was actually served.

All of the Christman staff had experienced similar events. They were seasoned and they knew their jobs. But they also knew that each Christman dinner was special enough to deserve the careful attention to detail of a theatrical premiere.

Word of the arrival of Vice-President Whitmore, ostensibly a stopover on his way to address the second session of the business executives group Christman had addressed the evening before, augmented the occasion. But it did not affect it greatly. There had been a dispute raised by the Secret Service men who arrived in advance of the vice-president, but mindful of Christman's stature, they graciously accepted the arrangements of his security staff. They would remain at the helicopter pad until the vice-president departed.

Soon after Alexander Christman was elected governor of the state of New York, he learned a simple political fact: the appearance of power is more important than the fact of power. He watched wealthy and powerful businessmen, many of whom sat in cubicles near the top of the American political structure, defer to men whose public office attributed to them the illusion of extraordinary foresight and power. Once, even Christman did obeisance to them. They wrote laws. They appointed men who administered them. And they appointed the judges who passed on them.

The fact of power was a lesser thing. At times, it

was even a mirage. Strong governors like Roosevelt,
Dewey, and Rockefeller often were no more than the
chief executive of a clearing house for petty power
brokers, union leaders, legislators, party contributors,
and others who helped elect him. In return, they expected personal service to them, before any notion a
governor might have of service to the people.

The exercise of patronage was one form of control,
and at first it did not come easily to Christman. His
initial impulse was to fight the power brokers and even
the ethnic pressure groups. But he swallowed the bit
and learned that to get along he had to go along. It
was easier to buy a man with a job than fight him in
public. And it was less painful to abandon a principle
if the final decision appeared an exercise in gubernatorial power rather than a defeat. Politics had, he
learned, only one objective: survival—and that meant
the constant expansion of power.

It sickened him to believe the power was not his
own. Now he ruled the state's political organization
with sixty thousand jobs. He controlled both houses of
the legislature and most of the men who served there
in both parties. But with all his power, it still did not
make it much easier to get the job done.

A year earlier, Christman found his own liberalism
challenged by a clear conservative swing in the state.
He reluctantly allowed the high cost of welfare to become a major election issue, though he personally de-
spised it as bigoted, anti-black, and anti-Puerto Rican.
He swallowed his gall and promised the voters a back-
to-work law and mandatory criminal sanctions against
fraudulent welfare recipients.

He was reelected. The legislature quickly drafted
and enacted new statutes. The welfare laws made him
physically ill. He knew he could not sign them. And
he did not—until he had absolute assurances in private
that the courts would declare them unconstitutional. He
even got himself a trade out of the legislature: the
upstaters agreed to support his new Atomic Power Authority.

He both liked and abhorred the professional poli-

ticians in the state because they never had any real
objective beyond the retention of power. And so before
Christman's administration, a New York general election had always been a battle between classes, the one
party representing the unpoor, the unblack, and the
uncommitted against the state's professed liberals.
Christman had changed that twelve years ago. He took
the nomination and moved to a centrist position between the two parties with a brilliant acceptance
speech:

"I believe in the New Politics," he told the state.
"Something for everyone. Government can't exist unless it is satisfactorily productive to all. Now can it? A
lot of people don't agree with me. But I think government has to serve all the people. And if I am elected,
it will.

"The fellas in the other party think you have to be
ardently for the disadvantaged. But unless you also en-
courage business, who is going to supply taxes to pay
for low-cost housing and sanitation and narcotics re-
habilitation?"

Christman even had a way with his enemies. When
a new cardinal was installed in New York, the two
powerful men met for the first time at a communion
breakfast. "You're not hitting me hard enough," the
governor told the clergyman. "Speak up when you
think I'm wrong."

But of all the political arts, Alexander Christman
was most successful at practicing the art of patronage;
for he had learned it was the *sine qua non* of politics
to see to it that people were indebted to you. He
learned that loyalty, purchased at a price, kept a man
in office and was far more reliable than loyalty based
on a common cause. If it were not so, an incumbent
would be destroyed if he ever found it necessary to
alter his philosophic position.

Of all the men he had known, none more personified
the pure politican than the man sitting next to him in
the basement sauna of Windy Meadow. He had known
Vincent Avrocanti, chairman of his party's state organization, for twenty-four years, but he had never seen

the ex-fight manager in the nude before. It shocked him. Rolls of fat, like excess filling in a layer cake, oozed from Avrocanti's chest, waist, and stomach. His thighs were so heavy they seemed to overflow his knees. Avrocanti's ankles were so swollen he looked like a penguin standing in a puddle. Famous as one of the great drinkers in the history of New York State politics, the obese real estate man looked by noon as if he had finished his first bottle of the day. The bags under his limpid green eyes sagged heavily, and he sweated profusely. He always seemed sleepy and inattentive, but Christman knew that nowhere was there a shrewder or more astute American politician. Avrocanti's understanding was deceptively simple: he believed politics was the art of using·favors to indebt anyone and everyone to the man in power. He functioned well. It was he who had taught Christman long ago that the appearance of power was frequently more important than the fact of power. Even for a wealthy man, Christman was a competent student. He saw clearly that what political people believed was often more important than any real power held by a public official.

Naked and sweating in the steaming sauna, Christman scratched an itch on his right thigh and looked at Avrocanti as he had not before, while they reviewed minor political decisions.

"To hell with him," Christman said, when they discussed one of a dozen of minor appointments. "I'm not going to appoint Prysox's nephew to anything."

"He's done a lot for the party, Governor."

The chairman had dealt with Christman's moods before, and so he knew the easiest way to get what he wanted was to minimize its value.

"It's strictly an honorary. Hundred-a-day, max two thousand five hundred dollars. We need him."

"The kid is a lush, Vinnie," Christman said. "I couldn't hire him as a ticket clerk for the airline. How can I put him on the taxpayers' back?"

"Governor," the chairman said. They had been together a long time.

Christman sighed. Avrocanti smiled at his reluctant acceptance.

"Jesus, do you ever get any exercise, fella?"

Avrocanti laughed, the mounds of flesh quaking obscenely.

Christman did not even smile. Avrocanti nimbly tried to find a way to please him. It was not like the early days anymore. Christman had gotten touchy. He knew they all got like that after a while, believing that they had been elected to office out of some divine perfection in themselves. They did not like to be reminded that the thirty thousand people who pushed doorbells before election day did it for a reason.

It was sticky. Avrocanti knew he needed a quick victory. It did not worry him. He had brought it with him.

He described to the governor the entente he had worked out, as he did each December, with the regulars of the opposition party: the legislature would create five new Supreme Court judgeships in Queens County. Two of the fourteen-year appointments would go to the legislative leaders, who would reciprocate with enough votes to give Christman a wafer-thin majority in both houses.

"Nice?" Avrocanti said. "And it costs us nothing, Guv."

Christman winced. "A little raw, isn't it?" he asked. It was softer than the words he wanted to use. But Avrocanti was the wrong man to give the slightest indication that he would not be running forever. One convincing hint, Christman thought, and this green-eyed wop will be conniving all over the state. Christman knew exactly how it would come out of the chairman's mouth: "I'm his staunchest. Right? I'm just saying *if* he doesn't go again."

Christman realized he was not listening.

"I said it's your legislative program, Guv," the chairman prodded.

"All right," Christman said dully. It was true that as governor he could veto the special interest bills of legislators in both parties. But some he passed. And Avrocanti was always ready to get them sideline jobs as directors of banks and insurance companies. That meant money, which he learned long ago was what politics was all about.

"Anything else, Vince?" he said, hoping it was over.

"Good?" The chairman grinned. He was not yet ready to let it go. It was good. But the sauna was hot and Christman was sweating. He stood and walked to the door. He returned with a bucket of ice water. He did not bother to offer it to Avrocanti. When Christman sat down, he dipped his hands in the frigid water and sponged his face and chest. He was still hot. Finally, he lifted the bucket and poured its contents over his head.

The chairman grinned, his bald head gleaming. Then the fat face opened into a vast smile that showed the gold tooth near the back of his mouth.

"The county chairmen are really busting it this time, Guv," he said, "but I got to know when you're going to go."

"I haven't decided I'm going to run, Vincent. You know that."

It didn't stop Avrocanti. "After you tell off the vice-president tonight, you're going to *have* to run."

"No, Vincent."

"A lot of people are counting on you, Guv," Avrocanti said.

Christman stood. He was unable to lie outright to Avrocanti. It would be suicidal to tell him the truth. He grinned as broadly as he could. But he could not bring himself to cuff the chairman on his fat neck. He did not want to touch him at all.

Avrocanti smiled back, sensing the governor's reluctance. He knew instinctively that there was something important he did not know. Or Christman was listening to someone he did not know. Or Christman had a new woman, which was something he should also know.

"Don't mention the Americana speech to me, Vincent. I can see it in your eyes."

"Never, Guv. I'm not the guy to talk about a three-million-dollar speech."

Christman did not react.

"That's what it cost you in campaign contributions," Avrocanti added. "But what the hell, it may have been worth it in the polls."

The governor did not even turn his eyes to acknowledge the bait. It was as if his consuming passion for the intricate undulations of political intrigue and response had died, like passion for a woman that has gone sour.

A sphinx, the chairman thought. The biggest gung-ho Yahoo on God's green earth has turned into a goddamn sphinx. He wondered if it meant Christman had finally decided to run and knew that, for a time, he had to hold it in himself. He knew he could double the three million dollars in contributions Christman lost, with the simple promise that Lieutenant Governor Walker would succeed Christman if he got to the White House. Avrocanti had always gone first for the guys who were hungry for a buck. Give me greed over ambition any time, he told his county leaders, in fighters, broads, or governors.

Christman sat down opposite the chairman. They squatted silently on opposite benches, each alone with his thoughts. The two men had been together a very long time, and so when they knew that words between them might injure their dependence on each other, they did not speak. But this was a time when Avrocanti could not leave it alone. Whenever it was time for change, enough was at stake to justify almost any risk.

"Guv," he said, finally, "can I help?"

Christman looked at him. "I'm getting there, Vincent," he said slowly. "I have to do it my own way."

Avrocanti was getting no closer to what he had come for. Any opening, any sign of real need or obligation on the part of Christman, even the slightest gesture of benevolent indulgence, might have opened the door. He was carrying a heavy contract, heavy enough so that if it were successful, he would have the cash in his treasury to finance a dozen party leadership fights. He would have been happier if the circumstances were a little bit better. But they never were when you caught White House fever.

"Governor," he said slowly, feeling his way, "I had a peculiar meeting with the Consolidated Electric people. A very peculiar meeting."

Christman came alert so quickly it startled the chairman.

"Usually they talk about power lines and variances, the crap pending before various departments and commissions. Don't get me wrong. They got to be able to talk to somebody unofficially. But this was different."

Avrocanti knew when Christman was really attentive. That had not changed in all those years since they talked about the first campaign. And he knew how to talk to the old Christman. Jeez, he could talk to anybody once he knew what they really wanted.

"What did they want, Vincent?"

"They want to help you, Guv. They really do."

"Oh?"

"It's something about auxiliary barges. They want to put gas generators on barges around Manhattan. Then if there's a power shortage, boom! They can fix it up."

"What's so special about that?" Christman said.

Avrocanti knew the tone of voice well. It had better be a good answer. The room was hot and the chairman hated it.

"What's special about that, Vincent?" the governor asked again.

The tone frightened Avrocanti. "It seemed like nothing," he said with a shrug. "I tried to handle it."

"Yes, Vincent?"

"I couldn't."

The chairman was wary of the famous grin, cursing his own instinctive reaction to Christman.

"Come on," Avrocanti finally said, "will you stop picking on me and tell me what the hell is going on."

"I'm going to break them, Vincent. I'm going to break every last one of those miserable sons of bitches."

"No-o-o-o," Avrocanti wailed, "we don't need a fight. We don't want that kind of fight, Alex," he said, standing painfully and waddling across the room. "Be president, be a good president. Then we can get *all* the sons of bitches."

There were times when the ex-fight manager became

confused or upset but these were rare, and then he would deal with the governor like any other fighter.

"I got to get out of here," Avrocanti wailed. "I can't take heat. I can't take moisture. I can't take it anymore."

Christman was laughing harder than he had in months. He took the chairman by the wrist and led him outside the steaming room toward the indoor pool, still laughing as the fat man tried to catch his breath.

"Vincent, jump," he said, through the tears in his eyes.

"No, no, no, I can't take water!" the chairman wailed. "I'm sorry I ever got into this insane business! Alex, if I have to swim only in Scotch whiskey! And with, God forbid, only Dorothy Fish of the Liberal party!"

The two men were laughing hysterically. Like children, they would look at each other's faces and laugh again. It was as if there were no urgent concerns here, no future, and only the insane sense of camaraderie of the past that had been so much in both their lives. If we were Greek, Avrocanti thought, we would be dancing gloriously together. Christman was only glad that they were alone.

"Alex," Avrocanti said hysterically, "if you want to believe all men are honest, then by Christ, you have to live as if they were."

"Bullshit, fella," Christman said. And they laughed hysterically again.

Both men tried to calm themselves but giggled as they peered at each other through tear-filled eyes.

"Vincent!" Christman shouted, "you are the greatest con artist alive!"

"Bullshit!" Avrocanti screeched. "Second greatest!"

Christman laughed hard, reminded, as Avrocanti wanted him to be, of the great wars they had been through together.

"Alex," the chairman said now, taking his hand, "do it for me."

Christman pulled his big paw out of Avrocanti's grasp. The chairman fell on the blue-white tile.

Christman tried to help the fat man up and realized

he was unhurt. "I'm sorry," he said. "I'm really sorry. I just can't help you."

The chairman moved his heavy thighs. He pushed himself to a kneeling position and then painfully stood up.

"Vince," Christman added, looking into his green eyes, his hand on the back of his neck, "I'll make you rich. I'll make your goddamned daughter rich, I'll even make your son-in-law rich. But I can't do it."

Avrocanti smiled wanly and shrugged. It was a heavy contract, but he would trade it for that kind of Christman IOU anytime.

"Do you really need a fight with Consolidated Electric now, Alex?" he asked. "They're a big contributor."

"I can't avoid this one."

"Why?"

"It's too big."

"Bigger than an inauguration at Sixteen hundred Pennsylvania Avenue?"

Christman stopped himself quickly. He looked at the fat man warily. "I guess you know," he said. "I never could fool you, Vincent."

"Know what?"

The governor grinned. Even the chairman loved him when he grinned. Talk about Ike Eisenhower. Or John Kennedy. Christman had it all over them. "I'm not going to do it," he told Vincent Avrocanti. Then he knew it was a very foolish truth to tell. The fat man damn well might believe him.

CHAPTER SIX

THE CHAUFFEUR-DRIVEN COURTLAND LIMOUSINE was
stopped briefly by a guard at the gate house. He in-
formed the Windy Meadow hidden command post of
their arrival.

In the rear compartment, Athena Courtland had decided to remove the other nylon. She stuffed the stocking in Roger's pocket. Then she stretched her
handsomely tanned legs and decided that it would be
impossible for anyone to tell she was not wearing hose.

Roger pushed his handkerchief into the corner of
the rear compartment cushion.

"I don't know whether it makes me happier that I
have you or that I am married to you," he whispered
in Athena's ear as they walked slowly up the three
tiers of white marble steps to the front door of the
immense Georgian mansion. She touched his hand as
if she were closing an electrical circuit.

As they reached the last stair, a white-wigged groom
in pink satin pants opened the door and bid the Courtlands good evening. Another groom in the eighteenth-
century costume of the court of France took Mrs.
Courtland's white mink coat. The large oval hallway,
with its white and off-white brocade walls, glittered
with gold filigreed candelabra that shone in the black
and white parqueted tile floor. In the center of the
foyer was a huge portrait of Governor Alexander
Christman. The cartoon style of the painting portrayed
the governor with tea rose cheeks and bright blue eyes,
as if Dick Tracy had traded his famous chin for Alex
Christman's crooked grin. The left eye of the full face
was closed in a wink. Staring at the picture, Roger

Courtland could almost hear Alex Christman's famous greeting, "Hiya fella!"

For perhaps forty seconds, but no more, the Courtlands were alone in the anteroom, captives of the portrait. Then the governor was standing in front of them.

"Hey, Roger, we finally named that park after you," Christman said.

Roger Courtland smiled. "It was a small park," he murmured, and they all laughed with him.

"You look as if you had a hard night, Governor," Athena Courtland said.

"Hey," Christman laughed, turning to her, "that's not nice."

The three of them turned as the First Lady glided into the room. She was a tall woman whose angular bone structure had pinched her face into a look of seemingly permanent disapproval. Her black hair was stretched back in a tight chignon at the back of her skull, which accentuated the haughty features that some people said came from living with a great deal of money for a very long time. She once had looked like Bette Davis, the movie star. The trouble was that not many years later, she had come to look like the kind of tense, overwrought character Bette Davis might play. Except that the enormous energy of her youth had become the nervous tension of middle age, and she no longer could control her fluttering hands or her feverish sense of disappointment. It had always seemed a trifle unfair to her that she who had rescued Christman from utter disaster should not thereafter possess him for life. And perhaps she was right.

If anything preserved her sense of identity in Christman's world, it was her roots in the establishment constantly reminding her that by talent, breeding, good taste, and the right of her inheritance, she would always matter. She belonged at the top of that special world of the cultured, the powerful, the accomplished; that very special board of directors of the American elite who ruled their private domains as they believed they should rule the public domain.

Their son, Joshua Morgan Christman, named for her father, was beside her. The brittle Morgan seriousness was in his face, but as his blue eyes set on his distinguished father, his face came alive with that unmistakable smile.

Christman turned away from them to grab his son in a bear hug. It was as if he had become so used to touching everyone that his son deserved something special. He squeezed him tightly in his arms, clapping his back fervently like a coach congratulating a victorious quarterback. Then he released him.

"Wow, that was some speech. Did you see the polls?" the young man said ecstatically. "I was right. I told you if you put it on the line we could start moving. Fifty-three percent! Fif-tee three pur-cent! This damn country is finally changing!"

"Fifteen years old," the governor said, pointing a thumb at Joshua and grinning proudly. "I'm not gonna run," he whined happily. "You just can't keep getting away with that kind of stuff. Nebraska isn't New York. You ought to know that. Right, Roger?"

"Alex," Roger Courtland said, "I don't think you could run third if it was a two-man race."

They all laughed, as if they had been infected quickly by the governor's special joy. Morganna Christman gently cleared her throat. The governor said, "Dear," kissed his wife warmly on the cheek, and then reached out to touch Athena Courtland's soft hand.

"Alex," Morganna Christman said, the moment she noticed his interest in the beautiful woman.

"She's a Harman," the First Lady added nervously, as if to tell him this woman was not his kind. Then she quickly led Athena toward the mansion's vast main hall. "Come along, Joshua," she commanded, calling her son without turning to look at him.

The governor patted Roger Courtland's generous stomach.

"Marriage," the executive replied, permitting himself to be taken to the small study Christman used as an office, off the main hall. In a box on the desk that had once belonged to Samuel Adams were the historic dueling pistols fired in the Burr-Hamilton duel. They were the governor's most famous stage prop, having been offered half in jest to anyone who disagreed with him. Whichever pistol was chosen, Christman would play out the joke by telling him, "Sorry fella, that was Burr's. He lost."

Roger Courtland eyed the pistols, and the governor lifted the lid. Courtland hefted a pistol and then sighted with a long, still forearm. "They were rough guys in those days," Christman said, shaking his head. "Really tough fellas."

The broadcast executive put down the pistol. He knew there were times when it was simpler to be blunt. "Well, Governor," he asked, "have you made up your mind?"

Christman groaned. "Not you, too, Roger."

"We can help. Any correspondent you want to cover your campaign. Money. Choice of time. Hell, I own the best political intelligence system in the country. Remember what we did to Gene McCarthy? The Kennedy guys had answers before his press releases were out, and the press patted them on the back for being well organized. And Agnew? We *really* had him going ape."

"You treat Griswold decently."

Courtland shrugged. "He's the president."

Christman laughed, knowing this was the kind of man who was flattered he had taken the time and trouble to charm him. "Roger," he said slowly, "let me be very frank. I think I'm just tired of being everybody's doormat. If you could do what you want in that job, that's one thing. But Jesus, when they wrote the Constitution, they tried to be damn sure no one would have any power at all." He shrugged. "Maybe it's a good thing. But I don't think it's really for me."

Christman poured them each a glass of Lillet, handed one to Roger Courtland and extended his arm in a toast. "To America. The greatest democracy in the world." Then he swallowed and said, "And that's one of the troubles with it."

Courtland ignored the bait. Slowly, he drained his glass.

"You're doing a big story on the power crisis, right?" the governor asked.

Courtland nodded.

"Now that's really something. That's what's going to change this country, nuclear power. Real nuclear power. Not all the talk we've had for ten years. Lower steel prices. Whole new cities across the country. Low-cost housing instead of political bullshit. That's where the twentieth century is coming out, not with a bunch of guys making policy decisions."

Courtland looked eager. "It's trouble," he said. "Three-quarters of a million in production costs and News keeps postponing the air date. They keep talking about conservation. The unions."

"Nuclear power is going to save the environment. Save it!" Christman said. "It's going to save this country. That's exciting."

They talked for half an hour, the chairman of the board eagerly absorbing the detailed information Christman had stored in his head. For both of them it was as if the party that was about to begin did not exist, and they were engrossed in a vision of the future that provided a feeling of exaltation, of an America that again led the world in thought, in deed, in its actions. Both men turned at the tentative knock on the door. The governor beamed when his son walked in. But he was less happy when he saw the orange sheets with the weekly public opinion polls in his hand.

"Jesus, fella," Christman groaned, "not again. I got the vice-president coming."

The three men laughed, and Joshua Christman took special pleasure in the company of his father. Roger Courtland had no children, and he envied the governor his son.

"Keep after him," he whispered. "Don't you dare let up."

The boy smiled broadly as Christman stood and motioned Roger Courtland to follow him, but the broadcast executive stopped the governor at the door.

"Will you take a look at the script, Governor?" he asked. "A three-part series is big for us. We would appreciate it."

"Sure," Christman said, "be glad to have the whole staff comb it over. Hell, they know a helluva lot more about the power crisis than I do. Send it over to Arthur Roe at Whitman, Gelman. He can handle it."

For three hours, Alexander Christman performed the amenities expected of a governor of the state of New York. There was the legislator who sought a favor no more complex than an introduction to a surgeon Christman had hired for the state university, whose skill could save the paralyzed leg of a nephew. There were bankers who, in return for buying state bonds, clearly wanted it known they expected something from him: approval of legislation that permitted bank mergers anywhere in the state. There were upstate manufacturers seeking loans from the state's Job Development Commission, although the loans granted were not always used to supply jobs.

"Leon," the governor told a Johnstown toy manufacturer, "you bought a company up in Canada, for chrissake, with the loan you got three years ago."

Leon Canaris shrugged. "Our distribution center is in Montgomery County. We make more toys, we need more people to distribute them."

"You got a pair of brass balls, fella."

Canaris grinned, but said nothing.

"I don't know whether to prosecute you or write you off, Leon."

"Suppose I just promise to elect you three new assemblymen."

Christman shook his head in disapproval, but he could not help liking Canaris. "Okay, fella," he said, clapping him on the shoulder. "You got yourself a deal."

Those who knew the governor well understood that this afternoon's backslapping performance was as polished as ever. But they also knew when his mind was far away, his concentration not wholly with the people or the words of the moment. He was like a well-skilled actor who, after playing Falstaff a thousand times in a hundred different towns, can tour *Waiting for Godot,* and then step back into the familiar role without an hour's rehearsal. It was as if he drew the substance of the character he played from the very substance of the people surrounding him. And he responded to them as they expected Governor Alexander Christman to respond: without hesitation or deliberation.

But the Alexander Christman with whom they had weathered three campaigns no longer existed, except as a character he had made out of the stuff of himself, and then found he could not abandon when he tired of the role. Politics, he knew, whether at the helm of the state of New York or in the pinnacle of power in Washington, was, for him, no longer creative or fulfilling. It was a game. When he was younger, he believed there were worlds to conquer. Now he could only see the new worlds that there were to be built.

. The men around him never seemed to learn to distinguish between the appearance of power and the fact of power. They saw him as nothing more than a great lord who could command the fulfillment of their private wishes. Twentieth-century rulers do not change the world. He sensed they shared with Morganna Christman the notion that nothing could actually be changed, indeed, should not be changed. So their objectives were drawn solely from the world they knew to be real: money, position, respect, and property. They were like men who experienced ultimate fulfillment in the purchase of a private airplane, as if they never learned that every bird in heaven already knew how to fly.

The grinding flutter of a large helicopter came through the open window. Arthur Roe immediately broke off his conversation with a major banker and moved quickly to the governor's side. Together the two men walked to the main hall to greet the vice-president of the United States.

"You ought to have a witness to your conversation with Whitmore," the lawyer told him.

"George isn't that bad," the governor said.

Roe was composed and the governor noted it. He also noticed how easily the lawyer slipped into the shell of the "faithful servant" when he was troubled, and Christman wondered why that familiar form of cowardice had never been identified in his mind with

Arthur Roe before. The lawyer did not leave. He waited, like a servant, for the sign from the master. Christman did not want to embarrass him.

The lawyer smiled wanly. He saw the winter sunset glistening in the dormer above the door as it was held open to admit the vice-president. George Whitmore was a short man, but with the sun shining at his back, he might as well have been the archangel of God, which was precisely at that moment what he looked like. Golden rays glistened in his pomaded stay-comb pompadour, as if the perpetual recognition of the small man's significance were, in fact, the will of God. And if Alexander Christman were not a believer, Vice-President George Whitmore had enough evangelism for both of them.

"Waal, Alex," the tiny man said, as he took huge strides across the foyer, his hand extended. "Ahm heah. Sorry to be late, but you know when I lost my wife, the late governor of our state, who succeeded me after two terms, I lost my good right ahm."

Christman took his hand as if it were an electrical switch.

"Stop that cracker shit, will you, George," he said, trying very hard to look as if he got the joke.

Whitmore looked about the foyer, his eyes moving slowly, stopping finally upon the face of Arthur Roe. Christman nodded to the lawyer and he quickly left them. Whitmore relaxed now, accepting the fact that they were alone.

Neither of them spoke. And as he rarely did, Christman felt the need of filling that void in time. So he said, "I am sure you know how much my family appreciates your lending the dignity of your great office to this occasion."

Whitmore laughed through his nose. With a wave of his hand, the gesture he had been taught, he indicated that the favor was less than a trifle. The vice-president was not only a short man, but like many short men, one addicted to pomades, exercises, sunlamps, and other devices that might make more of what he actually had, as if each square inch of his body had to do the work of twice the flesh of a larger man. He was the kind of man the sight of whom made Alexander Christman physically ill, and it was only under certain circumstances that Christman was willing to disguise his feelings. This was not one of those occasions.

Vice-President Whitmore did not extend his hand. "I hear you have some troubles," he said.

Christman shrugged. "We always have problems. It's a big state," he said noncommittally.

"I didn't say problems, Alex. I said troubles," the vice-president repeated.

The governor grinned at him. Then his big hand moved and grabbed the well-developed bicep in Vice-President Whitmore's left arm. Christman squeezed hard, but it brought no visible reaction.

"Well," the Tennessean said slowly, trying to match the Christman smile, "the president has asked me to tell you that he has heard a lot of stories, right out of the U. S. attorney's office here in New York. Some people seem to think there is hanky panky in your administration. He just wanted you to know he doesn't believe a one of 'em."

"He's quite a fella," Christman said. Then he stopped smiling and waited expectantly, not wanting to commit himself even to a faint interest, as if by wholly embracing the artificial casualness of the conversation, he could force Whitmore into more openly stating the threat. But the vice-president was no amateur. He had lobbed a grenade ever so gently into Christman's court. And the governor was either going to have to pick it up and throw it back, or let it explode.

Neither doubted what Christman would do. "I'm delighted," he said without a trace of sarcasm. "You mean the president wants to put in a good word for me?"

Vice-President Whitmore had his opening. He moved into it quickly and deftly. "I didn't say that, Governor. I didn't say that at all."

Christman did not like the game. Whitmore did. And so the vice-president said with amazement: "You know the president never interferes in matters of this kind."

"Bullshit, George," the governor told him, his voice hard and bitter. "Your boss is the worst shark we've been stuck with since Calvin Coolidge. He's raising the party's campaign chest by selling jobs in Commerce, in HUD, and you know it. Jesus, he's even got that millionaire's son running the Justice Department. The only trouble is that this isn't 1923. So let's stop horsing around."

The vice-president shrugged, unable or unwilling to suppress the trace of a smile. Christman had refused to second his nomination at the convention three years ago. But that was past. Whitmore raised his arm as he started to say something, but the door opened and Christman's son walked quickly to the governor's side. The boy shook hands with the vice-president and said, "The guests are ready, Dad. And a little impatient."

Josh started to press the point, but something in his father's face stopped him.

"We shouldn't keep all them nice people waiting, Alex," Whitmore said, patting the tight corset that held in his stomach as though he had just finished a banquet dinner, not realizing, perhaps, that he had told Christman who initiated the investigation in the first place.

"Is there any more, George?" the governor asked, still angry.

"Nope."

"He didn't say anything else?"

"Nope," he said smugly again, steering Christman toward the door.

Christman stopped for a moment and reached into his breastpocket for the handkerchief he used to clean his glasses.

"Mr. Vice-President," he said, his voice rasping out the words like a file moving across corrugated iron, "exactly what would you do in my situation?"

Whitmore fairly glowed with satisfaction, already forming in his mind the words and gestures he would use when he reported this to the president. He could see the dark-eyed man toss back his head and laugh with his strange har-har-har growl, jowls shaking, as

he told how he had jousted with a man the president
never liked, Alexander Christman of New York.

"Waal," Whitmore said, his hand brushing the
straight, graying hair at his temple, "now let me see. Let
me see. Governor, I'll tell you. The president asked me
to sound out your feelings on acting as Honorary National Cochairman of the reelection campaign. He's got
faith in you. Ah'd accept. Yes-sirree, I'd accept right
quick. An ah'd be willing to bet five dollahs to a
Bentley Silver Cloud, that U. S. attorney who's botherin'
you, he wouldn't want to make no trouble for one
of our own. Now you think about it, heah?"

Vice-President Whitmore's hand was at the door,
and he started to turn the ornate brass ornament carved
with the head of Thomas Jefferson. The governor's
hand shot out and he grabbed the lapel of Whitmore's
immaculate blue silk suit. The vice-president's hand
flew up to protect his face, reacting as if Christman
were about to strike him. The governor glanced at his
son, and then said slowly:

"You go home and tell that little cocksucker now
I know how scared he really is. And you tell him just
that way."

He released the little man and grinned now, as he
said:

"Thanks, George. Thanks a lot for coming."

And then he was gone, leaving the startled vice-
president standing in the doorway. Whitmore tried
quickly to decide whether it would be more embarrassing to avoid the party entirely. Then he turned
slowly on the balls of his feet until he was facing the son.

"Young man," he told him very slowly, "your
father is out of his goddamn mind."

"Do you really think so, Mr. Whitmore?" Joshua
Christman asked.

"Sonny," the vice-president told him, "nobody bucks
this president of the United States. You make sure
you tell him that."

The boy grinned. Vice-President Whitmore turned
on his heels and quickly walked back through the
foyer to the front door and was gone.

Later that evening, Governor Alexander Christman of New York received a telephone call from the White House. His son stood by the antique desk as he talked briefly with an assistant to the president. When he put down the phone, he said:

"Well, fella, I guess you won yourself a trip to Florida. It seems I have to go down and see the president."

"Dad," the boy said, "you can win. You can beat them."

This time Governor Alexander Christman did not reply. He was wondering whether anyone could force him to prove it.

CHAPTER SEVEN

GOVERNOR ALEXANDER CHRISTMAN flipped the radio switch on his throat microphone as the big jet idled under his hand. He identified himself to the control tower and was cleared for takeoff as if he owned the airport.

The young man did not take his eyes off his father as the two jet engines roared in response to his touch. The big plane shivered beneath them. When the engines whined to their peak, he released the air brake, and as if suddenly liberated, the silver dart leaped forward and sped down the runway. Outside the plane, landing lights whizzed past, holding his side vision until he saw the takeoff point less than seconds ahead. He pulled the wheel toward his belly, forcing the plane to climb steeply, like a bird suddenly escaping danger. They were breathless as the plane zoomed upward at half the speed of sound, not easing their lungs until he leveled at 18,250 feet with the green ball of the instrument panel stabilizer in perfect synchronization.

Behind them the cabin door opened and Christman's pilot, copilot, crew chief, and steward all pushed into the hatchway with Sergeant Devlin, the governor's bodyguard, following them.

"Very classy," the pilot said, the blood come back into his face.

Christman could not see him and he grinned, pleased with himself.

"You ought to get a license, Governor," the copilot ventured. "You really should."

The governor was beaming as he turned to look at the circle behind him.

"Well," he said happily, stretching his arms over

his head, "you fellas look tough, but deep down . . ." Then, glancing over his shoulder at them, he roared with laughter, unhooked the latch on his seat belt, and decided not to finish the sentence.

Joshua sat beaming beside him on the chrome settee designed for his plane. The governor leaned back in the chair and swiveled it to peer down at the eastern seaboard. Nothing ever cleared his mind quite so quickly as the lofty sense of solidarity he found within himself in an airplane. He could watch city lights vanish and sense the immediate concerns that pushed all else from the front of his mind evaporate with them. It was as if the height itself put events in his own life into perspective, and with a little effort he could squint into the distance and sense his own future. He found in himself no occult powers, and indeed if he could, he would not trust any perception of events to come that he might have. The sense of perspective operated on him in a different way. In the serenity of thoughts that were clear, he found precisely what he wanted and decided how he would go about getting it. He had long ago learned that deciding what what he did want was far more important than guessing what would happen. And so now he knew that he did not want to become a candidate, which meant that his meeting in Florida would be an easy one, for he had no quarrel with the president.

Christman turned to glance at his son. The boy was still watching his father. He had long since learned not to prod him when he wished to be alone with his thoughts. Their eyes met.

"Hi," Joshua Christman said, wanting his father to know how much he appreciated his attention.

The governor smiled warmly, slowly focussing on the boy's presence.

"It's that time of year again. Are you going to help me figure out what to get you?"

His son reached out to touch his father's knee, and then changed his mind. "You know what I want for my birthday?" he told the governor. "To be with you through the whole campaign. That's a real present."

He looked at the boy's face and held back a sigh,

telling himself that he had not been tough enough with anyone lately. Yet he was sensitive enough to understand that this was no place to start. He did not know how he could tell anyone his age what American Nuclear meant or why he felt it was the only path that would lead to real accomplishment. So the governor hid his feelings, wishing only to give his son a sense of the deep love he felt for him.

"Why do you want me to run?" he asked him.

The boy grinned as if the question were unreal. "I'm a part of you," he said. "I am you. So I know what you can do." He looked away in embarrassment.

"Suppose I do run. And suppose I win. And then suppose I am a very bad president?"

Joshua Christman looked back at his father, a touch of the Christman anger in his handsome face. "You don't really think that's possible, Dad?" he said. "Not with somebody who cares the way you do."

He became silent and his son was wholly engrossed in the expression on his father's face as he stared into the blackness outside the plane. It was rare that Joshua had seen the ever present gaiety disappear from him, for it had always seemed to him that there was very little that visibly touched his father. But he wanted to reach him now and this time he was unafraid of interrupting his thoughts. So he touched his shoulder and said, "Please run," knowing he sounded as if he were eight years old.

The governor turned toward him, the carefree grin back, his face mirroring the playful pixie the voters saw in him. "Sure," he said. "The only trouble is I don't want the goddamn job."

He was pleased that he was able to say it, not only to himself, but to someone else. But he still was inhibited enough not to be able to refer to it as anything but "the job," whether he was talking to his own son or anyone else. Occasionally, with the small children he frequently saw on a school visit around the state, he could be glib.

Alex Christman could still remember the boy at P.S. 81 in Riverdale, who he later learned, when he decided to write to him, was named Mark Johnman.

The eight-year-old waved his hand and very seriously asked, "Governor Christman, when are you going to be president of the United States?" He asked the boy his name and then replied: "Tiger, I don't think I'm going to get that far."

Now he told himself that if it could be done with a sense of joy and a feeling of achievement in the sheer doing of it, he might feel differently. But there were no answers in the black night outside the plane window. And unlike other men who he thought believed in the traditional aspirations that were called glory, righteousness, survival, honor, and country, to Alex Christman they had become empty notions in twentieth-century America. If other politicians were more honest, they too would acknowledge their total belief in one concept: the self. And quixotic though it seemed, he did not think his country was ready to be remade in the image of Alex Christman. Johnson, Eisenhower, Coolidge, McKinley, the second-rate presidents, had been second-rate because they tried to follow instead of lead. They believed in finding out what people wanted and then tried to deliver. Kennedy had been different, the governor thought, and realized quickly he had never admitted that even to himself before.

The boy struggled to find the words that would open his father's thoughts, but as he started to speak, the governor held up his hand to silence him. They both could feel the plane slowly descending in its long gliding path and, without thinking, Christman fastened his seat belt.

"Why?" the boy asked.

He had decided he had to answer him. And very slowly, he said: "Something's wrong in this country, and nobody knows what it is. That's the tragedy. It was easier when we could believe the war was the trouble. It wasn't. The trouble is with us. I can't solve that problem."

Alexander Christman stopped, as if he had answered the question. After the plane touched down and taxied to a private hangar and the first moist, hot breath of subtropical air touched his face, his spirit seemed to

change. Christman noticed the airport steward at the
foot of the gangway, and he stepped aside to permit
Devlin to pass.

Devlin jogged down the stairs two steps at a time.
He pried the attendant's fingers loose from the railing
and gently bodied him aside. The man pushed back
and Devlin gave him a quick frisk, still keeping his
body between the man and the governor, as the stranger
started to wave to attract Christman's attention. The
man finally turned and slowly walked away. Devlin
bounded back up the stairs.

"He says there's a phone call from your wife."

Christman looked startled. Morganna had not tele-
phoned him in years.

The look on Devlin's face reminded Christman there
was very little that had to be spelled out for Devlin,
and he grinned. Devlin carefully looked around the humid private airport which was dark now, except for a
few night lights inside a hangar. Satisfied, he walked
slowly toward the operations building, his eyes still alert
to movement in the shadows. Christman sat down inside the plane. A few minutes later, he saw Devlin
waving to him from the doorway of the clapboard hut,
and he moved out of the plane and quickly down the
metal stairway. There was a thin line of sweat across
his forehead by the time he reached Devlin.

"Couple of night attendants," he told Christman.
"They're all right."

Christman walked inside, waved and called, "Hiya,
fellas," to the operations men and picked up the phone.
The tiny baby voice was so familiar.

"Hi," he said.

"Is Josh all right?" she asked him. "I know what
happens when you get inside an airplane, Alexander."

"He's fine," he said, shaking his head with amazement. "It was a good trip."

"Is he flying back with you?"

It was as if he had suddenly been transported back
to the years when the boy was an infant and they
had been so very different with each other. He felt a
sudden warmth toward her. The telephone does that,

he told himself, forcing the feeling to disappear quickly.

"No," he finally said. "He's booked on a commercial flight."

"That's good," she said. Then she was silent, as if she had no other question to ask him. He sensed the awkwardness and said, as gently as he could, "Good night, Morganna. Sleep well."

"Thank you, Alexander," she replied.

His son was standing beside him as he hung up the phone. He turned and walked back to the counter and shook hands with the two night men. "Thanks for the use of the hall," he told them, "and let me buy you a drink." His hand was out of his pocket by then, and with two fingers he flipped them a hundred-dollar bill.

"Either of you fellas married?" he asked. Before they had a chance to reply, he told them, "I hope you're as lucky as I am. How many guys have an old lady who still calls him Mister Terrific?" All the men were laughing as Joshua Christman looked peculiarly at his father, shook his head reproachfully, and then followed him out the door.

The waiting limousine had hurried them to the yacht club. Neither the man nor his son wanted to talk, and so the younger one undressed quickly alone in his room and went to sleep, knowing that he had to rush through sleep as well if they were to be in the boat before sunrise. His father knew he must sleep too. But he also knew he had been so sensitized to the past that even the red gelatin capsules would not help.

"I'm alone," he told himself as he lay on his back, his arms behind his head, watching on the ceiling the play of moonlight reflected from the water. "I've always been alone."

He remembered the immense elation he had felt when five million voters in his state first elected him governor, and he wondered how he could repay them. He never was sure whether he fully appreciated their acceptance of him, or simply reveled in the opportunity they had given him to conquer the people in the world of his wife. He did not like men designated leaders before they were born, but he discovered at first they were surprisingly easy to do business with. They never shouted. Or became angry. Or carried a grudge. And when he later found they were ruthless, not polite; that they were acquisitive, not generous; that they gave only lip service to charity, not real concern, he found in himself the impotent outrage of the voiceless poor. But they had taught him well. He did not rant in his speeches. He did not openly attack the leaders in his state. He carefully did what he thought needed to be done for the hungry, the jobless, the illiterate, and the poor.

"And that is what I'm going to do now," he told himself. "I'm going to do what I know is right."

He had thought it was going to be a bad night. But his body suddenly felt charged with energy as he reminded himself of his meeting with the president. He buried it. Buried it quickly in a part of himself where he could reach it and use it, and then he thought of the boat and the pleasure of morning.

Alexander Christman rolled on his side and was surprised that he was consciously drifting into sleep. Even after his body relaxed, his mind was still functioning. And the last thing he remembered was that he had fallen asleep believing there was a grin on his face.

The boy woke him forty minutes before the red Florida sun began to move above the horizon. By 7:20 they were sitting opposite each other in the flat-bottom boat and the sun now, like an ancient, life-generating force, was high and hot in the blue-white sky. Both the man and the boy were conscious of the silence surrounding them, broken only by the light swish of fishing line cutting through water.

"There!" the young man shouted, as he saw the streak of silver cut through the shallows twenty feet away. Then he saw his father's arm cock at the elbow and throw the thin rod forward. The whirr-whirr of the reel and the plunk of the bait on water were the only other sounds between them. A second later, the light blue nylon thread jerked off the spool as the bonefish ran with the bait. Christman sweated through ten, then twenty, thirty, forty seconds, and then his thumb flicked the drag lever of the rod. The fish broke out of the water seventy-five yards from the boat and, for a moment, they both thought it had spit the bait. But the line drew taut again, and the older man lurched across the middle seat toward his son.

"Take it," he shouted, poking his shoulder with the elbow holding the rod.

"No," the boy cried out. "He's yours."

The big man sat down in the middle seat. The boy deftly paddled the flat-bottom boat in the direction of the fish. Christman would reel in slowly and imperceptibly tighten the drag. He was forcing the fish to extend itself, to struggle harder to take line. Then the line went slack, as the fish circled toward the boat.

"I'm going to lose him," he called, "back it off!"

The boy paddled away from the fish, which suddenly stopped, swished back and forth in the water near the boat, trying to disgorge the hook, and then began to run again.

For forty minutes, working together, they struggled with the fish, knowing that only when it had beaten itself could it be reeled home. The sun magnified by the glistening water baked their bodies a brilliant red, and both of them felt their skin becoming dry and scaly. Toward the end, the fish could barely hold its own, swimming in a wide arc beyond the boat. When the fish was alongside, Joshua deftly scooped it tail first, and then turned the mouth of the net to trap the fish before he lifted it out of the water.

"That's a real tough bastard," the governor said.

The boy said nothing, staring at the fish as it lay gasping, one huge black eye staring at them. He covered the bonefish with a towel and held it down as he extracted the hook from its upper jaw. Then he forced the steel bit of the stringer through the mouth and out through its gill and pulled it taut. The boy tied a double half hitch around the boat ring and slung the fish over the side. Then he rinsed his hands, splashing water onto his face, his neck, and his chest.

"We're both going to be too sore to walk in the morning," he said, cocking his head to grin at his father.

Christman sat up straight and looked at his son. "I've never seen you so happy," he told him. "It's good."

"Dad, we've never been together like this before."

"Come on, fella."

"It's true."

The governor turned away. "We're all one big family," he said, knowing that he did not want to permit his son to see his face now. And knowing as well that he had long since given up deciding for anyone but himself, and that he had learned too much by now to give up easily the luxury of selfishness. He remembered exactly when he had first given up depending on Morganna, given up the need for her opposition because she had made him wait for her too often.

"Josh," he said softly, "I can't give you what you want. So please cut it out."

"I always hated her," he said, looking into his eyes, "didn't you know that?"

Christman shook his head back and forth, his mouth only forming the words. No. No. No. No. Then he said softly, "You don't mean it, Josh. No," as if he were crooning, not speaking.

"When I was eight years old," Josh said, gritting his teeth, "you had gone away on a campaign trip. You called and said you had to stay an extra night. Mother was furious. She cursed you and cursed you. All I said was, 'Mother, he's working hard for all of us.' She turned on me, slapped my face hard, and screamed: 'Shut up, you little ass sucker!' "

His jaw muscle was working hard. He looked older than fifteen.

"Don't cry," Christman told him harshly.

Josh shook his head. "I never cry," he said. "And I never told anybody."

"You were supposed to tell me," his father murmured softly. "That was why she hit you. It was only to hurt me."

"I'm not an ass sucker," the boy shouted back at him.

The big paw caressing his neck calmed him. He heaved a deep breath of the moist Key West air into his lungs. "I knew that when I was eight," he said. "It didn't help. What could be wrong with wanting to be like you?"

Christman did not know how to reply, because he wondered now where he had been or who he might have been with on that night seven years ago. He also knew that it was not Morganna who had destroyed their marriage.

"She is a good woman," he told his son, because he did not know what else he could say.

His son's hand touched his wrist and he turned to look at him again, knowing fully now how little time he had given the boy in fifteen years. In their way, they were both alone. But it was too late to do anything about it. "What do you want?" he asked, not able to stop the touch of anger in his voice.

"To be with you, Dad. I want to help every step of the way."

"Josh," he told him heavily, "I'm not going to run. I told you that," knowing he had to end it quickly and with as little pain as possible. He picked up the oars and pulled hard, quickly stroking the boat through the calm water past the inlet. He kept pulling hard without missing a stroke the whole mile and a quarter to the marina. The boy was out first to tie up the light skiff. As he watched his father, he asked tentatively, "Are we going to have lunch together?"

"Sure, fella," the governor replied. "You sore?"

"Only in the arms and shoulders," the boy replied impishly, not wanting to push him again.

In the suite they shared overlooking the bay, the boy heard his father order a man named Arthur Roe to meet him at the Christman ranch, approve the interim appointment of a state Supreme Court justice, and instruct his chief counsel in Albany to see to it that all state funds were removed from the Rochester bank in which an appointee of his, who had that morning criticized the governor's state budget, sat as chairman of the board. Then he called Mayor Thayer's ex-campaign manager, who was now president of a mutual fund, and asked him to sell a large block of the Rochester bank's stock.

"I don't give a hoot in hell if it is going up," he

heard his father say. "If you're on the team, then listen to the coach. That bastard's got to learn his lesson." And it pleased the boy. Because he was learning how a man handled things when he was really tough.

He heard Sergeant Devlin tell the governor, "The Convair will bring her down," wondering who he was talking about.

"Great," his father replied. "If I ever needed her, it's now."

"Kids can be rough," he heard Devlin tell his father.

"You're not kidding, fella," the familiar voice replied.

The boy and his father, the older man wearing a loose, white lace shirt that barely touched his skin, sat across an immaculate tablecloth overlooking the bay. Beneath them was the helicopter pad and beyond that the clear blue water they both loved deeply. They had each finished an appetizer of Coquilles St. Jacques that was exquisite. The boy tried not to lean back in the chair. In front of them were bowls filled with spicy sauces and a tureen of large, iced Gulf Stream shrimp.

"This is the first time," Christman said in his nasal voice, "that two broiled lobsters ate a couple of pounds of boiled shrimp."

The boy laughed happily, pleased that his father was no longer angry. There were times when he did really feel like a man, he knew, but there would always be one man who could make him feel eight years old again. So they ate the shrimp and drank piping hot oolong tea, until the governor saw Devlin at the end of the terrace. He waved him away.

The boy saw the signal, knew his father was not using the available excuse to leave him, and leaped to its meaning. "Are you sure you won't change your mind, Dad?" he asked delicately.

"No," he replied. But he did not want to leave it that way, so he leaned over and grabbed his son in a painful bear hug. "You know, sometimes there's more of Mother in you than there is in Mother. You never give up."

He felt the boy become tense and then pull away.

Devlin was still standing in the doorway, and this time Christman accepted the chance to escape, almost jumped at it, as if he had decided that each step he took toward his son pushed him farther away.

"Give Momma my love and a big kiss, fella," he said, "and tell her I'm not mad at her at all." Then he winked at his son and followed Devlin down the winding steps from the terrace to the helicopter. He would do anything in the world he could to please the boy. Except run again for public office, including the goddamn presidency of the United States.

CHAPTER EIGHT

LEAP YEAR, like the election of an American president, comes every four years, and for both occasions, February is the crucial month. By February in a presidential year, the hopes of a half-dozen ambitious men, and a thousand others who would fulfill their own lives by serving another man's ambition, have been dashed to pieces. It is that time, nine months before election day, when a handful of serious candidates are left, each with a minimum of $1 million to spend in search of the nomination of his party, without which there is no possibility of election.

In a year when an incumbent president is completing a second term on Pennsylvania Avenue, the tensions are greater. Eight years of alliances carefully constructed by powerful groups, from major corporations to labor unions, suddenly fall into jeopardy. New relationships can be forged, but they take a great deal of time and a great deal more money. So in the corridors of power where men walk who do not hold public office but nevertheless come very close to ruling America, there is a desire to resist change. These are men who wish things to remain as they are. They want to forge nothing less than the kind of succession to the departing president that will least upset the structure of power they have helped to make.

As the helicopter moved north along the Florida Keys toward Miami, Governor Alexander Christman knew this. He also knew that the speech he had made in New York, in its calculated way, had served notice that he was not, nor would he be, part of any succession to President Griswold. There were men, he believed, who had to understand that he no longer wished to be a private or public servant. He wanted them to realize clearly that if he moved into the house on Pennsylvania Avenue, he would do more than upset the apple cart. There would not be any apple cart left. For he knew deeply that few people understood how much the nation needed change. And he knew that it would only happen if the men walking softly through the corridors of power in New York, Chicago, Detroit, Dallas, and Los Angeles wished it to be so. They had to understand the priorities that existed beyond profits. Or someone had to force them to accept them. If they did not, and Alexander Christman believed it was so, someone would force them to accept change at the point of a gun.

He came back to the physical sensations of the present as the Navy pilot swung the small four-passenger ship north over the Miami Beach Gold Coast toward West Palm Beach. The landing pad had been chalked off a few hundred yards from the big California-style ranch house the president used as a winter White House. Christman could see the presidential yacht, heaving to offshore. There was movement on the boat, and the tanned, handsome man sitting on a stern deck chair threw up both arms in a wave: President Griswold. On the yacht, Christman realized, he would be his host's prisoner. He would be there until he was dismissed. This was no courtesy call. Griswold wanted something badly.

The young Navy pilot touched down expertly and cut the engines, and the governor clapped him on the back.

"Nice flight," he said,

"My pleasure, Governor. We got a lot of feeling in Ohio for some of the things you've done back in New York."

Christman grinned and winked at the ensign, reaching quickly for his hand. He slapped it between his two big paws, winked again and punched him in the ribs.

"See you soon, fella," he told him.

Attorney General Carlton P. Fishman helped the governor out of the plane and greeted him warmly. He waved away the four White House staff members the governor recommended when Griswold was elected and steered Christman slowly toward the dock. The governor stopped, turned, waved, and called, "Good to see you. How's it going?" They did not smile. Christman grinned and winked at them. Virtually in unison, they broke into huge smiles, as if in the unspoken language they all understood, they had triumphed over the attorney general's desire to bar communication between them.

Pleased with himself, the governor walked slowly beside the bald man with the fringe of graying red hair at his temples.

"It's good to see you, Alex," Attorney General Fishman said.

"You too. What's he want from me?"

Fishman walked slowly, head down.

"He wants to keep it. He doesn't want to give up the job to anyone else."

The governor laughed. "I didn't help pass the two-term amendment. What does he want?"

"Your help. Your prestige. Your money. Anything he can get. For all I know, he wants you on the ticket." Fishman turned surreptitiously to catch Christman's reaction. There was none.

"I'm going to act in the best interests of the people of my state. That's the way I run things in New York."

The attorney general sighed unhappily. "Bullshit, Governor," he said. "If you don't mind the expression."

Christman pushed the shorter man's arm away and clapped Fishman on the shoulder.

"Don't get him angry, Alex. And please, for your sake, don't talk to him that way."

"Why not?" the governor snapped, wondering whether Fishman understood he allowed no one to talk to *him* that way.

The attorney general looked him square in the eye. "He can put an awful lot of heat on you in New York just through my department."

Christman stopped and turned to the attorney general. He was squeezing his shoulder hard and Fishman winced in pain, exaggerating the expression, hoping it would stop him. The attorney general knew the governor had not missed his signal.

"You're trying to tell me," Christman said slowly, "that he personally gave Guyman the go-ahead on the American Nuclear case?"

Fishman looked at the ground when Christman released his arm. When he looked up, the famous grin was spread across the governor's face.

"I don't know what I'm supposed to offer you," he told him, "but at least I know why you came down to the pier to meet me."

"It's not like that, Alex," Fishman murmured.

"Well, General, he isn't going to have that job forever. And neither will you."

The ensign at the wharf saluted smartly as they stepped aboard the presidential launch. Neither the governor nor the attorney general spoke during the brief trip, the bigger man using his anger to focus his senses on the coming meeting with the president, until it had cooled and finally was gone; the older man containing himself in an effort to avoid any trouble. Christman sensed the tension in the air.

They reached the yacht and President Griswold was on his feet, hand extended in greeting.

"Alex! How are you?" he asked warmly. "I'm certainly glad you could come."

"It's always a pleasure, Mr. President," he replied, noticing how quickly they had been left alone. Christman looked back to the gangway and saw that the launch had hove to at the side of the presidential yacht. The president stepped to the rail and took air deeply into his lungs, like a man who had just been released from prison.

"Jesus," he said, "after Washington this is really something. You know, this isn't the greatest job in the world."

Governor Christman flashed the big grin and clapped Griswold on the back. "I'm glad there's somebody in this country who agrees with me," he replied with a wink.

The president shook his head as if he were reproaching a recalcitrant schoolboy. He had come up through the party the hard way, from city councilman in Anaheim to state senator and congressman, and eventually junior senator from the most populous state in the Union. He was tall. He was handsome. And at sixty-one, except for the flecks of white hair at his temples, he looked not a day over fifty. California through and through, Christman thought. Nothing bothers him so much as a rainy day.

They sat down in two canvas chairs, and a black waiter in an immaculately starched white jacket brought steaming cups of coffee.

"The press bother you much?" the president asked.

Christman pulled the lace shirt away from his skin. "They don't even know I'm here, Mr. President."

Griswold laughed without joy and murmured, "That's the first time in a month one of my political visitors hasn't made page one. How do you do it, Alex?"

He shrugged. "I don't try to kid them, Mr. President."

The governor turned his head away and watched a small Chris Craft moving slowly toward the yacht. About five hundred yards off the port beam a Coast Guard cutter intercepted the blue and white boat and turned it away. President Griswold waved to the small craft, as if his instincts told him at least one tourist on the ship was watching him through binoculars.

Christman shook his head and asked, "When do you find time for the job, Mr. President?"

The president turned his head slowly to indicate he was not unaware of the insolence behind the governor's needling. He did not look placid anymore.

Christman popped his eyes open in unspoken apology, but it did not dissipate the irritation that was plainly visible in the president's face. "I'm sorry, Mr. President," he said slowly and reluctantly, "my son shook me up." Then he grinned, because he had not intended to offer acquiescence to the Californian, and added, "He's the only one who can do it."

Griswold refused the opportunity to pursue amenities. "Alex, the hardest part of this job is keeping things going on an even keel." His voice was gentle, mellifluous, as if he were making a speech. He looked at the governor again and this time his voice became harder, as the pretense of politeness between them was melting away. "You haven't really approved of me, have you, Governor?"

"I haven't kidded anyone when I disagreed with you," Christman replied mildly.

"Well," the president said sarcastically, "there are those who kept telling me everybody needs a conscience."

Both men had always sought the sunshine, and now they turned instinctively away from the tension between them to the blue sea around them. The Chris Craft was chugging slowly away, and they could see a half-dozen passengers in the stern of the boat.

The level on which they made contact was of little help to either of them. And both men accepted the distraction as an opportunity to face each other again.

When they sought contact again, they were as calm as the gulf.

"Politics can be worse than marriage," President Griswold murmured.

"Mr. President," Christman said warily, "I'm a loner. I thought everybody knew that."

The president threw up his hands. He leaned back and searched the cloudless sky as if the answer might be hidden there. It was a ploy Christman understood was made for emphasis by a man who one never doubted knew precisely what he was after and how he intended to get it.

Griswold looked back at him. "Alex," he murmured, allowing room for his voice to rise with the moment. "Loyalty! Unity! That's what I asked you here today to talk about, because that is what binds us together."

Christman was still listening, but the eczema on his cheek began to bother him.

"Mr. President," he said, controlling himself, "I'm one of those fellas who doesn't think he has to take a stand on everything. I don't have to take a stand on your guy Whitmore."

The president leaned forward and grasped Christman's wrist, but the governor pulled his arm away.

"That is a foolish notion, Governor," he told him, "for a man with plans so grandiose as yours."

"I have no political ambition, Mr. President," he said slowly, "except to oppose those people who subscribe to your methods."

Christman had issued his own warning now, but the president only smiled. It was the bitter, mocking smile of a powerful man who knows he can find pleasure in hurting those who displease him, and he did not have to remind himself that he had never liked the governor.

"Alex," he asked, "do you really mean to tell me there is nothing I can offer you?" His tone was mocking, irritating, as if he were trying to belittle the guest.

Christman grinned. If he had to fight, he would. But Griswold was not finished.

"Didn't anyone ever tell you it was a mistake to make enemies, Governor?"

"Yeah," Christman said, smiling.

Griswold looked away again. The gulf was calm and he turned his face toward the hot tropical sun. "Governor," he said, without looking back at him, "I expect you to give total and unqualified support to the vice-president. Is that clear?" His eyes opened and he turned his body sharply to fully confront Christman.

The governor said nothing, knowing he was foolishly taunting a man he should not offend without cause.

The president stared back silently, fully cognizant of the governor's mute defiance.

"Frankly, Mr. President," Governor Alexander Christman said finally, "I don't believe I can do that."

President Griswold stood and quickly stepped in front of Christman's canvas chair, blocking the governor from rising with him. His face was totally impassive as he leaned forward, touching Christman's thick forearm, until their eyes were but a few inches apart.

"Governor," the president said deliberately. But he did not finish the sentence. Instead, he straightened himself quickly, turned, and walked slowly away from Christman, leaving him alone on the afterdeck.

In the main salon of the presidential yacht, Griswold

was still angry as he gave his orders to Attorney General Fishman.

"Have Reeves tell the press I met with Governor Christman and invited him to act as national chairman for the vice-president's campaign. Have him tell the press the governor is thinking it over. Let the press make it hot for that son of a bitch. Then call the U. S. attorney in New York and tell him to move that case. And I mean move it. I want it into the grand jury now."

Fishman shook his head. "Mr. President, I'm not sure—"

Griswold stopped him cold. "I mean move it. That man is going to learn what happens when you quit the team if it's the last thing I do in this office. Do you understand me, Mr. Fishman?"

"Yes, sir," the attorney general said.

The following pages
contain an excerpt
from the one book
that is capturing
the heart
of America.

All Creatures Great and Small
by James Herriot

I got out and stood beside my battered suitcase, looking about me. There was something unusual and I couldn't put my finger on it at first. Then I realised what it was—the silence. The other passengers had dispersed, the driver had switched off his engine and there was not a sound or a movement anywhere. The only visible sign of life was a group of old men sitting round the clock tower in the centre of the square but they might have been carved from stone.

Darrowby didn't get much space in the guide books but when it was mentioned it was described as a grey little town on the river Darrow with a cobbled market place and little of interest except its two ancient bridges. But when you looked at it, its setting was beautiful on the pebbly river where the houses clustered thickly and straggled unevenly along the lower slopes of Herne Fell. Everywhere in Darrowby, in the streets, through the windows of the houses you could see the Fell rearing its calm, green bulk more than two thousand feet above the huddled roofs.

There was a clarity in the air, a sense of space and airiness that made me feel I had shed something on the plain, twenty miles behind. The confinement of the city, the grime, the smoke—already they seemed to be falling away from me.

Trengate was a quiet street leading off the square and I had my first sight of Skeldale House. I knew it was the right place before I was near enough to read "S. Farnon M.R.C.V.S." on the old-fashioned brass plate hanging slightly askew on the iron railings. I knew by the ivy which climbed untidily over the mellow brick to the topmost windows. It was what the letter had said—the only house with ivy; and this could be where I would work for the first time as a veterinary surgeon.

Now that I was here, right on the doorstep, I felt breathless, as though I had been running. If I got the job, this was where I would find out about myself. There were many things to prove.

But I liked the look of the old house. It was Georgian with a fine, white-painted doorway. The windows, too, were white—wide and graceful on the ground floor and first storey but small and square where they peeped out from under the overhanging tiles far above. The paint was flaking and the mortar looked crumbly between the bricks, but there was a changeless elegance about the place. There was no front garden and only the railings separated the house from the street a few feet away.

I rang the doorbell and instantly the afternoon peace was shattered by a distant baying like a wolf pack in full cry. The upper half of the door was of glass and, as I peered through, a river of dogs poured round the corner of a long passage and dashed itself with frenzied yells against the door. If I hadn't been used to animals I would have turned and run for my life. As it was I stepped back warily and watched the dogs as they appeared, sometimes two at a time, at the top of their leap, eyes glaring, jaws slavering. After a minute or two of this I was able to sort them out and I realised that my first rough count of about fourteen was exaggerated. There were, in fact, five; a huge fawn greyhound who appeared most often as he hadn't so far to jump as the others, a cocker spaniel, a Scottie, a whippet and a tiny, short-legged hunt terrier. This terrier was seldom seen since the glass was rather high for him, but when he did make it he managed to get an even more frantic note into his bark before he disappeared.

I was thinking of ringing the bell again when I saw a

large woman in the passage. She rapped out a single word and the noise stopped as if by magic. When she opened the door the ravening pack was slinking round her feet ingratiatingly, showing the whites of their eyes and wagging their tucked-in tails. I had never seen such a servile crew.

"Good afternoon," I said with my best smile. "My name is Herriot."

The woman looked bigger than ever with the door open. She was about sixty but her hair, tightly pulled back from her forehead, was jet black and hardly streaked with grey. She nodded and looked at me with grim benevolence, but she seemed to be waiting for further information. Evidently, the name struck no answering spark.

"Mr. Farnon is expecting me. He wrote asking me to come today."

"Mr. Herriot?" she said thoughtfully. "Surgery is from six to seven o'clock. If you wanted to bring a dog in, that would be your best time."

"No, no," I said, hanging on to my smile. "I'm applying for the position of assistant. Mr. Farnon said to come in time for tea."

"Assistant? Well, now, that's nice." The lines in her face softened a little. "I'm Mrs. Hall. I keep house for Mr. Farnon. He's a bachelor, you know. He never said anything to me about you, but never mind, come in and have a cup of tea. He shouldn't be long before he's back."

I followed her between whitewashed walls, my feet clattering on the tiles. We turned right at the end into another passage and I was beginning to wonder just how far back the house extended when I was shown into a sunlit room.

It had been built in the grand manner, high-ceilinged and airy with a massive fireplace flanked by arched alcoves. One end was taken up by a french window which gave on a long, high-walled garden. I could see unkempt lawns, a rockery and many fruit trees. A great bank of peonies blazed in the hot sunshine and at the far end, rooks cawed in the branches of a group of tall elms. Above and beyond were the green hills with their climbing walls.

Ordinary-looking furniture stood around on a very worn carpet. Hunting prints hung on the walls and books were scattered everywhere, some on shelves in the alcoves but others piled on the floor in the corners. A pewter pint pot occupied a prominent place at one end of the mantelpiece. It was an interesting pot. Cheques and bank notes had been stuffed into it till they bulged out of the top and overflowed on to the hearth beneath. I was studying this with astonishment when Mrs. Hall came in with a tea tray.

"I suppose Mr. Farnon is out on a case," I said.

"No, he's gone through to Brawton to visit his mother. I can't really say when he'll be back." She left me with my tea.

The dogs arranged themselves peacefully around the room and, except for a brief dispute between the Scottie and the cocker spaniel about the occupancy of a deep chair, there was no sign of their previous violent behaviour. They lay regarding me with friendly boredom and, at the same time, fighting a losing battle against sleep. Soon the last nodding head had fallen back and a chorus of heavy breathing filled the room.

But I was unable to relax with them. A feeling of let-down gripped me; I had screwed myself up for an interview and I was left dangling. This was all very odd. Why should anyone write for an assistant, arrange a time to meet him and then go to visit his mother? Another thing—if I was engaged, I would be living in this house, yet the housekeeper had no instructions to prepare a room for me. In fact, she had never even heard of me.

My musings were interrupted by the door bell ringing and the dogs, as if touched by a live wire, leaped screaming into the air and launched themselves in a solid mass through the door. I wished they didn't take their duties so seriously. There was no sign of Mrs. Hall so I went out to the front door where the dogs were putting everything into their fierce act.

"Shut up!" I shouted and the din switched itself off. The five dogs cringed abjectly round my ankles, almost walking on their knees. The big greyhound got the best effect by drawing his lips back from his teeth in an apologetic grin.

I opened the door and looked into a round, eager face. Its owner, a plump man in Wellington boots, leaned confidently against the railings.

"Hello, 'ello, Mr. Farnon in?"

"Not at the moment. Can I help you?"

"Aye, give 'im a message when he comes in. Tell 'im Bert Sharpe of Barrow Hills has a cow wot wants borin' out?"

"Boring out?"

"That's right, she's nobbut going on three cylinders."

"Three cylinders?"

"Aye and if we don't do summat she'll go wrang in 'er ewer, won't she?"

"Very probably."

"Don't want felon, do we?"

"Certainly not."

"O.K., you'll tell 'im then. Ta-ta."

I returned thoughtfully to the sitting-room. It was disconcerting but I had listened to my first case history without understanding a word of it.

I had hardly sat down when the bell rang again. This time I unleashed a frightening yell which froze the dogs when they were still in mid air; they took the point and returned, abashed, to their chairs.

This time it was a solemn gentleman with a straightly adjusted cloth cap resting on his ears, a muffler knotted precisely over his adam's apple and a clay pipe growing from the exact centre of his mouth. He removed the pipe and spoke with a rich, unexpected accent.

"Me name's Mulligan and I want Misther Farnon to make up some medicine for me dog."

"Oh, what's the trouble with your dog, Mr. Mulligan?"

He raised a questioning eyebrow and put a hand to his ear. I tried again with a full blooded shout.

"What's the trouble?"

He looked at me doubtfully for a moment. "He's womitin', sorr. Womitin' bad."

I immediately felt on secure ground now and my brain began to seethe with diagnostic procedures. "How long after eating does he vomit?"

The hand went to the ear again. "Phwhat's that?"

I leaned close to the side of his head, inflated my lungs and bawled: "When does he womit—I mean vomit?"

Comprehension spread slowly across Mr. Mulligan's face. He gave a gentle smile. "Oh aye, he's womitin'. Womitin' bad, sorr."

I didn't feel up to another effort so I told him I would see to it and asked him to call later. He must have been able to lip read me because he seemed satisfied and walked away...

Where the devil was Farnon? Was he really expecting me or had somebody played a horrible practical joke on me? I felt suddenly cold. I had spent my last few pounds getting here and if there was some mistake I was in trouble.

But, looking around me, I began to feel better. The sunshine beat back from the high old walls, bees droned among the bright masses of flowers. A gentle breeze stirred the withered blooms of a magnificent wistaria which almost covered the back of the house. There was peace here.

I leaned my head against the bark and closed my eyes. I could see Herr Farrenen, looking just as I had imagined him, standing over me. He wore a shocked expression.

"Wass is dis you haff done?" he spluttered, his fat jowls quivering with rage. "You kom to my house under false pretences, you insult Fräulein Brompton, you trink my tea, you eat my food. Vat else you do, hein? Maybe you steal my spoons. You talk about assistant but I vant no assistant. Is best I telephone the police."

Herr Farrenen seized the phone in a pudgy hand. Even in my dream, I wondered how the man could use such a completely corny accent. I heard the thick voice saying "Hello, hello."

And I opened my eyes. Somebody was saying "Hello," but it wasn't Herr Farrenen. A tall, thin man was leaning against the wall, his hands in his pockets. Something seemed to be amusing him. As I struggled to my feet, he heaved himself away from the wall and held out his hand. "Sorry you've had to wait. I'm Siegfried Farnon."

He was just about the most English-looking man I had ever seen. Long, humorous, strong-jawed face. Small, clipped moustache, untidy, sandy hair. He was wearing an old tweed jacket and shapeless flannel trousers. The collar of his check shirt was frayed and the tie carelessly knotted. He looked as though he didn't spend much time in front of a mirror.

Studying him, I began to feel better despite the ache in my neck where it had rested against the tree. I shook my head to get my eyes fully open and tufts of grass fell from my hair. "There was a Miss Brompton here," I blurted out. "She came to tea. I explained you had been called away."

Farnon looked thoughtful, but not put out. He rubbed his chin slowly. "Mm, yes—well, never mind. But I do apologise for being out when you arrived. I have a shocking memory and I just forgot."

It was the most English voice, too.

Farnon gave me a long, searching look, then he grinned. "Let's go inside. I want to show you round the place."

CHAPTER NINE

ARNOLD GUYMAN had fallen asleep at seven-fifteen, which made the sound of the telephone particularly annoying.

"Mr. Guyman?" A pleasant voice that he did not recognize floated through the phone.

He acknowledged, quickly struggling to waken himself.

"One moment for the president," the voice finally said.

That got him up fast. He had feared this. When the case first came to him, it occurred to him the president might merely be testing the loyalty to the Griswold administration of a man who owed his political career to Alexander Christman. He could not believe that anyone, even the president, would pursue a criminal case against Governor Alexander Christman. The president might hint at it. He might use it for political leverage to keep the governor in line. But to publicly prosecute Christman? Unthinkable.

As he waited for the president, Guyman wondered what he should do if he had miscalculated. Suppose the president was serious? Guyman's career, indeed his life, had progressed largely on his ability to wholly satisfy men with real power. And now he was caught in the middle and all he could do was continue to buy time with both sides. With luck, some new urgency would arise that would finally extricate him from this damn job into a set of black robes. Judge Arnold Guyman, he thought. And he no longer gave a damn whether he sat on the state or the federal bench.

He straightened himself up on the edge of the bed,

waiting for the president, modestly tugging at his pajamas to cover himself.

"Arnie, how are you?" the carefully measured voice said.

"Fine, sir," he replied. "I think I know why you're calling me."

"Well, that's good. As you know, I don't ever interfere in matters of this kind. But I did want to know that your office is moving ahead. The attorney general has convinced me you have a very significant case."

Guyman realized the president covered himself carefully. If the president had called him at his office, Guyman might have asked his deputy to listen in on the conversation as a witness. The Federal Bureau of Investigation did that. But President Griswold was not even taking a chance that he was audacious enough to record the conversation, and he recalled how he had been told in law school to be suspicious of anyone who opened a conversation with a disclaimer.

"I don't see how any member of your administration could consider a telephone call from you 'interference,' Mr. President," Guyman said. He knew now that Griswold had come upon the governor's involvement in American Nuclear from a Harvard chemist who had served as a consultant to the state of New York. Griswold was grateful enough to bring him to Washington as a White House assistant.

Griswold was silent for a moment, waiting for a specific commitment from the U. S. attorney.

"Sir," Guyman said hesitantly.

"Do I sense you have reservations, Mr. Guyman?"

"Yes, sir. I'm not sure the evidence is sufficient to bring this matter to a successful conclusion."

"You're not a very good lawyer, Arnie," the president said casually. "I had hoped you would be the kind of material we need on the federal bench. The bureau, as you know, is not happy with the way you're running things. They seem to think you're much too emotional. The director says his agents have prepared a report on your conduct, but, as you know, it's my rule, my general rule, that is, to ignore such criticism. I like to let a man set his own course."

"Yes, sir," Guyman said dully. He had learned the value of loyalty in politics because he had always done the right thing. But he had never been in a bind like this before.

"Arnie," the president said, "let's not play games. When can I expect an indictment?"

Guyman would have cried if he could, but even his wife was not there to see him.

"Within ten days, sir," he said.

"Fine," the president replied. "I'm counting on you."

And then he hung up.

Guyman held the dead telephone in his hand. He hoped the president's hint could be taken as a commitment, and that the commitment was as solid a coin of the realm as the word of Alexander Christman had always been. If he moved the Christman case, he knew one thing with certainty: he wanted to be on the bench damn fast, before anyone could touch him.

At noon, Arthur Roe walked down the wide, blue-carpeted corridor on the thirty-seventh floor of 345 Park Avenue to his suite of offices. He stripped quickly in his private bathroom, shaved, and stepped into the steaming shower. Esther Serene stood outside the door shouting telephone messages he had received over the noise of the steaming water, and Roe, in turn, shouted instructions back at her. His wife called from Montana; the children were fine. A bank president from Buffalo who had been bucking Christman. Too bad. Three executive officers of Christman corporations needing policy decisions of varying degrees of importance; he would make them. Ralph Deal, treasurer of the Christman gubernatorial campaigns, and U. S. Attorney Guyman.

"Who?" he shouted over the noise of the shower, his body suddenly tense.

"Guyman. He said he wanted to be sure you remembered to honor the subpoena at 9 A.M. tomorrow morning."

"That son of a bitch," he shouted. "He said that?"

"What's the trouble, Arthur?"

"Get him. Get him on the goddamn phone."

"Hughes wants to see you. Badly. He thinks he's found something."

"Will you get Guyman on the goddamn phone?"

He turned the single shower control to Full Cold and jumped at the quick change in the temperature. Unhappily he leaned forward and doused his head and neck in the frigid water. He turned off the control quickly and stepped out of the shower. As he put on a terry cloth robe, he could hear Esther Serene talking to someone through the open bathroom door.

Roe dressed in the small dressing room that was part of his suite of offices. Guyman. For a long time he had known the U. S. attorney was a party hack. If the son of a bitch tried to buck for a judgeship at any other time, Christman would drive him out of the state. But this was different, and he told himself it would be very difficult if Guyman had begun to understand that.

Esther Serene was still cradling the phone at his desk after he dressed, and her angry Irish voice had passed the conversational level.

"If he is out of town, give me a number where I can reach him. I told you this is important. Arthur Roe. Yes. He's right here. In the room. Yes, he will." She cupped the mouthpiece with her hand. "He's away. And this bitch won't even tell me where we can reach him."

Roe grabbed the phone from her hand. "Arthur Roe here," he said.

"Mr. Roe, the U. S. attorney is not in New York today. His chief assistant, Mr. Plant, will speak to you. One moment, please." The line was disconnected before he could reply.

"Shit," he said loudly, wondering if it made more sense simply to hang up. Guyman was enough of a flunky. He could only imagine what he demanded from subordinates.

The phone came alive. "Mr. Roe, this is Malcolm Plant, chief assistant to the U. S. attorney. We are glad you called. The U. S. attorney wanted to be certain he need take no steps to insure your compliance with the subpoena in question."

"Guyman vacated that subpoena himself."

"I'm sorry, sir," Plant said, "but I'm not aware of it."

"Ask him, for chrissake."

"Sir, unless I have your assurance as a member of the Bar that you will appear, my instructions are to have you brought to the grand jury room by a United States marshal."

"What?"

"I believe you understood me, sir."

Roe took the phone away from his ear and calmed himself.

"The U. S. attorney left very explicit instructions, Mr. Roe. I am certain there is no mistake. Do you have his order vacating the subpoena in writing?"

"No."

"Then I suggest you assure me you will comply. This office does not wish to embarrass you."

"Mr. Plant, I'm sorry. Your office has no right to ask me any questions relating to a client. You know that. The matter referred to here falls into that area."

"I believe, Mr. Roe, that is for a federal judge to decide. I am also authorized to tell you that papers compelling you to testify have already been drawn up and will be submitted forthwith if you fail to cooperate. I am certain you are aware that such papers would become a matter of public record and would, therefore, be available to the press."

That was it, Roe thought. They were mousetrapping Christman. It would be page one news across the country if Roe refused to testify and his client was named. No one would have to prove any allegations. Guyman's office could simply enumerate in its petition to the court any questions they wished. Roe would be bound by client privilege to refuse to answer.

"Mr. Plant," he said calmly, "I think the status of the client involved in this matter warrants that I talk to the U.S. attorney himself."

"Counsellor," Plant replied, obviously savoring the opportunity to answer the question, "I am certain you know this office treats everyone equitably, no matter what their status in the community might be. It is not the U. S. attorney's desire to try this matter in the press. And if you will give me your assurance that you will guard against, shall we call them, unauthorized leaks, you will have similar assurance from this office."

"Yes," Roe said weakly before he hung up the phone. "Yes. I guess that's all right."

He stared at the telephone console for a moment. Then he looked at Esther Serene. "Put in an absolutely urgent call for the governor," he said.

For four hours Roe buried himself in paperwork, sensing that the outside world had closed itself to him. Governor Christman did not return the call. Neither did the U. S. attorney for the southern district.

Roe dismissed Esther, instructing her only to double-check his appointment with William Connor O'Breslin, the firm's criminal law specialist.

"I want to see him before five, while there is still an O'Breslin to talk to."

When he was on trial, which was all the law he practiced now, O'Breslin touched no spirits more intoxicating than Saratoga Vichy Water. But in the months between the three or four cases he was able to manage each year, he became a lost soul. He was committed to three Irish whiskeys at lunch and sipping through the afternoon at a leisurely pace. It was as if he needed a vacation from reality between engagements to flush his system of the enormous quantity of facts, hunches, testimony, statements, and data he wholly committed to memory each time he went to trial. And there were few prosecutors who did not know that O'Breslin's memory could quote accurately, by page number, from the trial transcript record and the vast body of law relevant to the trial.

"Mr. O'Breslin will see you at five-fifteen," Esther said.

Roe went back to work. At precisely 5:15, he pushed aside the papers on his desk and carefully focussed his attention on the matters he wished to discuss with O'Breslin. He combed his hair carefully in his private washroom, and then walked out of his office.

Jack Clarity tried to attract his attention as he passed through the outer offices, and he stopped briefly enough to say: "Good brief you did. See you at the staff meeting." He left the young lawyer, who was the son of a federal appeals court judge, grinning from ear to ear, which was precisely what he intended to do.

Roe walked with his head bowed through the wide hallway, partly because he was deep in thought, but more certainly because he wanted no interruption. There was neither a secretary nor a receptionist in the anteroom outside O'Breslin's offices, and Roe stopped to press the buzzer of the intercom, deciding it would be better to announce himself. One never knew. As he waited for the older lawyer to answer the phone, his toe pushed idly at the small circle of empty peanut shells on the carpet near the desk of O'Breslin's receptionist.

"Criminal law," he muttered with disdain.

Finally, O'Breslin answered the buzzer and in a sleepy voice responded, "Oh, it's you, Arthur. I gave the girls an afternoon off. Sorry. Come in, will you? If you're going to be formal, then the mausoleum is doomed."

O'Breslin sat, legs up, on the deep cushioned green leather settee in his office, a tumbler of Irish whiskey by his hand and a leatherbound copy of *The Hound of the Baskervilles* in his lap.

"How can you do it, Bill?" Roe asked, flicking a manicured finger at the glass of amber liquid.

"It's not a bad book."

"Not that."

"I was born deficient to the extent of two Irish whiskeys. Get the cards out of my top drawer, Arthur."

"It's a heavy day," he protested.

But William Connor O'Breslin, with a wave of his hand, lurched up from the leather couch and walked to his desk. He took the Bee playing cards from the drawer and slowly began shuffling them, one hand forcing the cards into the cards held in the other.

"You look as if you're in trouble, and I can't think unless I'm doing something," O'Breslin explained, reaching now into the bottom drawer for the quart of

Irish whiskey. "Deal first. Then talk. Usual stakes."

Roe took the cards, riffled them twice, and alternate-
ly dealt ten cards each to O'Breslin and himself. He
felt like a small boy helping his bedridden father pass
the time of day. Even the hand was bad: two kings
that were different suits from a pair of queens, three
sevens, a nine of spades, a seven of hearts, and the ace
of clubs. If he kept the picture cards, he could be
caught with more than forty points. If he broke the
pairs and discarded them, it would signal to O'Breslin
the kind of hand he had. Who cares, he thought. This
hand is as bad as the last three days: a high risk with
the probability of winning decreasing all the time.

"Fine." O'Breslin sighed. "Now what's on your
mind?"

"Play cards," he replied. He picked a king from the
top of the pack, felt a trifle elated, and discarded the
nine of spades. O'Breslin chortled, took it, and flipped
a six of clubs on top of the discard pile.

"Have you ever gone in against Guyman?" Roe
asked.

"He's your man," O'Breslin grunted, a little surprised. "What's the trouble?"

Roe did not reply. A part of him was again a boy in
Florida, sitting at his father's bedside while his mother
ran the dress shop. It made it that much harder to
hold back. But as it became more difficult, his certainty increased that he must keep his own counsel. Too
much was at stake. On his next turn, he discarded the
ace of clubs and realized quickly that he would have
done the same thing with his father.

O'Breslin's eyes bulged as he popped open the lids
in mock astonishment. "Arthur," he shouted, snatching
the card, "you know better!" He spread four sixes, the
eight, nine, ten of spades, a four of hearts, a two of
diamonds, and Roe's ace of clubs in front of him on
the desk and said, "Seven."

An hour later, Roe had lost three straight sets,
some seven thousand points, and the $350 bothered
him, but not as much as Christman's failure to return
his call. The elderly lawyer had tried a dozen times, in
as many ways, to open the young man's thoughts, to

convert what he sensed was on his mind into speech. But each time he tried, no matter how deftly, Roe turned the questions aside. As they played cards, he watched the old man sip slowly and steadily at the tumbler of raw Irish. Not the faintest trace of an effect appeared. But in Roe's constellation alcohol was a sign of weakness, as it had been in his father, and he could not bring himself to trust O'Breslin.

"Arthur," he said, waggling a finger after the third game, "you know it's really the money that's bothering you."

Roe laughed softly. He begrudged the time. It was wasteful. "Deal," he said.

"Double the stakes? Ten cents a point?"

Roe nodded.

As O'Breslin again mixed the cards like an old gypsy, Roe was angry with himself. He had come to the old man for professional counsel, but he had stopped himself from asking him, as if he could make the threat of the U. S. attorney's office go away. He held the cards O'Breslin dealt in his hand, barely glancing at them. Slowly, he began to ask his colleague questions regarding the legal situation of an attorney who refuses to testify before a grand jury investigating the affairs of his client.

O'Breslin did not look up as he answered Roe's questions slowly, carefully, and without involvement. His face revealed neither understanding nor even casual interest. When he did look up, he said:

"The real question is how serious are your problems with American Nuclear."

"What problems?" Roe lied defensively. "We've never been in better shape."

O'Breslin groaned as he leaned forward to pick a card. "You're not really candid with me, are you, Arthur? Gin," he said, fanning his cards face up across the edge of the desk and reaching, in virtually the same gesture, for the tumbler of whiskey.

He held the cards motionless in his huge hairy paws and stared at Roe. The younger lawyer had laughed when prosecutors muttered in dismay at O'Breslin's ability to create a moment in a courtroom by the sheer magnetism of his own concentration. Now he knew it was true. If was as if, in those few seconds, the two men existed motionless in the vacuum of the universe, without sound, without the myriad visual, oral, and tactile sensations of existence. Now the older man lifted his hairy hand from the playing cards in a gesture of silence. Then it descended on Roe's wrist.

"Hold this thought," O'Breslin said in a whisper so soft, his companion wondered for a moment whether he had spoken or he was only hearing the voice inside his head. "You can get hurt very badly, Arthur. The truth is you don't *really* need Alexander Christman anymore."

Then he lifted his hand. The spell was broken. O'Breslin was shuffling the cards, stopping only to poke Roe's arm with a thick forefinger. "When they decide to gang up, the big fellows can cream anyone. Even Alex Christman." He stopped and flipped over a jack of spades. "Hell. Especially Alex Christman."

Both men looked up as the recessed neon lights overhead flickered, sputtered, and died. O'Breslin pushed the black button on his ancient desk lamp. Nothing happened. The electric clock on the maple desk had stopped at 6:14. Roe walked over to the window and opened the floor to ceiling louvered shutters as the street lights below flickered and died as far north as he could see. The Pan Am Building, like a huge steel tombstone burying the graceful nineteenth-century beauty of Grand Central Station, was black.

"What in the blue hell did you do, William?" Roe said in awe.

"Play cards," the old man barked with amusement. "The lightning comes later."

But the younger man had already reached for the phone.

He called his own office. Esther Serene said the lights were not only off in the building, but the whole eastern seaboard was blacked out.

"It's a power failure."

"Did you get Christman yet?" he shouted, letting out the tension.

Roe slammed the receiver and knocked the phone off the desk. He found the telephone cradle with his left hand and replaced the phone. As he started to move toward the door, O'Breslin grabbed his wrist, and he sat down again in the leather chair. It was quiet again. The two men, without speaking, sensed each other's presence in the darkness, and the silence between them was louder than any noise measured in decibels, as it always is, Arthur thought, when the mind wholly focusses on silence. He was again back in Florida, again at his father's bedside in the darkened room, the heat rising in the airless dawn as the temperature in the office became stifling without the air conditioner. In the darkness it seemed easier to tell the other man about Christman's reluctance to run, the American Nuclear mess, and the rest of it. He was terrified now, as he had been when he was a boy. Except that this time he was frightened of things that were very real.

The two men sat silently for five minutes, twenty minutes, it might have been an hour. They did not know. Finally Arthur Roe straightened the crease in his trousers with two fingers, and stood.

"Let me help," O'Breslin said.

"No," he replied, realizing he had almost called the old man Papa. "Christman is my pigeon."

"Everyone has to let it all out to someone," the deep voice whispered softly.

"Only in your religion," Roe said.

The younger man stood, walked to the desk, and turned on O'Breslin's transistor radio.

"In other news, President Griswold, as expected, expressed his unqualified support for Vice-President George Whitmore today. The president indicated that he had asked New York's Governor Alexander Christman—considered the only other serious contender for the party's nomination—to act as national chairman for the campaign.

"In a statement issued from his Albany office, the governor's press secretary, Harvey Kuhn, indicated Mr. Christman was too busy to comment. Kuhn indicated the governor would broadcast a statewide mes-

sage from his office in the capital regarding the power
crisis later tonight. Right now, Kuhn said, all the governor is concerned with is getting power back to the
people of the state."

Roe shook his head and turned off the radio.

"You don't need him anymore, Arthur. You're going
to be running this firm one day. And that's enough
for any lawyer."

Roe stood quickly. He was glad O'Breslin could not
see his face. Gently he touched the older man's arm.

"It's something to think about," he said politely, as
he started out of the room.

O'Breslin could not be stopped. He was walking toward the door with him in the darkness. "You can go
down with him, Arthur. Don't forget that. And it's a
long way down. It's always a long way down."

Roe stopped and turned toward the older man. He
could not see his face.

"I've got a lot to do, Bill," he said. "Somebody's got
to get the lights turned back on." And now he also
knew what would happen if Governor Alexander
Christman of New York decided not to accept the
bidding of the president of the United States.

CHAPTER TEN

GOVERNOR ALEXANDER CHRISTMAN SAT in the canopied golf cart like a boy awed by his first circus, as Athena Courtland put the pure white Lippizan stallion through its paces. He had seen the horse, but he had never seen this woman look so beautiful before. She was wearing whipcord breeches, a black hunting jacket, and a diamond clasp in the ascot about her neck. In her gloved right hand, she held a rhinestone-studded whip, but it never moved in her grasp as the horse shifted easily from a gallop to a trot, then halted before the governor and bowed his head.

"Wow," he said, "that's really something."

"It's quite a horse." She laughed happily.

Devlin stood next to the groom holding Truman, the governor's big chestnut stallion. The detective caught his eye, shrugged, and held his hands out, palms upward. Christman shook his head to indicate a negative reply.

"I'll call him back," he said, ignoring the detective's gesture of urgency. Devlin did not press him.

It was nearly five o'clock on the Arizona desert, and the brilliant red sun had begun to touch the mountaintops beyond the valley. It was cooler and the shadows were longer now, and he gingerly straightened his sunburned back as he sat on the very edge of the golf cart seat, almost all of his weight on the base of his spine.

He watched her buttocks, held tightly in the breeches that laced down the inside of each leg, as they bounced in perfect rhythm against the tiny flat saddle, and slowly he pushed himself off the seat.

Athena trotted back carefully on the show horse,

controlling its pace with the movements of her body. Devlin shook his head as the groom boosted the big man into Truman's saddle.

"The switchboard is going crazy," Devlin told him. "Roe says it's urgent."

Christman laughed. "Roe always says it's urgent. And tell the other fellas to stay sober. I'll be over in half an hour."

There were four huge main buildings on the 7,200 acre. Christman ranch that covered the most verdant corner of the Arizona desert. There was the elegant old main house with its forty rooms that he had rebuilt and modernized twenty years ago. Since then it had been fully automated; a single button could produce a three-course meal in the kitchen's microwave ovens in less than fifteen minutes. He had even automated the sixty-foot pole in front of the old building. At sunrise, a photoelectric cell automatically raised the flag. It was lowered at sunset or the first drop of rain. A senator from Arizona had been struck by the gadget, and Christman ordered a similar one installed at his home. He still remembered the gesture had cost him $17,384.

Beyond the main house there was a hunting lodge, two large buildings to house the staff of seventy that raised three thousand head of cattle on the ranch, a smaller building for his staff of twenty men that patrolled Eden's vast fences, a squat two-story office building that a magazine writer said housed the Christman papers, but was in fact a series of offices and communications center. He had also commissioned an artificial salt marsh and duck blind, for which six hundred birds had to be imported each year, three tennis courts, two Olympic-size swimming pools with cabanas in the cool blue and white Christman colors he had always used in his campaign posters. An electric railroad connected the buildings, each of which had a closed circuit television system that could be hooked into telephone cables to receive any program broadcast by any station in the country. There was an underground bomb shelter, that he now knew had been a wasted investment. But he did not regret it. He had set out to build a city for the use of one man, and that was precisely what he had done.

Christman dug his heels into Truman's flank until the horse galloped alongside the Lippizan.

"Where did you learn to handle a horse?" he asked.

She wet her lips with her tongue. "Are we going to talk, Alex? Or did you bring me here just to watch my butt?"

He reached over and grabbed the bridle of her horse, but the Lippizan shied away. Then Athena Courtland came to him, and without moving her hands, the horse stopped and stood quietly. He leaned over and kissed her fully, his tongue touching her teeth. Her gloved hand went around him.

"You've really got a burn," she said, her hand on the back of his head.

Christman grinned. He felt free now. It was the first time that day since he left the president that he no longer regretted what he had done. Maybe it had been a mistake, he thought. But if he were going to face the boy again, or himself for that matter, it had to be done.

They had stopped under a tree a few hundred yards from one of the big swimming pools. Athena started to dismount.

"I can't," he told her.

"Alex," she said, leaving him uncertain whether she was angry, "send them away."

He laughed and said, "No," spreading his arms in a helpless gesture. Then he stopped laughing. "I really have to talk to these guys," he told her, moving toward Devlin. "This is important."

She brushed her hair angrily away from her face and jerked the Lippizan's reins. "I thought you really had to talk to me," she called.

"Hey," Christman yelled back, but she was gone. He dismounted, turned the reins over to the groom, and got into the golf cart beside Devlin.

"The lady likes to whip," Devlin muttered, pushing down hard on the accelerator. The detective was quiet. In front of them, the sun had begun to brush the mountaintops, casting hard, black shadows across the landscape. Devlin decided he could tell him. "They have big problems in town, Governor. Real big problems. Mr. Roe is trying to get you. It's the sixty-five blackout all over again."

The smile on Alexander Christman's face began around his eyes and crept downward until he was taken fully by the exhilarating thought. His hand moved to Devlin's thigh, squeezing it for confirmation.

"You're kidding, fella," he said.

Devlin shook his head.

"Jesus! Right in time for the meeting." He pulled the steering bar toward him, turning the electric cart away from the office building where his guests were waiting. "Hey," he cried, "I've got to talk to Arthur."

Devlin shook his head again. "He's been trying to get you for an hour."

The governor slapped his leg again. "Okay, okay. It's not your fault. I just hope Mayor Thayer isn't getting a snootful in the backroom at Sardi's this time. He is going to have his hands full."

Devlin saw the governor's face light with the kind of intensity he had not seen since they left New York. He knew that Christman was pleased with himself. The governor remembered the warning from his own Power Commission when he had them turn down the power company's request for auxiliary generators on river barges surrounding the city. They told him he was risking a massive blackout as severe as the big blackout of 1965. And he knew immediately it was precisely what American Nuclear needed to dramatize the state's and the nation's vulnerability unless they replaced outmoded equipment with his company's nuclear generators.

Christman moved quickly into the house and showered in the small bathroom adjoining his study, still uncomfortable with anything touching his skin. Above the roar of the shower, he could hear the voice of a secretary struggling with a long-distance telephone operator. The governor shut off the water quickly, stepped out of the glass stall, and pulled on a terry cloth robe. Still dripping, he walked into the study and took the phone.

"Operator? Operator, this is Governor Alexander Christman of New York. I'm calling on a national priority matter."

Whether the girl in Tuscon believed him or not, something in his voice told her to obey, and he heard the familiar electronic bleeps as she dialed his private number on the Irvington switchboard.

"This is the governor," he said. "Connect me with Mr. Roe."

"Yes, sir. Sir? Everyone is trying to reach you. The press. The office in Albany. Apparently no one knows where you are."

"Fine. Get me Roe. And Ellen, make sure you personally tell people in all our offices that no one is to speak to outsiders without checking with Mr. Roe. That includes the chairman of the Power Commission, the state police. Anybody. Tell them to disconnect their phones if they have to. Can you handle that?"

"Of course."

"Now get me Mr. Roe."

He dried the back of his neck with the nape of the terry robe and then wiped off the telephone. The lawyer was on the line quicker than he expected.

"All hell's broken loose here, Alex. It's 1965 all over again. Subways. People trapped in elevators. Nearly all the goddamn radio stations are out. And that's not all."

"Calm down, fella," Christman told him. "Is anybody hurt?"

"No. As far as we can tell it's being handled as well as it was in 1965. But *The New York Times* is trying damn hard to find you. They've got a guy up in Albany, another one at Irvington, somebody else camped outside your office in New York. Jesus, they even have a guy assigned to me."

"Hey, that's terrific."

"Alex."

"What's the matter? We knew this was going to happen, right? Now that it's happened, we know how to handle it."

"Alex," Arthur Roe told him, "don't get carried away."

Christman laughed. "All right. It's important no one know I'm out of the state. Draft a message for me that can be recorded in Albany and broadcast live from the capital. As far as anyone is concerned, I'm in Albany. Have Kuhn set up a press conference for eleven tomorrow morning and make sure those guys from Consolidated Electric are there. That's not all. Harvey should have an announcement ready every hour. You both know what to do. At ten o'clock, let him tell the press I have ordered the state guard assembled and put at the disposal of Mayor Thayer. He'll turn down any help, but it will keep the press guys busy for a while. At eleven o'clock tell them a series of meetings have begun with the State Power Commission. By midnight they can announce a full-scale investigation. Give them something at one A. M. and again at two. By that time, they'll be too tired to care. The point is I'm too busy to meet with them. The Albany broadcast should be on the air by ten-thirty. Might as well do it before everyone goes to bed. Is there anything else, Arthur?"

There was a long pause on the New York end of the line, and Christman began blotting his chest with the robe. He stepped away from the cold puddle of water he had left on the floor tiled with Persian jasper.

"Alex," Roe said slowly, "apparently my meeting didn't stop Guyman. Or he changed his mind. I'm ordered to testify tomorrow. It just doesn't make any sense if you're going to back the vice-president."

"What?" Christman roared.

"The president announced today you had agreed to become national chairman for the vice-president's campaign."

"No," he said angrily, "that isn't what happened at all."

"You saw Griswold?" Roe asked in amazement.

"You're damn right."

Neither man spoke for a moment. Then Roe told him, "If you turned him down and he made the announcement anyway, then I assume they are really going to try and bite your ass. It doesn't look like they're kidding."

Roe heard Christman laugh in his hard, bitter way that told him he might not want a fight, but he would be more than ready for it. "That son of a bitch," he told Roe, "is not going to mousetrap me."

"We don't need this fight now," the lawyer pleaded.

"Well," Alexander Christman told him slowly, "I think the time has come when you're going to get one."

Roe still heard Christman's laughter as he put down the phone. And he wondered how the sound of the governor's voice could be enough to reassure him, when his mind told him clearly that everything they worked for was jeopardized.

The governor dried himself and dressed quickly. It did not escape him that he could have easily avoided this. If he were more sensible, he knew, he would have traded stroke for stroke with the president, responded to his flattery, and deferred anything that resembled a firm decision. In his first term as governor, he remembered, he had been stunned enough by his actual election to try to respond to everyone: ethnic groups, contractors, labor unions, and most of all, the more powerful editorial writers in the state. If their suggestions made sense, he tried them.

Two years later, he found that when a program failed that had been ardently promoted by a newspaper or a labor union, they blamed him anyway. Some even attacked him for doing precisely what they had first recommended. Christman learned then he had to deal with all pressure groups equally, whether they were newspapers or individuals.

Midway through his second term, he had become so familiar with his own state that the pattern which marked his political career became set, much as cement hardens in its own specific time after it is poured. But Christman knew he was more of the stuff that steel is made of than cement. He could be bent when the heat was on, but he was yet to encounter anything that might have made him crack.

Devlin was waiting in the foyer of the vast, white Georgian house. He rose quickly, held the front door open for the governor, and then walked around the electric cart and climbed in beside him. The sun had turned a blood-orange red behind the mountains.

"It's getting late," Christman said laconically.

They approached the U-shaped two-story office building he had added to the ranch. Its cellar was shared by a massive steel vault, containing the Christman art collection, and row upon row of computer banks that were the nerve center and storage vault for Christman Data Systems. The first floor contained a series of soundproof office suites with the center of the U serving as a conference room. Above the command post, which had been built eight years ago when Christman had seriously considered the possibility of a national campaign, were the building's living quarters. They served as guest rooms for visitors not invited to the main house. We may have to use it yet, he thought.

All of them were waiting in the conference room. Foreman, the Philadelphia banker who with his crew cut and tight, muscular physique always looked more like a longshoreman than a millionaire; McCloud, the tiny, boyish Texan; the perennially tanned Californian who was his closest friend in the group, Dick Siemanowski, who met Christman's eyes and then nodded toward Julius Gutstein to remind the governor he had to deal with him. The Chicago banker nervously ran his manicured fingers through his hair. Alexander Christman quickly turned away from Gutstein, as if he had not noticed his extended hand.

"Hey," he said, banging Siemanowski's shoulder with his fist. "Wow. I'm sorry I'm late."

Gutstein hung back from the group surrounding the governor, his eyes on the blue-carpeted floor. "Julius?" Christman said.

The banker looked up. "We've been waiting for more than an hour, Alex."

Siemanowski, McCloud, and Foreman watched the governor carefully, as he again avoided Gutstein. The fat man wiped his forehead as the five men moved slowly around the conference table. Siemanowski left his glass of ginger ale where it was. The others took their drinks and set them on the yellow pads in front of them, waiting for Christman to indicate how he wished to proceed. Gutstein sat in the white contour chair farthest from the head of the table, and Christman did not take his eyes off him.

He could control Gutstein or any of the others any time he wanted to, but he had learned each time the power of absolute fiat was exercised, the corpus of his power was diminished. So he had chosen to find other ways.

"Governor—" Gutstein murmured.

"What the hell are you so defensive about, fella?" he asked the fat man, as he put on his oversize glasses and looked around the table.

"Have you seen the president?" Siemanowski asked.

"Yeah. Yesterday," Christman replied.

The conference room was absolutely silent. The air conditioning equipment might have sucked the air from the room and left a vacuum. Christman did not offer to fill it.

Finally McCloud spoke. "Is it true you have problems in New York?"

The silence was shorter this time. The governor tilted his chair back from the table and stared at them.

"Jesus," he said, smiling, "I'm beginning to think this thing is so big you're all getting scared. Have you ever seen anything I can't handle?"

He did not wait for a reply. Instead he slowly took them back up to the mountaintop they had seen six years earlier, when they were first brought together in this room.

"We've got the engineering company. We've changed the Atomic Energy Commission rulings. We've succeeded in accomplishing a major shift in this country, so that people no longer consider nuclear power a threat to the environment. Through the Friends of the Earth, we have convinced a majority of

Americans atomic power is going to be the salvation of the environment. And the blackout that hit New York a couple of hours ago won't hurt either."

It was difficult for Christman to tell whether he had won them back or they were simply enmeshed in his performance. But he did not stop.

"Fellas," he told them, "let's move along. Once around the table."

Siemanowski's detailed report dealt with the status of private and public nuclear sites across the United States. McCloud tediously outlined the condition of bond issues subsidized by subsidiaries of the consortium. Foreman reported equally favorably on the recruiting program the partners had decided was essential. Cutbacks in the government's space exploration program, he said, had made a buyer's market in engineers and scientists. Gutstein was scheduled to deliver the treasurer's report for the consortium.

The governor stood and walked slowly around the conference table until he was standing directly behind the fat man. Gutstein had to twist his neck uncomfortably to see Christman.

"Well, Julius," Christman said, as he held up his hand to the others.

The fat man opened the manila folder in front of him and extracted a sheaf of orange papers. He lifted them, as if he were about to begin reading, but Christman's big paw slammed them down hard.

"I don't want to hear the numbers," he said harshly. "I know the numbers. I want to hear about your meetings."

At the other end of the table, Siemanowski had opened his heavy black briefcase. He pulled out three reels of recording tape and they clattered on the center of the conference table.

"May I have a glass of water?" Gutstein asked.

McCloud poured it from the silver carafe on the conference table. It slopped over the sides, leaving a wet pool in front of Gutstein.

"One is not always interested in money," he said slowly, trying to reach them.

Christman shrugged. "Okay," he said, "tell us about it."

"Governor," the fat man said, leaning forward, his fingertips spread on the table, "one understands the terrible mistake you are making."

They both sensed the tension in the room. "Okay," Christman said, "we're all listening."

"I believe in your powers and your ability," Gutstein said. "Unquestioned. Your sincerity? Unquestioned. But I do not believe even you can change the economic or political structure of this country. The moment American Nuclear becomes visible as a political force," he said, his hand rising in the air as if he were trying to catch a puff of smoke. "Even the magnificent Christman. As nothing."

"That's your reason?" the governor said, pointing to the tapes.

Gutstein was sweating. "I think that if this venture is to fulfill our expectations, you must become president of the United States."

There was silence in the room, and the governor knew exactly what it meant. And he also knew there was nothing to be gained now by punishing Gutstein's disloyalty.

"Jesus," Christman spat at them, "you guys made me give you my word eighteen months ago that I would under no circumstances get involved in any more politics. Damn it, I agreed with you," he whined, the pain and irritation rising in his voice.

Christman stood, the smile automatically returning to his face. But he was not happy as he folded his glasses and dropped them into the breast pocket of the lace shirt. The faces around the table told him they agreed with Gutstein.

"Alex?" Siemanowski called. Christman did not reply. "What are you going to do?"

"Read it in the newspapers," Alexander Christman said. He turned and walked out, but Siemanowski followed him. The two men were outside the building before Christman said a word.

"You know," the governor murmured, looking at the

black sky, "no one ever gets what they really want in politics."

"Can you really say that, Alex?"

"I guess," Alexander Christman replied, "it finally caught up with me."

Siemanowski grinned, as if to say that somewhere there had to be a woman. They had known each other a long time.

"Yeah, fella," Christman replied, "I've got to take care of that, too."

It was darker now, and the governor was quickly driven back to the main house. In the study, Devlin was wearing a headset wired to the telephone. Both instruments were connected to a voice-activated tape recorder. The detective handed Christman a typed copy of the brief text Roe transmitted.

"The situation is about the same," he told Christman. "The city seems to be calm. No catastrophes."

"Where is the lady?"

Devlin grinned. "I think she's sore at you. She ate alone and then went upstairs."

"Did you get anything to eat?"

Devlin shrugged away the question. "Roe is on the open line," he said. "Press six-o-four."

The governor moved to the desk and set the brief statement in bulletin-size type in front of him. He did not need his glasses to see it. With his left hand, he pressed the button for six-o-four and picked up the phone. "Put through that line to Albany," he ordered Devlin. "I want to get this over with."

A white-jacketed waiter quietly set an oversize cup of steaming bouillon in front of him, and he winked his approval. "Thanks, Ralphie," he said. "I'm not going to eat tonight." The waiter nodded and left the room, closing the door behind him.

"Alex? Alex? You there?" he heard the voice calling on the other end of the line.

"Yes, Arthur," he said.

"Governor," the exuberant voice of the lawyer said rapidly, "Mayor Thayer called a little while ago. He wanted to know whether he could issue a statement saying he had met with you. I told him it was fine and as far as you were concerned he could go ahead and do it."

Christman laughed deep in his chest. "Is there anyone who can say we are both liars if anyone finds out?" He sounded certain the charade would work.

"Are you ready to record, Alex? It's all set on this end," Roe pushed him. But the governor had not yet left his sense of amusement with Mayor Thayer.

"Do you think Thayer's coming around?" he asked. "I could tell the truth at the press conference tomorrow. Jesus, that would embarrass him."

"Alex!" the lawyer cautioned.

"Okay. Okay," he said. "The meeting here went fine. The draft of the statement looks fine. What's happening with Guyman?"

"I've been trying to get him since one o'clock this afternoon."

Christman was silent. He took a deep breath and when he spoke again the tense edge was back in his voice. "Do what you think is best, Arthur."

The governor nodded to Devlin who instructed the switchboard in Irvington to patch Roe's line into the Albany call, as the governor sipped the steaming bouillon. He heard Roe ask for Harvey Kuhn when the patch was completed, and his press secretary was quickly on the line.

"How is it up there?" Christman asked him.

"We've handled this kind of problem before. The press guys are no problem. But that Power Commission of yours doesn't know when to shut up."

"What happened?" he heard Roe ask.

"It's well in hand," Kuhn replied. "Governor, we're set on this end. They'll put you on live from Albany at ten forty-five our time. Jesus, there are only three stations still operating in the city anyway. All the newspapers are knocked out. But the four motorcycle guys we use to deliver press releases in the New York office can hand-deliver the text just to keep us covered. You'll top this story at the press conference in the morning."

The governor finished the bouillon and it relaxed

the muscles in his throat. "I still think it's worth doing."

"No argument," Kuhn told him. "I'll introduce you before you read the statement. Let's do it three times so we can pick the best take."

"Right," Alexander Christman said, lifting the text to his eyes, "whenever you're ready."

He heard Kuhn clear his throat. "Ladies and gentlemen," the press secretary said solemnly, "from his office in Albany, the governor of the state of New York."

Christman read the statement three times, and each time, Kuhn introduced him. When he was finished, he stood, stretched his arms over his head, and tried to soothe his back by rolling the aching muscles under his shirt. Devlin was waiting for instructions.

"Tell the Irvington switchboard to keep a telephone line open for the WOR broadcast. Pipe it up to the speaker in the master bedroom. And get yourself something to eat. We try to run a pretty good establishment here."

Devlin nodded. "Do you want me to pipe the running news accounts upstairs?"

"No," Governor Alexander Christman said, as he walked out of the study toward the stairs.

She was in the bedroom and without a word, he undressed quickly and sprawled on the bed.

His back was peeling and he could feel heat, even on the cool, white satin sheet. Athena Courtland hesitated for a moment and then knelt beside him on the immense round bed and trailed a nylon stocking across his body as he stared through the skylight at the stars sputtering brilliantly in the Arizona sky. He sighed and moved his arms behind his head, opening his sensitive rib cage to her caress. His eyes were closed as his mind sorted out the accelerated events of the past twenty-four hours. It was all different now. And he wondered whether he would ever again regain absolute control of his own future. He had no doubts whatever about what he must do, and he knew he had fought it so long it would no longer cause him pain.

"Can we talk now, Alex?" she whispered softly, touching his lips with her long fingernail.

"No," he told her, as he squirmed on the bed.

She slapped his chest hard and his eyes opened quickly. Athena Courtland was sitting straight up, her hands on her hips, glaring at him.

He grinned at her, happy to elude the conclusion forming in his mind. "Hey," he told her, "I've never seen you really angry before."

"What do you think a woman is, Alex?" she said, lifting her hand to swing at him again. Christman grabbed her wrist and pushed her backwards onto the bed.

"Lips. Hips. Breasts. Hair. Thighs," he said softly, kissing her mouth as he held her hands over her head. "Fingers. Toes. Ears." She began to squirm beneath him, twisting and turning her head to avoid his kisses.

"Please, Alex," she begged.

He sat up and held his hands in front of him and said innocently, in the nasal voice she had learned to recognize when he became defensive, "Later. I promise."

The incredibly beautiful woman looked for a moment as if she were about to cry. He touched her cheek and smiled gently at her. "Be Athena," he said softly.

She seemed confused, as if she did not know whether to hit him or kiss him. They were both startled as the bedroom speaker suddenly squawked and then they heard Harvey Kuhn's deep basso announce:

"Ladies and gentlemen, from his office in Albany, the governor of the state of New York."

She looked at him for a moment and laughed.

"I've been saved by a pretty good fella," he told her sheepishly. She smiled back at him. As though he were explaining a magic trick, he said, "It's a recording."

Christman put his arms around her and pulled her down beside him, as if he were offering protection in the warm curve of his body. Then he propped his head on his hand and listened carefully to the broadcast.

"Ladies and Gentlemen, My Fellow New Yorkers," Alexander Christman heard himself saying, "it is a distinct pleasure tonight to pay tribute to each and every man, woman, and child within the sound of my voice."

The sound of his voice made Athena Courtland sit straight up and stir in the governor's arm.

Together they heard him speak of the heroism of city dwellers and the rapid, cool-headed response of police departments throughout the state. She giggled once, and then she saw his face. It silenced her quickly. He explained that the blackout had been caused by massive "load shedding" that resulted from unexpected drains on the interstate power pool.

"I am determined," he said, as her hand touched his thigh, "that this potential for disaster to life and the property of the people of this state will not occur again. New York's power companies for too long have established themselves as feudal monarchies, whose only purpose is to produce greater and greater profits for investors who care nothing for the general welfare of the people.

"They have fought the development of inexpensive, safe energy produced from atomic power. They have deprived seventeen million New Yorkers of the rightful benefits of modern technology—increasingly less expensive power.

"Accordingly, I have instructed this state's Public Service Commission to reexamine and revise downward all electric rates in this state. Future rates will no longer be based on inflated corporate costs that support malingering executives at exorbitant salaries. By next year, New Yorkers will pay no more for electricity than they should have to pay if these companies were producing the same commodity using atomic-powered generators.

"In conclusion, Fellow New Yorkers, I pay you tribute. It will continue to be a long, black night which we will endure together. God bless you and goodnight."

"Okay," he told her, "now we can talk."

"Shut up," she said, pushing him flat on his back as she shoved a large satin pillow under his buttocks.

She kissed the inside of his thighs and ran her tongue gently through his groin as he groaned on the bed. He sat up and straddled her body, balancing himself on his knees.

He watched as her fingers moved to her crotch and spread the clean-shaven pink lips to receive his kiss. Then he moved forward until he was poised over her. She opened her lips with two fingers and he slid inside her.

"I love you, Alex. I love you so damn much," she groaned, angry with herself for responding, when she did not wish to, to the power she felt in him.

She did not move at first, careful not to touch his sunburnt body. With muscles inside her vagina, she squeezed him inside her until the ring at her entrance imprisoned him. She wished to hold him prisoner forever, and so she squeezed hard enough until the groan she heard from him was more pleasure than pain. Her ankles locked behind his back forcing him deep inside her.

Christman flung out his arms, forcing her legs apart, and then pressed her knees back against her breasts. He moved in and out of her rapidly, almost viciously, pounding her flesh with his pelvis. His hands went under her buttocks and he lifted her with both his arms, trying to possess her, trying to prevent her from moving without his permission.

"Ride me," she shouted, the sweat covering her body, as both their bodies pumped at each other. They were in battle. "Ride me hard," she screamed, when he thrust into her. She stiffened again and her heels pounded on his back and shoulders. She could have been spurring a horse. She was driving him, taunting, pressuring, and forcing him to an effort he had not known he could make, for she knew how deeply it would please him.

When her breath returned, he was still above her. She took his face in her hands.

"You're marvelous, old man," she said, for she had learned that pleased him, too.

He moved off her, carefully wiping his loins with the top sheet that had been kicked to the foot of the bed.

Christman was grinning. "Thank you," he whispered happily, his hand sliding on the inside of her thigh. "Thank you so goddamned much."

"That's nice, Alex. But you promised me we would talk."

He looked at her as if she were an adversary instead of an accomplice now, and Athena DeWitt Thompson Woodward Courtland, who loved men with power as she loved nothing else, knew inside herself that it was time to stop. She knew that this was neither the time nor place to pursue it, because if she did, she would lose him to the mood she did not understand that possessed him in this moment. But she could not help herself, she knew, any more than a politician can help taking a campaign contribution, even from someone with an unsavory cause. But the cause was herself. And she did not know how to stop.

"Tell me," she said.

"I thought about it," he told her, trying to be as gentle as he could, knowing he did not want to hurt her.

"What do you think a woman is?" she asked him.

"I told you before," he said, smiling, but not touching her this time. "Hips. Thighs. Buttocks."

"Alex," she complained indignantly.

He looked at her and told himself he wanted to be gentle, knowing that he had never been very good with words when it came to women. "You just got married," he said.

She sat up and lifted herself off the bed, as badly beaten as any creature who had ever played a role in her fantasies. Her shoulders sloped. Her head hung low as she wiped her thighs with a corner of the sheet. He reminded her of her first husband, the one who called her an ugly slut before he went after her with a shotgun. But disappointment and pain did not make her afraid anymore.

"You son of a bitch," she said.

He smiled, but it did not calm her. He knew there was no way to be gentle, and he knew he could not permit himself to be brutal with her. Inside himself he felt the kind of pain he had not allowed to touch him for longer than he wished to remember. But he did not wish to show the pain, and he did not wish to be untruthful with her.

"I can't divorce her," he said, looking at the sheets because he could not tolerate the unhappiness he knew would be mirrored in her face. "Everything is different now."

Athena Courtland said nothing. She still felt the pleasure of him in her loins. But she felt pain too. For she did not wish to have anyone but him inside her ever again. Her hand reached out and grasped his chin and turned his head, forcing him to look at her.

Sheepishly, he stared into her eyes, knowing he would not allow himself to tell her what she wished to hear. "I can't do it," he said. "That's the way it is in politics."

She did not respond, for she still did not wish to hurt him. And when he caressed her cheek this time, she smiled, and he told himself he could not do this if he was forced to run.

"Hey," he said gratefully, "I'm starving to death." Then the small boy crept into his voice and he asked her if she would sneak downstairs with him to get something to eat. She nodded, and he looked at her again. For him, she had always been a goddess. And it had disturbed him that in the last half hour he found that she had become something less, something more human, someone who made him feel that he was in love in a place other than Olympus. Now she had become a goddess again: aloof, untouchable, superior, perfect. And he was pleased and grateful that he had not hurt her.

CHAPTER ELEVEN

ARTHUR ROE KNEW Foley Square and he knew the
U. S. Courthouse well. Even the cracked wooden
benches and the labyrinthian hallways of the old
federal building were familiar to him. But he had
never been inside a grand jury room before.

The grand jury is one of the most ancient bodies in
Anglo-Saxon law. It is comprised of twenty-three citizens, including a foreman, who hear evidence presented by a prosecutor. It is the function of the grand
jury to sift the evidence and decide whether a majority
of them believe arrest and indictment is warranted. No
judge presides over a grand jury. Lawyers representing
clients called to appear are not permitted inside the
room to hear testimonay. It is a secret proceeding in
which testimony is sealed, under penalty of law, unless and until the seal is broken and the testimony
made public by a judge, based on an application by
the prosecutor or a defendant.

It was precisely such a petition that Arthur Roe
feared U. S. Attorney Guyman would bring. The legal
purpose of such a petition would be to compel Roe to
testify. The petition's real purpose would be to destroy
Alexander Christman, because Roe knew well that
Guyman could cite sufficient evidence in a petition
presented in open court fo force American Nuclear
into the headlines and smear the governor. It did not
matter at all that Roe had an absolute legal right under
the long established lawyer-client privilege to refuse to
testify concerning any of his clients' affairs.

Assistant U. S. Attorney Martin Soshin seated Roe
at a bare wooden desk. In front of him, the grand jury

138

panel sat in a raised semicircle that looked like a medical amphitheater. Soshin walked up the steps and paced slowly in the back of the room, while the panel stared at Roe. He wondered what they already knew about him.

"May I proceed, Mr. Foreman?" Soshin asked.

A white-haired, gaunt-looking man in the second row signaled with the forefinger of his right hand, as if he were telling the pilot of a small plane to take off.

"Would you state your name and occupation?"

"Arthur Roe. I am an attorney and a partner in the firm of Whitman, Gelman."

"Among the many clients of your distinguished firm, do you include Alexander Christman, now governor of the state of New York?"

"I am certain that the fact that an attorney represents a particular client is not included in what the law would consider privileged information. The answer, Mr. Soshin, is yes."

"Thank you."

"I don't believe there is anything else you can ask me."

"Let me be the judge of that, sir. You are testifying pursuant to a legal subpoena issued by this grand jury now investigating certain matters related to the affairs and methods of the state of New York."

"I am not an employee of the state of New York."

"Thank you," Soshin said sarcastically, hoping that Roe was irritating the panel. It made it that much easier to persuade the grand jury to go along with him. He could not take any action without their approval, and he knew how important it was to stay in control.

"Mr. Roe," the foreman asked, "have you ever been an employee of the state of New York?"

"No, sir."

Soshin permitted the interruption to pass as he paced the back of the room, sorting his notes. The panel was waiting for him and he was ready.

"Mr. Roe, as I understand it, you also serve as legal counsel to the corporation known as American Nuclear Energy?"

"That is correct."

"And Governor Christman is one of the principal stockholders in that company?"

"I believe that is a matter of public record," he said, knowing it was not, hoping it would induce the jurors to believe no conflict of interest was involved on Christman's part.

"And that American Nuclear Energy has received some six hundred and forty thousand dollars in research grants from the State Atomic Energy Agency?"

"That is also public information, Mr. Soshin."

"Have you ever discussed these grants with Governor Christman?"

"I decline to answer that question, sir, on the grounds that it constitutes a privileged communication between an attorney and his client."

"Sir?"

"You heard me."

"Did you recommend for appointment several members of that agency?"

"No reply. Same grounds."

"Has American Nuclear Energy accepted gifts of property from the state of New York?"

"Same grounds."

"Is their equipment and personnel owned or paid for by the state of New York now used solely for the benefit of American Nuclear Energy?"

"Same grounds." Roe recognized the men and women in front of him were a lay panel that did not understand the legal argument. He could not have cared less, as he pushed the chair away from the table and started to stand.

"Please remain seated, Mr. Roe," Soshin blustered. "This isn't a staff conference in your Park Avenue law firm."

He carefully avoided reacting to the slur. "Mr. Soshin, members of the panel, with all due respect, I believe my position is quite clear."

"I'm not finished, Mr. Roe," Soshin shouted, immediately sorry he had raised his voice. He walked quickly to the front of the room, as if that would force

Roe back into the chair. Roe was angry, but he was well under control.

"I think my answers," he said slowly, "are sufficient to establish a pattern indicating that I will continue to reply in precisely this manner. I am not interested in your creating a record that can be used to harm an innocent man. Do you understand me, Mr. Soshin?"

"Counsellor," he snapped, playing to the panel, "you know as well as I do that proceedings before a grand jury are secret."

Roe uttered a sound of disgust and began walking toward the door.

"It is our intention," Soshin told him, "to bring proceedings that will compel you to testify, sir."

Roe spun around and turned on him. "I think we better see Mr. Guyman," he said. "You have more than exceeded your authority in this matter."

Soshin smiled. "I think we had better."

They walked down the wide marble staircase to the musty fourth-floor office of the U. S. attorney for the southern district of New York. Soshin did not stop at the receptionist's desk, nor did he present himself to the redheaded secretary seated outside the U. S. attorney's office, beneath an overpowering portrait of President Griswold. He rapped sharply on the heavy wooden door. When he heard a whining grunt of acknowledgment from within, he opened the door for Arthur Roe and then followed him inside. Guyman had the *Daily News* Sunday comics lying flat on his desk. He was resting his head on his hand. He did not look up, and Roe could see the bald spot that was beginning to grow in the center of his crew cut.

"What is it, Soshin?" he asked harshly, as the assistant U. S. attorney stood in front of the massive desk, his hands on his hips.

"I think you had better give this matter your fullest attention," Roe murmured, happy to see Guyman's head pop up from the desk. He saw Roe, stood quickly, and walked around the desk to greet him warmly. Guyman's face showed that he was beginning to realize why Roe was there.

"May we speak privately, Arnold?" Roe asked, glancing at Soshin.

The U. S. attorney's face flushed a bright red and he ran his fingers through his crew cut. He walked to the small closet near his desk, rolled down his shirt sleeves, and put on his suit jacket. When he had seated himself again behind his desk and removed the newspaper, he finally addressed himself to the visitors. Soshin sat down on the green leather sofa, a yellow legal pad on his lap and a pencil in his hand.

"This is not for the record, Martin," Guyman said with a glance toward his young assistant. "Arthur," he said, a look of anguish on his face, "I think you will understand the decisions made in this matter were not mine to make. That is to say, I am acting under specific instructions."

"Stop the bullshit, Arnold," Roe told him. "You're the U. S. attorney for the southern district."

Guyman's face was brick red.

"Mr. Guyman," Soshin said, "this man refused to answer certain questions before the grand jury today. He refused to cooperate in any way with this investigation. He refused to respect the right of the grand jury to ask him questions. And he even refused to remain in the grand jury room until the record was completed."

"Soshin," Arnold Guyman said, waving his hand at him, "be quiet."

Guyman held his head in his hands. If he had a greater political debt, it was to Alexander Christman. But he was trapped between two immensely powerful men, and he still was not sure of anything, except that he could only get hurt choosing sides between them.

"Arnie," Roe began gently, "the questions I refused to answer would have violated privileged conversations with my client."

"I think that is a matter for a federal judge to decide," Soshin shouted. "I don't give a damn who Arthur Roe is or how powerful his client may be. Mr. Guyman, I had your word this case would proceed."

Guyman's face was filled with irritation as he tried

to wave Soshin quiet. Then he turned to Roe. "I would like to be fair with everyone, Arthur."

It was precisely the opening Roe waited for. "I have no objection, providing," he said, hitting the word very hard, "that the Petition to the Court drawn by your office is not used to embarrass my client."

Roe eased himself back in the soft leather chair. He had prevented the prosecutor from asking him any further questions until the issue was decided by a judge. And if Guyman agreed, he had blocked an overt attempt to get the story into the press.

"Which judge did you have in mind, Arnold?" Roe asked.

"Paul Falkenburg is sitting in motion part."

Roe could not restrain the grin. When Griswold was elected, Falkenburg was Christman's first recommendation for the federal bench. The lawyer, for the first time, found himself admiring Guyman's ability to carry out orders from Washington in a way that would not make an enemy of Governor Christman.

"This is highly irregular," Soshin complained. "This man cannot be allowed to participate in drawing a court order demanding he produce information."

Guyman waved him once again into silence and called for a stenographer. He played with a paperweight while they waited, and then motioned the thin brunette into a chair. Guyman did not say a word as his assistant and Roe negotiated the language of the petition to the court. The lawyer would object to the slightest allusion to his client by name, position, or even county of residence. Soshin complained bitterly, but without support from Guyman, who occasionally muttered, "That's fair," there was little he could do. For thirty-five minutes, the two men argued matters of language until Guyman's telephone interrupted them.

"What?" he roared, his face turning blotchy, glancing angrily at Roe. "Bring me a copy!"

The door opened. An assistant walked briskly to Guyman's desk and handed him a typed slip of memo paper. He put on his glasses, read it quickly, and looked again at Roe.

"You son of a bitch," he said. "You dirty son of a bitch!" And flung the paper at Roe.

"Arnold," Roe said softly.

"Read it," he sputtered. "I have gone out of my way, out of my way to be fair, and jeopardized my goddamn job—for that?"

Roe read the typed memorandum. It said:

WINS News reported that Governor Christman denied he would act as national chairman for the presidential campaign of Vice-President George Whitmore. In an interview at Butler Airport, he said, "The president is using his power for personal gain. I won't tolerate it and I don't think the people of this country will tolerate it."

"Can you give us some specifics, Governor?"

"Ask the stooge the president has used to black-mail me. And I mean the U. S. attorney of the southern district of New York, Arnold Guyman."

Roe looked up.

"Don't just sit there, Soshin," Guyman screamed, "Go and get a goddamned radio!" He picked up the phone. "Miss Berlin. No calls. I don't care what you say. Say I'm meeting with the attorney general."

Roe was on his feet moving toward the door, and Guyman stepped toward him quickly, as if he were about to tackle him.

"Where do you think you're going?" he shouted.

The lawyer opened the door and turned, smiling broadly at Guyman.

"Arnold," he said, "you know something? Suddenly I don't give a hoot in hell what you put in that petition to the court."

"But Arthur, he shouldn't have done that to me. It isn't fair," he whined. "I was doing what I could."

"Sure," Roe told him. "My advice to you is to get back on our team quick. Think about it, Arnold."

Roe left quickly. Walking down the stone steps of the Federal Building two at a time, he knew that Christman had found his own way to protect his dream. And he wondered whether the governor knew that the surest way to avoid prosecution was to be elected president of the United States.

CHAPTER TWELVE

THERE WERE forty-six microphones by actual count, as the Associated Press reported. Governor Alexander Christman's twelve-thirty press conference the afternoon following the blackout brought to his New York City office on West Fortieth Street no less than five metropolitan reporters from *The New York Times,* including the paper's chief political reporter, environmental correspondent, and its urban affairs correspondent, and all the "in-depth specialists" from all the other papers as well. The three major television networks assigned camera crews to cover the event, in addition to those already assigned by their local news stations. Even newspaper editorial writers, who simply wanted to hear firsthand the governor's account of the blackout, were there. And so were reporters from the news magazines, the Washington *Post,* the Los Angeles *Times,* and the Chicago *Sun-Times.*

Kuhn, press secretary to Governor Alexander Christman, followed Arthur Roe's instructions to the letter. He was sure of his handling of the details. He held up announcement of the press conference until 10 A.M., certain the short notice would help produce a large turnout. He also took it upon himself to tell the state attorney general and the lieutenant governor that the governor wanted them present. Then he personally called Mayor Thayer and told him to stay in City Hall, which he considered a stroke of genius only Christman would appreciate.

Kuhn knew Roe had called the chairman of the board of Consolidated Electric, a man who had been stunned to learn the executive vice-president he appointed had bribed the commissioner of water supply

of the city of New York to obtain permission to build
new power lines to the city. The press, Kuhn's instincts
told him, would want to show their toughness by roast-
ing someone for the second major blackout in ten
years. That would be enough to deflect hostile questions from Alexander Christman.

Christman came in the Thirty-ninth Street side of
the office at exactly 12:25. Kuhn had no time to brief
him. He led him to the sitting room where a butler
had provided the chairman of the board of Consolidated Electric with a glass of ginger ale. The ruddy,
athletic executive was wearily chatting with the public
officials who had been elected to office on Christman's
ticket.

"We warned you, Alex," he told the governor, handing him a copy of the statement he planned to read.

The governor slipped the oversize glasses on and
quickly scanned the single, typewritten page. Then he
folded it, tore it lengthwise, and then tore it again. He
handed the bits of paper to the bald, ex-liquor lawyer
who was the state attorney general, and turned back
to the chairman of the board.

"Whit, I'll shut you down."

"Sure, Governor." His voice was heavy with sarcasm,
as if he was trying to say he had taken this kind of
punishment for the last time.

"I not only can do it, fella, I can justify it. The people that pay your bills don't like the electric company."

Parsons said nothing.

"Do you want me to shut you down?"

The board chairman was so angry he found it difficult to look directly at Christman.

"What's in this for you, Alex?"

Christman eased himself away from the private confrontation. "I'm just acting for the people," he said.
"Somebody has to act for the people."

The governor put his arm around Kuhn's shoulders
and walked slowly toward the small room lined with
rows of metal folding chairs. It had been designed for
press conferences of fifteen or twenty reporters. More
than a hundred were packed inside today.

"Good job, Harvey." The governor grinned. "I appreciate it."

Kuhn's expression never changed. "Toward the end, as a sort of a topper, the *Newsday* guy will ask you whether this was your worst crisis. I thought you would want to downplay the blackout. Why not tell them they ought to see you on election night?"

"Right," the governor said. Then he took off his glasses and dropped them in his breast pocket. "What did it cost us?"

"I gave him a look at that pisser of a report on missing equipment in the city hospitals. Thayer will go up the wall when it leaks out."

Christman had wondered whether Mayor Thayer might be coming around. He punched Kuhn hard on the arm.

"You're worse than I am!" he said happily.

The governor stood just outside the door as Kuhn walked to the dais in the packed room.

"Ladies and gentlemen," he said, "the governor of the state of New York, Alexander Christman."

Christman knew they were curious. At least as curious about how he might look, or act, or feel, as they were about the blackout. Political reporters, he learned, considered themselves not only students of the men in power they wrote about, but also very special insiders. They always needed some bit of news, an impression, an anecdote that would serve privately to prove their status and privileged knowledgeability with wives, family, and friends. It was not the kind of thing that appeared in print. And Alex Christman gave it to them blithely, with the same careful attention he did everything else.

He appeared somber to them. A trifle drawn. The pouches under his eyes were heavier than they remembered, and perhaps the eczema on his cheek was a little worse. He did not bounce onto the platform on the balls of his feet, as he usually did, but rather seemed to shuffle to the podium like a tired left fielder taking his position in the last inning of a double-header.

Christman carefully established the mood of serious

concern until he decided it was time to demonstrate
he was the same man they had always known. He
placed his hands on either side of the rostrum, leaned
forward, and winked at a reporter in the front row.
Then he had a "hiya" for a minor local television
correspondent. He leaned into the microphones, the
familiar smile on his face, and said:

"Some turnout. You guys all got a piece of a
winning lottery ticket?"

Christman grinned, almost certain he had rewon
their affection, as he tried to do each time he faced
them.

"Okay, fellas," he said. "Quiet down. I've got
a statement. The chairman of the board of Consolidated Electric is here, Whitney Parsons, and if you
don't think that takes some guts, you're wrong. He's
got a statement. Maxie," he said, waving to the state
attorney general, "has no statement. He just came by to
complain I don't give him enough to do."

They laughed again, like Romans acknowledging an
imperial promise of a minimum of one live Christian.

Arthur Roe entered the back of the hot, crowded
room and Christman winked at him. The lawyer
watched him return a reporter's question with the
mechanical victory smile of a Cheshire cat. Then the
governor turned quickly back to the audience, as if
they were a roomful of unruly children.

"All right," Christman said, "how do you want it?
My statement, then Whit, then questions? Or statement, questions, statement? I think, for the moment,
we should defer any political questions."

Most of the press groaned. But the NBC man pro-
tected the governor.

"Let's get the hard news in the can first," he yelled.

In whatever manner men who run meetings learn to
perceive the majority consensus, Governor Christman
simply proceeded, having adequately demonstrated
what appeared to be his democratic penchant for con-
sulting everyone. He looked straight into the cameras,
knowing they were turning, and said:

"Let's look on the bright side of the blackout."

Laughter exploded, as a hundred sweating reporters

let loose the tension of twenty-four hours without sleep that ended here, in this uncomfortable room.

"Well, there's the quote of the day," whispered one of *The New York Times* editorial board members. "He can't top that one."

"Come on, fellas," Governor Christman said, holding up his hands in mock anguish, "if you'll let me start again, I promise to fire the guy responsible for that line."

It was not a blooper and he knew it. He also knew it delighted the press to catch him off base. Score one for us, he thought, knowing that if he gave them something to tease him with, the questions to which he would be subjected would hardly be fierce at all. He also reminded himself to protect Parsons as best he could.

"You guys never take me seriously," he said, to more laughter. "There is a bright side to the blackout." Again they laughed. "Come on, Abe," he said in anguish. "Shut that camera off. This isn't on the record."

"Sorry, Governor," Abe Peterson came back, as Christman held up his hands and waggled his head in despair. The press had beaten him once again.

The governor's statement was the kind of masterful performance they had come to expect from him.

"It's easy to say New Yorkers behaved magnificently," he said, his voice bordering on a high nasal whine. "That's not good enough. The people in this state pay for electric power and they are entitled to full service. It's not enough to tell them to shut off their air conditioners or conserve power in other ways. People are entitled to service. Right?

"What happened last night was no freak. It can happen again. Now I don't like to say this, but I've been fighting for at least six years for conversion to atomic generators in this state. I've tried to educate the conservationists. That's taken some time. Now we know we are out of time. We have to move quickly in the interests of the people. As for the power companies, I have been tolerant. I have been patient with their problems. And I made a mistake."

His eyes scanned the room, and he knew they were ready.

"Early this morning, I asked the State Public Service Commission to appoint an Atomic Power Site Selection Committee. That committee will choose eight locations. If Consolidated Electric and other companies will not undertake building these facilities, I will ask the legislature for permission to issue special state bonds to finance them. If the power companies refuse the option of financing construction of these facilities, I will order appropriate statewide rate reductions to compensate the taxpayers of New York State."

Governor Christman stopped, waiting for questions, but before the reporters reacted, he had introduced Parsons to distract them.

The board chairman of Consolidated Electric was on his feet quickly, as Governor Christman offered him the rostrum. In a flat uninspired style, he talked of "grid systems," "the interstate power pool," and kilowatt consumption as causes of the blackout. Less than half a dozen of those present understood a word of it.

When he finished, as Kuhn predicted, the questions were all directed at Parsons. Christman, standing by his side, merely ran the meeting. Christman finally pointed to a redheaded reporter with a pockmarked face in the third row.

"Governor," he said in a high nasal voice, as though the last letter of the word was an *a*, "let's give the boogy man there a breather. I'd like to ask you a question."

"Shoot, fella," Christman said, noticing that most of the cameramen were too busy reloading to care. They had all gotten the best of Parson's squirming.

"Governor Christman," he said, "don't you have a personal financial interest in the development of atomic power in this state?"

Christman was startled by the question. But he did not permit himself a moment's visible awkwardness.

"My interest," he said easily, "is in the welfare of all of the people in this state. The proposal I made here today is in the interest of meeting their needs."

The governor's eyes quickly scanned the room looking for a raised hand. He found one. Abe Peterson knew a rescue cue when he saw one. Motioning his cameraman to start rolling, he said:

"Mr. Parsons, there's one question I think you have to answer. Will your company accept the governor's proposal and build those plants at your own expense?"

Parsons glanced behind him for help, but there was no one but Christman. He looked at the governor, whose grin was easily the best moment on the evening news. Then he turned back to the microphone and said:

"I don't know, Mr. Peterson. I can't answer your question."

"Sir," Peterson said belligerently, pushing hard as he always did when he knew it was safe, "you are the chairman of the board of this company. Certainly you have some reaction? Some notion of what you will recommend? Frankly, I don't understand how you can face your customers in this city."

"That's uncalled for, sir," Parsons said.

All the cameras were rolling now. Even the pencil press was alerted. To a man, they disparaged Peterson's baiting in an interview, but they always enjoyed it.

"Sir," Peterson said again, "I think the people deserve an answer."

"Mr. Peterson," Parsons responded, with what sounded like a heavy sigh, "I'm not sure this is going to be my decision to make."

"Do you mean, sir," he pursued, "that you plan to resign as board chairman?"

"I—" Parsons began to say and glanced at Christman for help. He was flustered. "You, sir," he began, "are an impertinent—" No one heard the word. To Peterson, it sounded like "yid."

Christman took command. "Hey fellas, take it easy. This guy's been up all night too."

Peterson looked angrily at Christman, but kept his mouth shut. The governor saw Kuhn give his signal to the *Newsday* reporter with whom he had planted the question, and it came back as if he had punched a button on a tape recorder.

"Governor, it sounded as though, like everybody

else, you had your hands full last night. Can you tell us whether you've ever faced a greater crisis?"

"Sure. Election night. When the returns start coming in from those upstate counties, I really grit my teeth. And it was even worse the second and third time."

The room rocked with laughter, and Alexander Christman knew he was playing with the press corps in the half-joking manner they loved best. He had given them the story, and now by entertaining them, he could insure its being told in precisely the manner he wished.

He let the laughter and the rib-poking in his audience continue, delighted that those cameramen he could see from the rostrum had all decided to start filming this portion of the press conference. Instinctively, and it had taken him a while to learn it, the television producers of the evening news shows liked to have a tag of twenty or thirty seconds to match up with the filmed section of his prepared opening statement that had been carefully timed to a minute and twenty seconds. Together, the two segments would make a two-minute film clip package. The only variations that would exist from station to station would depend on whether the producer decided to use a question and answer put by the station's own reporter.

They were all laughing and tears were in the eyes of some of the press. He heard one cameraman say, "He's a pisser, all right." The question was a perfect plant. Off to the left side he saw the pockfaced, redheaded reporter, whom he did not know, waving his hand. Stay away from that one, he told himself, he's going to try to clip you again. But as the laughter died, the working press had, as they often did, seemingly lost the thread of the conference. And there was the redhead, hand waving above his flushed face, the croaking Irish voice shouting "Governor, Governor," over the din as if the title was a dirty word. He looked down at the redhead, who had moved between the microphones held by the CBS and NBC reporters, and his hands were on both of them as he said:

"Can you tell us, Governor Christman, precisely where *you* were through the blackout last night?"

The cameras had stopped rolling with the first wave

of laughter, and someone had cut the spotlights. Without hesitation, as he caught perfectly the last wave of laughter, he said, squinting his eyes and then popping them open, as the huge grin came over his face again, "Sure. I was in my pool on the ranch in Arizona. Somebody told me to go jump in the lake and I couldn't resist."

They began laughing again, and as it had been before, it was the warm laughter of a band of men who believed they had shared a common experience the night before and had not slept in twenty-four hours. In Christman's response, they recognized the mocking tone of someone who always performed well in adversity, and they knew that soon they would imitate it themselves.

"Is the floor opened for those other kinds of questions now?" Abe Peterson asked, and they all laughed as Christman rolled his eyes toward the ceiling. Peterson was, without question, the best man in the room to frame the question, and the governor knew it.

"Okay, Abe," he said with resignation, the mock anguish clear. "Shoot."

"Governor Christman, yesterday President Griswold announced your appointment as national chairman of the Whitmore for President Organization. This morning at Butler Airport you had some unkind things to say about the president." Peterson was holding the wire copy in his hand and now he read it. "You said he was, and I quote, 'immorally using the investigative powers of the Government for political purposes.'" Peterson read it as if he did not understand the words. "Am I quoting you correctly, sir?"

"Yeah."

"Well, what did you mean, Governor?"

"Just what I said. The president is using the U. S. attorney's office and the Justice Department to intimidate people into supporting the man he has chosen as his successor."

No one coughed. The room was absolutely silent. If reporters respected anything, it was their own presence at a moment they thought was history. Christman waited in the silence for the next question.

"Is he trying to intimidate you, Governor?" Peterson asked, the awesome disbelief evident in his voice.

Christman's hands were raised in supplication. "I am saying that he is attempting to use that particular office in an effort to blackmail me into supporting his candidate. I can think of no greater danger to this nation than the abuse of power by the most powerful man in this nation."

He slapped the rostrum with the palm of his hand and started toward the door as Kuhn took his place before them.

Peterson almost asked it as an afterthought. "Governor, one last question."

Christman turned and waited.

"Is it still accurate to say that you are not an active candidate for president of the United States?"

Christman blinked as his eyes scanned the room. The smile began slowly, as if he could not control it, and spread across his face until the monumental grin was as warm as they had ever seen it. He was like a man bursting with a secret he could no longer contain, and every eye in the room was caught up in the moment.

"Nope," he said, the smile gone and the muscle working hard in his jaw. And then smiling again, he stepped out the door.

The room was bedlam. Reporters turned to each other and shouted, "What did he say?" Someone replied, "Nope. What's nope?" A man from the Newark News said, "He couldn't have announced. You don't do it that way." The room rocked with shouts as somebody called to Kuhn, obviously as stunned as everyone else, and asked him what the governor meant. For the first time in his life, the press secretary was flustered, and he shook his head and said, "I better go ask him." Five of the television cameramen did not have it on film, and one got angry at the reporter working with him. "You told me not to shoot any of Abe's questions," he screamed. "Go fuck yourself," was the reply. Peterson's cameraman signaled an O.K. sign to his boss, and the squat, dark reporter wiped his forehead in relief. It was one of the rare times he needed no one to congratulate him. The network would damn well have to come to him if they wanted film.

As Arthur Roe moved around the back of the room, trying to avoid the crush of bodies around him, the red-headed reporter said, "That's some piece of work," to no one in particular. The *Times* man heard him and turned, removed the pipe from his mouth, and said, "He's beautiful."

The lawyer wrenched his way past a burly sound-man, trying to reach Christman. "We're in it," he told himself. "Goddammit, we're in it."

Kuhn was back at the rostrum, wiping the sweat from his face, and the room quieted quickly as reporters and newspapermen glared at bustling camera crews.

"What did he actually say, Harvey?" the man from the *Times* asked.

"I think," he said, and then stopped himself. "The intent of his response was crystal clear."

"Come on, Harvey, get him back here. Be fair."

Kuhn looked across the room, for the first time realizing the total pleasure of being precisely where he wanted to be, delighted with an audience that hung on his every word. His joy was as much in his own style as his feeling of competence, and now he held up his hand and pursed his lips, as if he were tasting a fine dry Bordeaux.

"Governor Christman will make a formal declaration of his candidacy for president of the United States at eleven A.M. tomorrow," he told them flatly. "That is all, gentlemen." He turned and strode off the podium.

"Nice job, Harvey," Roe whispered to Kuhn as he passed him in the hallway on his way to the knot of people surrounding Christman. The attorney general was at the center, slapping the governor on the back like a football coach. It annoyed the governor, but he said nothing, pulling away only when he saw Roe. The lawyer would not have wished to restrain the joyous look on his face, even if it were possible.

"Cut it out, fella," the governor said, breaking loose to take Roe's hand and cuff him softly on the cheek. "We got a lot of work to do tonight. Let's move."

Governor Christman started toward the rear door of the building, followed by Arthur Roe. Two dozen staff members, elected officials and advisors waited to be summoned. It was the kind of moment the governor clearly understood and once thoroughly enjoyed, until he found himself contending with the feelings of far too many people. He could not satisfy them all. And so now at crucial moments he thought only of what needed to be done.

Devlin held the door open for the governor, and Roe followed him to the waiting limousine. Devlin smiled mockingly at the men who watched them leave and then followed them out the door. When they reached the curb, the governor put his arm on the lawyer's shoulder.

"Okay," he asked him, "are we or are we not ready to go?"

Arthur Roe grinned. "It's going to take twenty-four hours."

All three men turned at the sound of a commotion one hundred yards down the street. A young man, shirttail flying, raced from Fifth Avenue toward the governor's car, and the four-man uniformed patrol permanently stationed on the street rushed to stop him. Devlin stepped in front of the governor and pushed him hard into the back seat of the car. The governor looked down the street and shoved back as the beat patrolmen grabbed the young man.

"Let him go," Christman shouted.

The startled policemen released the young man in order to salute the governor. The boy, who had run all the way from the family townhouse two blocks away, wrapped his arms around his father. Christman caught him in a bear hug and kissed him hard on the cheek. Joshua Christman looked up at his father and said, "I did it. I really did it. I convinced you, didn't I?"

"Are you with me?"

"All the way, Dad," he replied. "All the way."

The governor thought he saw tears in his son's eyes.

CHAPTER THIRTEEN

THERE HAD BEEN MEN before who rocketed to the national pinnacle of American politics, but none like Governor Alexander Christman of New York. The years of preparation, planning, and research, combined with the recruitment of extraordinary, loyal, and able personnel, paid off. To the public, it was as if Christman suddenly filled a vacuum they had not previously been able to identify: they saw in him an honest, open man with a sense of purpose. A single word activated the most powerful political machine yet constructed across the broad reaches of the American continent. The word, on that cold January day following the most serious blackout New York City had ever seen, was "Nope."

Forty-eight hours after the word was spoken, no less than three hundred offices manned with six thousand paid workers were opened in major cities across the United States. Magically, Christman literature appeared. A hundred advance men fanned out across the country, carefully organizing "spontaneous" rallies wherever the governor's staff of scheduling experts decided his foot should touch earth. The Minority Group section of Christman for President, Washington headquarters, by the end of the week had purchased hundreds of thousands of dollars' worth of newspaper and radio advertising in Yiddish, Polish, Italian, Arabic, and Spanish, that no one ever saw but the readers who cared most about the promises the man from New York made in Yiddish, Polish, Italian, Arabic, and Spanish.

Before the week was out, the nightly television news broadcasts showed three thousand students organized to picket the White House with placards and buttons that read: NO THIRD TERM. The man from United Broadcasting had his instructions straight from Roger Courtland: get a response from the White House. He got it on film at the next regular briefing by the president's press secretary:

"President Griswold is not a candidate for reelection," the young man said. "He is supporting Vice-President Whitmore."

The spontaneous laugh that followed from the White House press corps meant more on the one hundred million television sets across the country than a dozen political speeches, or the cleverest campaign commercials Madison Avenue could produce. And it gave Governor Christman an issue as potent as tax reform, atomic power, or the president's alleged abuse of the powers of his office.

There was the Christman charm. And even the Christman luck. He had walked into the midst of a fire bombing four days before the Florida primary, followed only by a camera crew from United Broadcasting that had been permanently assigned to the governor's campaign. Across the nation, men and women saw the governor of New York face down three bearded black leaders carrying shotguns. And few people, whether they were in Northville, New York, or Eugene, Oregon, had not heard his confrontation with the blacks and few could not remember what he said.

"I don't agree with you fellas at all [grin]. You're breaking the law. But *somebody's* got to have the balls to sit down and listen to what you've got to say."

There were people who pretended to be shocked at the word, and there were some who were, but even they did not fail to admire either Christman's virility or his courage. And if liberals credited the governor of New York with honest feeling for the problems of blacks, conservatives did not downgrade him for having the guts to tell them off.

If the public image of the Christman campaign was one of spontaneity, impulsive honesty, and broad grass roots support, nothing could have been further from the facts. The huge computers in the basement of the office building at the Arizona ranch churned out voting data at the rate of 470 words a minute. They began with a precise profile of the American voter by age, sex, income group, and nationality. The statistics were further refined by state, locality, and the particular area scheduled for a campaign swing.

The Christman engineers had developed CDFS, Constant Data Feed System, that not only combined the results of five thousand in-depth interviews conducted daily across the country but the raw data produced by pollsters working for Gallup, Roper, Yankelovich, and a half-dozen specialized regional polling companies. It provided the campaign managers with clear reactions from each group in the voter profile as an issue was developed in the campaign. Christman had rebelled more than once.

"Jesus," he told Roe at one briefing, "aren't there any issues we really care about?"

Roe did not hesitate. "Winning," he said laconically.

Out of the data, staff researchers developed a theory that it was not so much the position a candidate took on political issues that mattered, but the words the candidate used to describe his position. Conservatives, he pointed out, no longer attacked ancient liberal hobgoblins like social security and free medical care for the elderly. Public housing was less of an issue than where you placed the housing. All voters opposed crime. But words like law and order had a special meaning.

Roe permitted the researchers to work closely with Christman's staff of speech writers. They found that in most suburban areas near large cities, like Grosse Pointe in Michigan, and upper New York State, candidates who referred to "the people" were out of touch with voters. Most wealthy suburbanites thought of "the people" as blacks, Puerto Ricans, welfare recipients, and minority groups in general. Wherever a Christman speech referred to "the people," Roe changed it to "the taxpayers." He devised a rationale that placed Christman as an ardent advocate of constitutional law, thereby convincing the liberals that the governor broadly supported civil liberties and at the same time telling conservatives that Christman well knew every American had the right to bear arms, as the Constitution stated.

Each phrase, each sequence of words, virtually every position, no matter how obscure, was tested overnight against reams of raw data fed into the computers at the Arizona ranch. At first, there was nothing but sheer delight in the Christman entourage. These were seasoned politicians who had been through the touch and go, test and prod, of campaign wars before, and they glowed in the pleasure of every play, like football fans happily second-guessing a superb quarterback. The lone dissenter was the governor's young son, Joshua Christman, who sensed first that the student volunteers were asking the same questions over and over again about the candidate:

"Sure, he's great," they would say. "But what does he really stand for?"

As for the governor, his days were spent using fully the immense physical energy that had been given to him. Wherever he went during those days, his son was with him, asking the same questions.

There were nights when Alexander Christman lay between the sleek thighs of Athena Courtland until she rolled him over and rode him to the high heaven of her world. Except that after he found the most total release he had ever known, instead of falling into a gentle, dreamless sleep, his mind was obsessed with questions put to him by a fifteen-year-old boy. It became so absurd he even sought the consolation of Athena.

"I've got to tell people exactly where I stand," he told her, his huge paw reaching for her hand.

"Why? Is your son at it again?"

He shrugged. "When you get to be fifty-six years old, there are certain kinds of contracts you make with yourself."

Her hand released his. She twirled her finger in the hair inside his thigh and pulled gently enough to hurt him.

"You don't really want it, do you, Alex?" she said. There was that too, he knew, but it was easier to roll on top of her and push his face into her armpit. She held him as if he was a huge baby. Gently, he caressed the side of her breast with the tip of his tongue. When she could no longer withstand the pleasure of his caress, she rolled him over again, and this time rode him until he was senseless.

If it was important to keep the governor's hands off the machinery and the thrust of the campaign, Roe was the man who knew it. He scheduled him hard. Fourteen- and sixteen-hour campaign days became usual, and Roe allowed the candidate surcease only in the arms of the wife of the chairman of United Broadcasting. That presented a different problem. The relationship was no secret among the thirty to forty reporters who regularly traveled in the press plane Christman provided. Roe, perhaps out of fear, or more likely his own prudishness, concluded he had to deal with it. When he did, Christman looked at him as if he was demented. And then, for the first time in the months since it had begun, there was the old familiar grin.

"Do you really think anybody is going to write it, fella?" he asked. "You're in the big leagues now."

Roe dropped it, though he was less than certain that Christman was right. For he had come to understand, perhaps better than the governor himself, how dependent Christman had become on Athena Courtland. It was Athena who kept him going through the long, impossible days because she was always there when they were over to play whatever role he wished. Roe had come to understand the incredible ability of this beautiful woman to assume whatever role evolved in the fantasies of the man she loved.

The lawyer and his staff also knew the campaign had not gone badly at all. There had been ups and downs. But in recent weeks, the polls indicated they were very much in the race against a candidate everyone assumed would wholly dominate the convention and the party machinery at the convention.

To nonprofessionals, it seemed any candidate would win his party's nomination by capturing the 729 delegate votes that appeared to be at stake in twenty-one primary states. The "magic number" needed was 667. But Roe knew there were primaries that were no more than popularity contests that did not bind delegates to the candidate who won in their states. In other states, the primary ballot carried the names of pledged delegates, but not the presidential candidates. And no matter how they fared, in the three months that had passed, Roe knew Whitmore still had a big bomb when he need it: American Nuclear.

Privately, in the rare moments when they were away from the staff and the campaign schedule, Christman and Roe would deal with it.

"Arthur," the governor argued one day, "I think it's time to brazen it out. I'm proud of American Nuclear. It's not as if I formed the consortium to make money."

"You can't do it," the lawyer told him. "The campaign has momentum now. It has a rhythm. Only losers try to upset that. And you're not a loser."

Christman would shake his head unhappily, never actually agreeing with Roe, but yet conceding to defer the question again. For the lawyer, it was enough.

But the same message, the threat of American Nuclear, was in the IBM computer printout capsulating the nineteen primaries that were past. Christman had not been on the ballot in New Hampshire, the nation's first primary, but he campaigned vigorously up and down the windy hills of the state. The governor criticized harshly the president's sense of justice and the American corporate structure that swallowed independent businesses into giant conglomerates, in a state dotted with mills that had been purchased and then relocated, shut down and obliterated from the state's economy. Even reporters were stunned by the write-in votes registered by the governor in a campaign where the vice-president was the only candidate on the ballot.

	CHRISTMAN		WHITMORE		OTHER	
	Delegates	Vote	Delegates	Vote	Delegates	Vote
N. HAMP.	0	31,241 write-ins	8	47,231	0	3,231 scattered write-ins

In Florida, the administration kept the vice-president off the ballot in hopes that he would begin to lose his southern tinge. Instead, Whitmore strategists ran a "no preference" delegate slate led by Governor Edward K. Gottlieb. He served as a superb stand-in for Whitmore.

	CHRISTMAN		WHITMORE		OTHER	
	Delegates	Vote	Delegates	Vote	Delegates	Vote
FLA.	5	149,318 (delegate slate)	29	(Not on ballot by name)	0	234,612 (For Gottlieb)

Deference, or fear, or the certainty their side could win the convention support of Mayor Powell of Chicago kept both candidates out of Illinois.

	CHRISTMAN		WHITMORE		OTHER	
	Delegates	Vote	Delegates	Vote	Delegates	Vote
ILL.	0	23,612 write-ins	0	6,614 write-ins	58	742,318 Mayor Powell uncommitted slate

The real head-to-head confrontation seemed to come in Wisconsin's "force" primary that permitted state election officials to list the name of any man on the ballot they considered a serious candidate. But it was only the beginning of an eight-week seesaw struggle through eleven primaries. By mid-May, Governor Christman and Vice-President Whitmore each could claim 189 delegates.

As the press reported in the middle of May, administration forces were supremely confident. Governor Christman had not swept the primaries. And with 604 nonelected delegates at the convention, the pressure an incumbent was able to bring to bear was overwhelming.

Governor Christman thought he was finished. But the staff analysis of constant polling contradicted what had passed. The analysts believed that voters across the country had only begun to perceive the governor as a president, and their response had not yet caught up with the polls. Christman was ready to quit. But late one night, alone in a suite in Fort Lee, New Jersey, the call came from President Griswold.

"Are you really joining my team?" the governor asked, sensing what was coming. He knew very well that he was not the only politician in America who read polls.

	CHRISTMAN		WHITWORTH		OTHER	
	Delegates	Vote	Delegates	Vote	Delegates	Vote
WISC.	25	401,601	4	256,733	1	42,705 President Griswold
R.I.	14	37,003	0	32,612	0	
MASS.	34	27,744 write-ins	0	31,469 write-ins	0	391,242 for Sen. Bock committed to Gov. Christman
PENNA.	5	169,313 write-ins	58	262,313	1	47,603 former Gov. Stassen
ALA.	0	14,212	23	26,701	6	18,907
DIST. COL.	4	48,612	5	52,311	0	
IND.	9	328,411	17	606,211	0	
OHIO	58	476,311	0	372,601	0	
NEB.	0	50,655	16	81,116	0	
W. VA.	35	82,212	3	53,007	0	
MD.	0	not on ballot	26	62,171	0	

President Griswold made no effort to be gentle. "You can't win, Governor," he said in his gritty, metallic voice. "You know that. But you can still help the party."

Christman heard Griswold take a deep breath before the president said it: "And the party can help you."

"No."

"The party can also hurt you, Alex. It can hurt you badly."

Alexander Christman was not a man easily given

to anger. But it began to boil inside him. "Go to hell, Mr. President," he said quietly.

Griswold laughed. "I think you are liable to be sorry you said that, Governor." And then he hung up.

Christman had learned never to ignore that kind of threat. He began to take the steps that were necessary. In a telephone conference call the following morning, Dick Siemanowski was elected chairman of the board of American Nuclear. He sent Roe to meet privately with U. S. Attorney Guyman, and late that evening, the two men had one of their rare moments alone since they last discussed American Nuclear.

"Guyman's a bag of jelly," Roe told him. "And that's dangerous when he is in the middle."

Christman smiled. "All those guys carry black robes in their briefcases. He's no different. The trouble is the president can't promise him a judgeship. Because if he delivers, he will be proving my charges that he uses the law for political purposes are true." There was a glint in the governor's eye. "If Guyman backs me up, Griswold will make him a hero by demanding his resignation. Then I can give him a judgeship."

Roe's face was impassive. "Do you really believe that, Alex?" he asked.

Christman shrugged. "I think Arnold Guyman will," he said.

Roe quickly dropped the subject. There was something else on the governor's mind and it shocked him. For the next twenty minutes, they discussed American Nuclear. And in those minutes, the lawyer felt in himself the pain he knew was somewhere in Alexander Christman.

"You can't do it to yourself," he told him.

"Sell it, Arthur. Every share."

He threw up his hands. Christman punched his shoulder. "Fella," he said, "you got to fight the fight you've got. And it isn't always the one you want."

Christman touched all the bases, including a private meeting with Martin Soshin, the U. S. attorney who had developed the case against him. It was brief, it was to the point and it took place in the back of the Christman limousine late one night.

"I need you," the governor told the young lawyer. "Come and work for me."

"Governor," Soshin complained, "I disagree with everything you stand for. Make no mistake about that."

"Fine. Fine," Christman came back, clapping him on the shoulder. "What's wrong with that? Everybody needs a conscience."

The crooked grin spread slowly across the young man's face in disbelief. He shrugged in acquiescence, knowing that if he wished, he would never have to deal with Arnold Guyman again. Three days later, he was appointed chief counsel to the New York State Commission of Investigations, with a mandate from Christman to clean the politicians out of the state's banks.

The governor for the first time since Roe had known him was tired, and he was irritable. He was like a man who had struggled harder than anyone alive to control his destiny, only to find he had become a puppet, programmed by a computer analyzing five thousand daily interviews. As he let them fit each new public position into his campaign strategy, he donned the new hair shirt like a man accepting his proper punishment, knowing that it would soon be over. But he was determined to win.

Only Josh made it difficult for him, only Josh mattered to him now. He stood in front of his father early one morning in a Beverly Hills hotel room, outraged at the press release in his hand. He refused to sit down at the rolling breakfast table two bellmen left in the suite.

"You can't talk about the 'sanctity of the neighborhood,' " the fifteen-year-old told him.

It made him feel absurd. This was the weekend before the third Tuesday in June. Four primaries, California, New Mexico, South Dakota, and New Jersey, were at stake. One hundred and fifty-four delegates. And after that there were only New York, his home state, and Tennessee. And he was here taking guff from a fifteen-year-old boy.

"You can't do it, Dad," Joshua said. "That's the goddamn code."

"Don't use that kind of language," his father told him.

"You're saying fuck the blacks. Don't you know that?"

Christman poured a cup of steaming black coffee. "I make a lot of people edgy. Sometimes you have to reassure them."

"Reassure me," the boy pleaded.

The parental role had a newness for him. He did not know precisely how to accomplish what he wished to do. He stood up and tightened his robe.

"Calm down," he told him, the huge arm going around the boy's shoulders. "We are going to win."

"Not this way. Jesus, but you don't have to do it this way, Dad."

To hell with him, Alexander Christman thought. He squeezed his shoulder hard and told him the truth.

"Any way is better than losing."

Losing was also very much on the minds of the two men who watched the primary returns that week with Governor Alexander Christman of New York. They sat in the office above the candidate's vast New York City headquarters and listened to returns that said he had won easily in the neighboring state of New Jersey, won in New Mexico and South Dakota, and then crowned the early hours of the morning with a 36,350 vote plurality in California. It was not only total victory, but as Roe delightedly pointed out, a perfect computer predicted sweep. And while the hordes of volunteers shouted for Christman from the floors below, there was no joy in the thirty-second-floor command post.

"If the bombshell is going to do them any good, Whitmore better throw it now," Roe said laconically.

Christman lifted a glass of port and tried to cheer him. "We can handle it," he chortled.

"He'll throw it," Roe said. "If he doesn't stop us now, he can't stop us in Miami."

In one night, four primaries had given the Christman forces a sweep of 172 delegates. The governor already had a total of 361 pledged or committed

first-ballot convention votes, and victory in New
York and Tennessee, the last primaries, would give
him no less than 479 of the 667 delegates needed to
win.

"Whitmore can count on the nonprimary states,
Governor," Roe said.

"He can count on most of them. But not all of them.
He's got to throw it or give up."

He finished the port and put down the clipboard.
He stood and walked to the desk and lifted the single
page containing his victory remarks to the volunteers
who would whoop it up in the ballroom below amid
cascading balloons and a blaring fifty-three-piece band
staged for coast-to-coast television cameras.

The governor was tense and he was tired. But he
had followed directions to the letter, and Roe did not
want to disturb that. And it was time to reassure the
governor as best he could. "Maybe Whitmore won't
use American Nuclear," the lawyer told him.

"No," Christman said dully as the lawyer fell in
step with them. "It's not a possibility at all."

He was right. But when the bomb came, it came
unexpectedly. And from an unlikely quarter. It was
ten days to the last of the primaries, and it was a
Sunday none of them would ever forget. The governor
had gotten six hours sleep for the first time in almost
as many months. And after he left Athena Courtland's
apartment that warm Sunday morning, the staff briefing
was as thorough as any he had. Unlike most political
candidates, Christman needed no statistical impacting
of facts when he appeared on a network television
news show. He did not need a careful rationale for each
position he took. Instead, a dozen of his ablest researchers and press people played devil's advocate,
firing questions calculated to embarrass him for two
and a half hours. The more antagonistic and hostile
they became, the tougher the challenge for him. He
loved the give-and-take, the way a home run slugger
likes to face the toughest batting-practice pitcher on
the squad.

The lines he would use on the show came naturally, and they came from him.

Typical was his easy answer to one question on his proposal to eliminate the oil depletion allowance:

"That's a question you ought to ask the fella over here," he replied, gesturing with his thumb to the chair where Vice-President Whitmore would be sitting. "He carried Texas. I didn't."

The staff roared.

When it was over, Athena Courtland was at his side. She patted him on the bottom. He winced. "Nice job," she whispered in his ear, as the staff crowded around him. He was tired, but he had come to thrive on their dedication, their feeling for him, and their concern for his well-being.

"Splendid," Roe told him, as the group continued to congratulate him. "If the real thing is as good, you'll cream Whitmore."

At the network's Second Avenue studio in mid-Manhattan, the governor of New York and the vice-president of the United States sat in barber chairs opposite each other, as the makeup man each of them retained directed the union makeup man employed by the network. The vice-president took a touch more eye shadow than the governor, and a lighter powder was used on his neck and jaw to mask a double chin. Whitmore's heavy tan gave his tiny body a sense of vigor almost as strong as Governor Christman's. Network executives, newsmen, campaign workers, and the eight invited visitors each candidate was permitted milled about the room. The two men were of one party, and there were those among each of their staffs who wanted to be certain a job was waiting for them when the primary was over.

"Alex," the vice-president called, "you know you are still the numbah one choice on mah ticket."

"Thanks, fella," Christman called back, as he shuffled through the index cards on his lap.

Roland LaStarza, the blond coauthor of a syndicated "Inside Washington" column, could not resist.

"Is it accurate to say, Governor, that the sentiment is mutual?"

The governor did not even open his eyes. "I stand in the center," he said, as LaStarza picked up the often repeated line and said it in unison with him, "with my arms stretched out on either side welcoming all elements in the party."

The small audience roared, and Roe began to relax. Christman was loose.

"How do you really feel about the vice-president, Governor?" LaStarza pressed.

"George?" the governor said, opening his eyes. Roe shook his head back and forth, but Christman for the first time in months was not able to resist. "He belonged on President Griswold's ticket. He does not belong on mine."

The movement of the people in the room had stopped. There was the sound of a sharp intake of breath as they turned as one man to watch the small, dapper Southerner in the barber chair opposite Governor Christman pop up and slowly lean forward.

"The voters are not going to let you do in this country what you have done in the state of New York, Governor Christman," Vice-President Whitmore said. Then he threw the striped barber's sheet on the floor, stood, and walked rapidly into the adjoining studios, followed by the full press entourage.

"What did the vice-president mean?" a reporter asked.

"The governor knows what I mean."

"Are you making a specific charge?"

"Governor Christman's record is a sufficient indictment."

Five minutes before air time, the two candidates consciously ignored each other as they were seated at adjoining desks in the cavernous studio. Staff aides for both men scanned the studio monitors and then hurried to give instructions to the lighting engineer and his assistant assigned to the show. At four minutes to air time, Roger Courtland was on the set to express his appreciation to both candidates for accepting United Broadcasting's invitation. He shook hands with Governor Christman first and was rewarded with a grin. Then the chairman of the board walked, hand extended, to the side of the set occupied by the dapper vice-president of the United States.

Roger Courtland was as effusive as a grand dame hostess who has snared the prize guests of the year.

"I'm not here because I like what UBS has been saying," Whitmore growled no louder than he was certain Courtland could hear.

"You may be in for a small surprise, Mr. Vice-President," Courtland replied calmly.

There was a moment of confusion in Whitmore's eyes and then a flutter of recognition. He had wondered whether the rumors about the governor and Roger Courtland's wife had come home to roost. Courtland was not a man blessed with a poker face, and so the vice-president did not wonder anymore. It happened so quickly only the show's director, focussing his attention on the monitored control room close-up of the vice-president, noticed it.

"What the hell did the old man tell him?"

"Beats me," Alvin Smilon, the producer, replied. "But if R.C. is for him, you damn well better kill that low-angle shot that shows his heavy jowls."

"Right on, boss," the director came back, indicating he would follow orders. He had been at UBS a long time.

Then it was air time. Three reporters, UBS Washington correspondent, George Farmer; LaStarza, the syndicated columnist; and a *Newsweek* editor questioned the two candidates. It was a "soft" panel, as advisors on both sides expected, permitting the candidate to communicate in terms of the way they looked, rather than by means of the issues they discussed.

Vice-President Whitmore: Neat, precise, competent, a man of the farm and the suburb, whose wit might even be a shade quicker than his opponent's.

Governor Christman: Tough, warm, determined, a virile man's man with a sense of joy, who brings hope to some viewers. A self-made man with contempt for those who only inherit position.

General reaction: Whitmore looks like a vice-president; Christman, the stronger leader.

It was twenty minutes into the show. The questions,

by and large, had been so general each candidate had refined his answers to them a dozen times before. And for the moment, both men seemed content to avoid direct confrontation between them. To some observers, it was as if Governor Christman had read his own rising polls and believed them, while the vice-president had decided the nomination was his at the convention.

Then UBS's George Farmer woke up the audience that stretched from the canvas chairs in the cavernous studio to living rooms across the nation.

"Governor Christman," he asked, removing his glasses, "you have been one of the leading proponents of commercially produced atomic power in this country. Is that correct?"

Roe thought he was the only one who saw the governor tense. But on the monitors, Camera Number One had moved in for an extreme close-up.

"Yes, that's correct," the governor replied. "This nation has got to begin moving into the twenty-first century. And it has got to do it now."

He turned away, assuming the subject was closed. It was not.

"Is it also true, Governor," Farmer said, picking up on the answer, "that you have done a great deal in New York toward the goal? I refer to underwriting research, subsidizing private construction of atomic power plants, and the like?"

The governor smiled and eased back into his chair.

"Sure," he replied, a trifle stiffly. "My state leads the nation in the development of nuclear power. I don't even think the vice-president would debate that."

Whitmore grunted. But Camera Number one never left the governor's face. Farmer's question came very fast this time.

"Governor Christman," he said very slowly, certain that no one would interrupt him, "is it not also true that a corporation named American Nuclear Energy is the leader in the field of the commercial development of nuclear energy? And you, sir, are the principal stockholder in that company?"

There was a gasp in the darkened corner of the studio. Athena Courtland looked into the lighted control room and saw her husband grinning like an animal about to pounce.

"Mr. Farmer," the governor said, leaning forward toward the camera, "I have consistently advanced the cause of nuclear power in the best interests of this country. I've never denied it. And the very nature of the suggestion you are making, I'm afraid, raises some serious questions about your fairness and competence as a journalist. I do have an abiding interest in the future of this country. It has been very good to me."

The camera switched to Farmer. He looked frightened, as if he had not fully understood the implications of the questions he was given to ask. His head turned toward the control room where Roger Courtland was nodding vigorously.

"You know and we know, sir," he reacted, "that your affairs have been under federal investigation for six months."

Christman remained calm, as if he were talking to a schoolboy.

"I answered that question when I announced my candidacy for this office, and you know it. And I assumed President Griswold, rather respectably, I thought, had ceased to use the law to further his own political end—the election of my opponent."

It was Whitmore's moment. Thirty-five years of Senate training were not wasted on him.

"That's an evasive answer. You're not being truthful, Governor Christman," he said gently, "and you know it."

Alvin Smilon, the show's producer, had his orders and he whispered them quickly to the moderator through the hearing device hidden behind his right ear. He quickly cut off the debate as the monitor cut to Christman's outraged face and then to Whitmore, who seemed no more than mildly reproachful. The vice-president knew clearly that he could not permit the charges to become in any way his charges, and he handled LaStarza's follow-up question carefully.

"Mah campaign staff and I am aware that Governor Christman is the founder and major stockholder in this company. But I have not heard the charges you speak of before, sir. I have not heard them from mah staff. I have not heard them from the attorney general, and ah have certainly not heard them from the president of the United States."

"Bullshit," Christman retorted.

They all heard it. Roe held his head in his hands. The reporters thought a fist fight might break out in the studio between the entourage of the two candidates. But if there was murder in the air, it was in the galling anger with which Athena Courtland searched out the face of her husband.

When the show was over, reporters tried to corner both candidates. Roe and Devlin, with the help of two burly advance men, surrounded the governor and forced him out of the studio. Another phalanx of reporters were in the UBS lobby, and Christman was pushed past them and into the limousine.

Vice-President Whitmore was also anxious to move along, but he understood that anything new he said after the broadcast would get prominent attention from newspapers and the other networks.

When the lights in the lobby were set up and the cameramen were ready, there was only one major question.

"Governor Christman," he replied blandly, "has to mah knowledge always been an honorable man. Ah have no knowledge that he has committed any crime, sir. Whether there has been some impropriety heah"— he shrugged—"that would disconcert me very much. Ah lak the governor. If these charges are groundless, why, he'd make a fine running mate for any member of this party."

Vice-President Whitmore made the mistake of smiling when he finished. It led reporters to wonder whether he meant what he said. And then they wondered, if he meant it, how far was he willing to go? And if he were willing to go that far, could any reasonable observer expect Alexander Christman to accept the number two spot on a Whitmore ticket?

Governor Christman wondered, too. He wondered whether the sudden thrust of American Nuclear into the news after four months was nothing but a transitory flash in the long campaign. And Josh Christman wondered. He wondered whether his father was really the man he always thought he had been. Arthur Roe did not wonder. He merely wished it would blow over, for it was his job to reassure the staff, the press, and the world that there was nothing to the story. Yet he knew it would not blow over.

He was right. The bulk of the American Nuclear story and Governor Christman's involvement began the next morning under a two-column headline on page one of *The New York Times* and continued for eight columns on page 42. What *The New York Times* may have missed when their reporter illegally culled grand jury testimony supplied by an undisclosed source appeared in the afternoon editions of the Los Angeles *Times*. It was all there. Neither of the major wire services bothered to check the story themselves. It was sufficient to quote two reputable newspapers and let it go at that. By mid-afternoon 1,200 newspapers, 640 television stations, and another thousand AM and FM radio outlets wrote, broadcast or transmitted summaries of the story.

Arthur Roe had more than a hundred requests for interviews with Governor Christman. Twenty or so reporters, who had followed the campaign closely, asked Harvey Kuhn for interviews with Arthur Roe. At 11 A.M., the hour of the daily morning briefing, Kuhn had only himself to present to the press.

"Why has the governor cancelled his trip to Tennessee?"

Kuhn did not have to hesitate. "It was never firm," he replied. "Our schedule has always been tentative up to twenty-four hours in advance, and everyone who has covered this campaign knows it."

"Where is Governor Christman at this moment?"

"Next question," Kuhn answered sourly.

"Is he going to answer these charges?" Abe Peterson wanted to know.

Kuhn held up his hands. The hundred cameramen,

reporters, and technicians were silent. There was only the whirring of the sound camera motors indicating that what Kuhn said next would be the ninety-second film clip seventy million Americans saw on the six o'clock news. He did not like it. No one at headquarters liked it. But he did his best.

"Governor Christman based his announcement that he would become a candidate upon the issue of presidential abuse of power. He has spoken often of President Griswold's proprietary use of investigative agencies to further his own ends. And he does not believe it is necessary to honor these outrageous charges with a reply."

They were stirring. "Come on, Harvey," someone shouted from the back of the room, "that kind of garbage isn't going to wash. Where the hell is the governor?"

Kuhn was sweating. "One. The governor has never acted except in the best interests of the people of this state. Two. The governor has taken a very real interest in the development of commercial nuclear power. I think it's very clear that if the public utilities in New York had been more responsive, we might have avoided the blackout last February. Third and finally, Governor Christman has said he holds no interest in American Nuclear. I think he made that very clear." He knew they were not satisfied and that he could only make it worse. He cut it off quickly. "Thank you, gentlemen," he said. "Check in with me later today."

He heard them grumbling behind him as he left the room, but there was nothing he could do. It took him less than five minutes to bound, taking two steps at a time, up the staircase in the Fifty-fourth Street converted brownstone that Governor Christman used for a New York City office since he had been elected. Arthur Roe was waiting for him in the private penthouse office. With him was Dr. Freeman White, chief statistical analyst for the campaign. Dr. White sat in an overstuffed, green leather chair balancing an oversized cup of tea on his knee as he talked on the telephone. He made notes on a thick pad of yellow legal paper.

"Did you see it?" Kuhn asked.

Roe gestured without looking up toward the bank of television screens, one of which received video-tape replays of the governor's press conferences. He shrugged at Kuhn as he stood up. "A disaster. Did you expect anything else?"

"The press guys like Christman," Kuhn replied defensively, but he knew there was no defense. "What did he say?"

Roe stared at the press secretary.

"You still can't get him?" Kuhn's tone was a mixture of outrage and disbelief.

Dr. White waited until his audience acknowledged that he had their full attention.

"How bad?" Roe asked the statistician.

"One is not encouraged by the overnight samples."

There was a silence between them, Roe annoyed as he always was by the pontifical manner of the doctor, who again was waiting to be asked.

"Will you stop playing, Doctor," the lawyer complained.

White smiled. "One cannot remove oneself from a lifelong habit, my friend." He looked down again at the numbers on the pad. "Eleven percent of the voters interviewed now perceive Alexander Christman as no different from any other politician. Fourteen percent believe he should withdraw. Twenty-three percent think he should answer the charges more fully. Forty-four percent did not understand the series of questions. Eight percent never heard of Governor Alexander Christman."

"That's funny," Roe said. "His name recognition is down all of a sudden from ten to eight percent."

"One must understand it is far too early to measure the full effect of this event. The attention span to news events of most voters is relatively low on Sunday. They are less angry than when they are at work. The negative aspect of those figures, those voters who now dislike Governor Christman, may double in two weeks' time. The indication from a very small sample is that they are already double in New York State."

Kuhn was trying to light his dead pipe. "Who is to

say it is not just an instant reaction that will blow over by Wednesday?"

"I do," Dr. White told him.

"But we've seen this kind of thing before," Kuhn said.

Dr. White waved the press secretary silent. Roe looked squarely at the big man. "Doctor," he said, "three options are clear. One. He can withdraw or accept the vice-presidency from Griswold. It is the same thing. Two. He can ignore these allegations, in which case he will lose the primary in his home state and with it the nomination. And finally," there was a moment of hesitation now, "he can attempt to re-affirm the original perception of him on the part of the voters as a man like other men, a self-made man, a selfless man."

"How, for Christ's sake?"

"Nixon did it in 1952. Kennedy also did it after Chappaquiddick."

"You mean a Checkers speech? Alexander Christman—a Checkers speech?"

Dr. White pursed his lips. "One must make him understand there is never humiliation in victory."

Roe's mouth was open when they heard the knock at the door. He turned quickly. Esther Serene peered into the room.

"I said no calls, dammit," Roe told her.

She ignored him. "It's Mr. Guyman. The U. S. attorney."

Roe wondered whether it had finally occurred to Arnold Guyman that no matter what happened to Christman, Griswold would no longer be president. Nothing, he understood, could possibly frighten the present U. S. attorney more than the thought of being out of a job with nowhere to turn.

"It's about time," Roe said, as he hastily ushered both men out of his office, closed the door, and walked quickly to the phone.

"Arthur?" Guyman sounded like a frightened boy. "Is this line safe?"

"What do you want?"

"I've been trying to reach Alex. He won't take my calls. Christ, he knows how I feel about him, and he knows I would never do anything to hurt him. I owe everything to that man."

"I'm sure that's going to help him a lot."

"Arthur, I'll do anything."

Roe took a deep breath, pleased that Christman was right. Guyman had come around. But who really knew what might help now?

"I didn't leak that stuff. I didn't authorize it. You met Soshin. He walked out of here with the goddamn files. The funny thing is that Whitmore may be telling the truth when he says he didn't know anything."

"Bullshit," Roe said. "Soshin didn't leak anything to anybody."

"What?" Guyman said.

Roe decided to give it to him straight. "If you want to straighten yourself out with the governor, resign now, Arnie. It's as simple as that. President Griswold personally instigated the investigation. You can publicly say that. When you found nothing, he insisted you impanel a grand jury. You're resigning in the interests of justice, fair play, whatever the hell you like."

"But what do I do about Soshin?"

"Forget him," Roe shouted into the phone. "And do what I told you."

Roe thought they had been disconnected, but Guyman was still on the line. "Will you protect me?" he asked sheepishly.

"Arnie. Do it now. To do any good you've got to get it out at a press conference by four o'clock, so we can turn this thing around before the six o'clock news."

"Tell Alex I'm grateful," Guyman mewled.

"You'll do it then?"

"If you promise he will take care of me."

Roe reassured him, wishing Christman could be persuaded to renege, but he knew he would not. After the lawyer hung up, he called White and Kuhn back into his office and told them what had happened. There was a peculiar smile on the doctor's face as he listened to Roe.

"One salutes you, Mr. Roe," he said. "But," and now he held up his hands, "it will not change the essential problem. We have only escalated the issue."

Kuhn started to say something, but he was beginning to understand this was out of his league.

"I better go see the governor," the lawyer said.

"I don't like to say it, especially to you, Mr. Roe, but if you want my advice, better wait until he calls."

Dr. White watched them almost eagerly, waiting for Roe's reply. He might have been writing his own history of the campaign.

Roe looked at the press secretary. "We haven't got that kind of time," he said. "In fact, I'm not sure we have any time left at all."

He decided to walk. But by the time he crossed Fifty-ninth Street, the heat from the pavement, combined with the rising June humidity in New York, began to make him sweat. Arthur Roe wanted to calm himself, for despite his own ambition, he wanted to be certain he did not push the governor. He was dealing with a man who had become so physically drained by the rigorous demands of a long campaign that he could bounce hard in any direction without warning and Roe knew it.

He crossed Fifth Avenue, glancing at his wristwatch, and allowed himself precisely five minutes' rest on one of the green hard wood benches outside Central Park. A boy with a helium-filled balloon being led by a governess waddled past him, and Roe's eyes followed them into the park. In the final two minutes he allotted himself, he sat still, his eyes shut, and blotted out of his mind the statistics, the campaign people, his staff, his colleagues, and Alexander Christman. Then he rose as if he were a man without a care in the world and quickly walked to the Christman triplex apartment overlooking the park. He passed the gold-braided doorman, who saluted, and walked quickly to the governor's private elevator at the end of the long foyer. Detective Devlin sat on a large striped settee, reading the *Daily News,* and he stood up when he saw the lawyer.

"He call you?"

"Sure."

The detective shook his head. "I'm glad he's coming

out of it. She's up there. I guess she left her husband."

"Fine," Roe told him, stepping into the self-service car.

"On top of everything else, he had a fight with the kid last night." Devlin hesitated. "Is he going to quit, Mr. Roe?"

He had now answered the question a hundred times in the past forty-eight hours. It came by rote. "Alexander Christman?" he said.

The detective let the elevator close behind him, and the car lifted Roe swiftly to the twenty-eighth-floor penthouse. Roe stepped out into the private hallway and shook his head, as he always did, when Hals's "Rosenkavalier" stared back at him. Two million bucks, he thought, as he had before, and my turkey hangs it in a foyer.

He knocked three times on the white-paneled double doors, but there was no answer. Roe knocked again, louder and harder this time.

"All right, who the hell is it?"

"Me," he said.

"Jesus, not now. Come back at four o'clock."

"Alex," he said, not able to hide the irritation in his voice.

Christman was wearing a yellow short-sleeved golf shirt and light tan pants. He was barefoot. The governor turned and Roe followed him into the vast living room. Athena Courtland, in a white satin robe that left her knees bare, was sipping tomato juice on a green brocaded settee. The lawyer had never felt so utterly alone in his life.

Christman walked to the desk in front of the window and found his oversize glasses. He pushed some papers from the center of the desk, discovered what he was looking for, and handed a single sheet of paper to Roe.

IT IS MY DECISION ON THIS 12TH DAY OF JUNE TO WITHDRAW AS AN ACTIVE CANDIDATE FOR PRESIDENT OF THE UNITED STATES.

Roe glanced at Athena Courtland. She was smiling. He found the handwritten sheet difficult to read. He looked up at Alexander Christman.

"Fix it," the governor said gently, "and get it out."

The lawyer nodded and turned to leave. There was nothing to say.

"Don't you know what will happen if I quit now?" the governor growled, trying to antagonize Roe.

The lawyer suddenly was tired again. He started to say something, changed his mind, and walked past the governor to the windows overlooking the park. It was a brilliant, sunny day, but the air conditioning in the apartment made the glass cool to the touch of his forehead, and his breath formed a light mist on the pane. The reflection in the glass showed him Christman, hands on hips, staring at the back of his head.

"You don't want it now, Alex, and you never did."

"And you won't tell me to fight?"

"No. Not this time."

He turned to look at Christman's tired face and, in himself, felt as lifeless as a man who has lost all feeling in his arms and legs.

For an instant, the governor flashed the famous grin. In that moment, the lust for life, the joy of being Alexander Christman, was alive again. Then the governor scowled and said, "You won't tell me to fight?" The hands were back on his hips. "What kind of a goddamn friend are you, fella?"

Arthur Roe wanted to put his arms around the big man and hug him. There were tears in his eyes as he crossed the living room and took Christman's hand.

"Jesus," Alexander Christman said, "what the hell do we do if we win?"

"Fella," Arthur Roe said, mocking him, "do you really think there's still much chance of that?"

Four days later, Roe was still wondering. The governor's public schedule had been cancelled. He had granted no interviews. He had spoken to no one outside the campaign family, with the exception of Arnold Guyman, a "thank you" call.

Roe had spoken to the governor twice. The first

time Christman approved the purchase of a half hour of television time and agreed to broadcast from Windy Meadow with his wife, Josh, and even Violet, the family cat.

The second conversation was even more cursory. No, he did not want to see the script for the show.

"You fellas know what you're doing," he said.

"Alex. This is your career we're talking about."

"Right."

"You don't object to the American Nuclear proposals?"

Christman laughed. His voice was hard and angry. "Sure I object."

"Are you paying attention, Alex?"

"Right."

"Then please read the script."

"You have the research. You know what you're doing. If it was up to me, I would lay it on the line and tell them what kind of country this really is."

Roe did not press him. "Mrs. Christman doesn't like what we planned."

The governor sounded almost cheerful. "When they have you boxed everyone takes. All you can do is minimize the losses."

"Alex?" Roe said.

"Forget it. There are times when you can lead and get something done. And then there are other times when you just have to wait until they tell you where to go."

"You can still get out."

"No," he told Roe. "You know what Caesar said, 'I'd strike the sun if it insulted me.' We're only talking about Griswold."

Roe had to conquer his own feelings first. In four hours a major candidate for the presidency of the United States, his candidate, would deliver the most important speech he had ever made, a speech he had not even read.

It was a maudlin, sentimental, pleading kind of apple pie appeal calculated to humanize a man whose feelings and intellect were far above its content. Yet it was a brilliant political exercise. But as he

drove north toward Windy Meadow on the Henry
Hudson Parkway, Arthur Roe wondered whether Alexander Christman would so demean himself to the level
of this speech.

June had turned Westchester deep green. And the
winding road past the guard house at Windy Meadows
was lined with late blooming daffodils and Mrs. Christman's brilliant Red Emperor tulips. The side of the
huge Georgian mansion had been turned into a parking
lot, and rows and rows of cars surrounded the bulky
color television van that would be used to transmit
the telecast. Christman had agreed at the outset to
broadcast "live" to the nation. In front of the house,
Detective Devlin was leaning against the custom-built
white Chevrolet.

"How is he?" Roe asked.

"Beat to hell. I've never seen him so tired."

"He hasn't done anything for three days."

Devlin shrugged, then grinned broadly at the lawyer.

"Is she here?"

"Nope. He's even being nice to the missus."

Governor Alexander Christman had closeted himself in the second-floor study. His eyes seemed half
shut as he studied the orange script in his hands. Roe
thought he saw the governor wince painfully as he
mouthed the words, trying to decide upon the inflec-
tion he would give each.

The governor looked up at him over the top of the
big glasses.

"Rough, amigo, no?" Roe asked.

There was no reply.

"I'm proposing to federalize the commercial production of nuclear power to cut rates forty percent.
Well," he said slowly, "it'll do great things for the
economy."

The governor took off his glasses and turned his
head to look up the river he loved. A small tugboat
was pushing three long coal scows so slowly his eye
could measure their slow progress in inches. When he
turned back, his face was solemn and drawn, as if all
that had once been partly a game was no longer fun.

"Maybe we just moved too fast, fella," he told the

lawyer. "Maybe we just didn't realize how slow you have to go to accomplish anything in this country."

Roe did not want his mind to drift off now. It was less than an hour to air time. "Did you talk to her?" he asked.

The switchboard located Mrs. Christman quickly, and while the governor waited for her, Roe was silent. Finally he stood up and moved to the door, taking his leave before the unwanted confrontation.

Christman waved his hand without turning. The tugboat and scows were almost out of view, and he had to crane his neck to watch them move past Tarrytown into the narrows of the river.

"Good day, Governor," the familiar voice said imperiously from the doorway.

He had listened to her for many years, and with every year he liked it less. She had been his wife for twenty of those years, and her voice still startled him enough to shake him into the unpleasant reality of her presence.

"I was beginning to think I had to call a press conference to get you to visit me."

"Hey," the governor of the state of New York said, "that would really be something. I bet even the *Wall Street Journal* would come."

"I'm not joking, Alexander."

"No," he replied, turning to stare again out the huge bay window of the seventy-five-year-old mansion above the Hudson River they had remodeled together. They were younger then, and she had been flexible. Then she changed. The ugliness, the demand for obedience that had always been there, attacked her spirit. And then the hunger for life in her, which had always been small, died of starvation.

"Are you still busy trying to take over the country?"

"No. That's the lawyers." He held up the orange script. "I need your help, Morganna."

"Of course you shall have it, Alexander."

She looked like a tall, thin bird, who in twenty years had grown from a sparrow to an angry crane.

"Thank you."

"And I have something to ask of you."

He turned away again, knowing what she was about to ask as quickly as he knew he did not want to hear it.

"Voters don't like divorced men in this country."

"I can't help that," he replied.

He sat down on the air-cooled window seat. By twisting his head, he could still see the river.

"Alexander?"

"All right," he said flatly.

She knew well enough not to press him when he was in agreement. But she could not resist walking to the window seat and gently touching his cheek, as if she were consoling him.

"What happened to us?" she asked.

He did not know how to reply. So he tried to be gentle. And without any thought for the words, he said softly, "You got old. That's all." And then he knew it would have been less cruel to say nothing, because he had forgotten that he was stupid with all women. And then he did not wish to answer again, for he did not wish to force her to do anything they would both regret, so that it was even pointless to apologize.

Behind him, the river had not changed. At sunset, the orange-red ball sinking behind the Palisades still played on the river's surface, turning it into a palette of green, gold, orange, and blue-gray.

He wished to will her out of his presence, and having gained more than she had lost, she sensed his desire and obeyed.

"Your son wishes to see you, Alexander," she told him.

His mood was broken, and he walked silently with her to the door. A dozen staff aides, television technicians, and family domestics were standing quietly in the large hallway outside. Joshua pushed his way toward his father.

"Can we have you in makeup?" a young man with a hearing aid asked Morganna Christman. She nodded.

"Thirty minutes to air time, sir," he said.

Joshua Christman had the blue copy of the air script in his hand. He followed his father back into the study. They stood facing each other just inside the door.

"Are you really going to do this?" the boy asked indignantly.

The governor tried to shrug it off. "The fellas that work for me know what they're doing."

Joshua's face was red as he shook his head back and forth. Christman grabbed his shoulder and held him. "Say it, fella."

"It isn't worth it," he shouted. "This just isn't worth it."

He threw the blue copy of the script on the floor, opened the door, and walked out of the room. Christman hesitated long enough to turn again and stare for a moment at the blackened river. Then he took a breath deeply into his lungs, bent down, picked up the script, and looked at it again.

Page 11 was on top. "My father hung drapes for a living," it said. "He was an honorable businessman, but not a rich one. The Christmans were not Rockefellers."

"Jesus," he muttered, as he shuffled the papers.

Page 2. "I would like you to meet my family. This is my beloved wife, Morganna, my son Joshua, and our dog, Hoover." Then the script said, "DON'T FORGET TO PAT THE DOG, GOVERNOR."

He shuffled the script in his hand again. It had not seemed quite this awful when he read it before.

Page 31. "Ladies and Gentlemen, I do not own a single share of stock in American Nuclear. The allegations made against me come from men who would pervert all that is sacred in the American system of law to justify their own lust for power."

The governor dropped the script back on the floor and walked out of the room.

The speech had been carefully hand-lettered on giant-size "idiot cards," that could be read twenty feet away. The text was repeated on a rolling teleprompter atop each camera lens. Technicians persuaded the governor to wear a hearing device behind his right ear to permit communications from the control room during the broadcast.

In the living room, the Christman family was seated

like a Grant Wood group, hands folded in their laps, on a wide Victorian sofa. Mrs. Christman was stroking Eleanor, her pure white Persian cat. Hoover, the family's Dalmatian, was at her feet.

"Exquisite," someone murmured. "It's pure Kansas City."

Christman looked quickly around the room. "Get me Roe," he ordered someone he had never seen before.

The floor manager took off his headset and raced for the makeshift control room. It was a minute-ten to air time. Movement in the room stopped. Technicians, campaign staff, and his wife and son stared at him. Roe walked quickly toward him, sweat visible on his face.

"Fifty seconds," the floor manager called.

Christman grabbed the lawyer by his bicep.

"Get all this crap out of here," he said, waving at the idiot cards.

"Alex. No."

"I said get it out of here."

No one stirred.

"Thirty seconds," the floor manager said.

Roe called quickly to an aide and whispered Christman's instructions.

"Get somebody to introduce me. I'm going to stand behind the desk."

"Twenty seconds."

Christman walked quickly to the Samuel Adams desk and stared out for a moment at the dark river below. He turned and squinted into the lights as cameramen and dolly operators jerked the cameras into position.

"Ten seconds."

The governor picked up the orange, first copy of the script that had been placed on the desk for him.

"We're on the air," he heard the stage manager say. And then he heard Arthur Roe's voice.

"Ladies and Gentlemen, the governor of the state of New York, Alexander Christman."

Christman stared straight into the camera.

"A speech was prepared for me. It talked about

my life, my family, our pets. It made me appear to be a humble man, a man with whom you would be sympathetic.

"I'm not going to read that speech. Because I do not believe this country can survive by electing men who paint that kind of picture of themselves. Any more than I think we can survive by electing the man who draws the most untrue picture of this country."

He was shaking his head back and forth, the right hand chopping downward, his concentration absolutely compelling.

"It's wrong, my fellow Americans. It's that kind of gap between the facts and the American dream that's put us where we are. Because," he said, waggling a finger at the camera, "we are at a point in this nation where if the Bill of Rights were introduced in Congress tomorrow it would be defeated overwhelmingly."

"Jesus," the director said, touching Roe's shoulder.

"Shut up," he responded harshly, "and listen."

Christman stopped for a moment to collect his thoughts. He poured a glass of water from the silver carafe on the desk and sipped it slowly. Roe almost believed he was enjoying himself.

"The problem," he said slowly, "is that our principles have given way to the gold standard in our country. Money has become the standard for justice, for special interests, even for measuring the worth of a neighbor. A good man is a rich man. By that measurement," he said, the idea and the grin coming at the same time, "there is no question who our next president should be; I've got more money than anyone else running. So I've got a bigger stake in this country than anyone else."

The smile was gone.

"But that's wrong," Christman said. "It's the kind of thing that has given us two sets of rules in this country. We have written rules—thou shalt not steal. Thou shalt not kill. You know them.

"The unwritten rules are different. If a company sells a defective car that kills its driver, that's not murder. It's product failure. If all the companies in a single industry are caught price fixing, that's not restraint of trade, it's negotiated competition. If a man avoids taxes on hundreds of thousands of dollars in income, that's no crime. It's a loophole in the tax law. And if an officer in the United States Army orders the execution of a hundred and four civilians, that's not murder. It's war.

"The unwritten rules have a real purpose. They keep the same gang perpetually in power. Things only appear to change."

He stopped again. "The accusations you have heard against me are simple enough to understand: I tried to break some of those unwritten laws.

"I was disloyal to my social class . . . the rich.

"I was disloyal to influential special interest groups."

Christman grinned broadly, with a sense of pride. "And the president of the United States believes I have been disloyal to our political party. So here I am," he said, the sweeping hand indicating his predicament.

"I believe there are times, my fellow citizens, when a man finds it more important to be loyal to his planet and this nation than to the special club that runs it."

The governor hesitated for a moment, glanced at his son and then back at the camera.

"Six years ago, I formed a company that would control the development of private atomic energy in the United States. Money and talent appropriated in New York State played a part. It was plainly and simply a vehicle to gain power because I wanted to change priorities in America. Power that would force creation of new housing. Power to create new cities, instead of new weapons.

"I wanted the power to change. And that is a power that in two hundred years no president of this nation has ever really had."

The governor looked down at the desk, again as if no cameras were present, and lifted the silver carafe. Slowly he poured three-quarters of a glass of water and drank it. The director quickly cut to Morganna Christman stroking the cat.

"No," Roe shouted, "get back to the governor!"

Christman put down the glass and looked back into the camera.

"I did not develop American Nuclear for personal profit. In fact, I have already taken steps to deposit my entire interest in the company in a public foundation. The material benefits of American Nuclear belong to the people of my state and this nation.

"By the same token, I did not initially wish the office I now seek. Now I have no choice. The next president of the United States is the man who will decide the future of American Nuclear. I believe we should elect the man who will use it to re-shape this nation."

Christman had fallen into a monotone. But he looked more vigorous than he had in a week.

"Ladies and gentlemen," he said, a touch of the nasal Brahmin "a" creeping into his voice, "President Griswold has asked me to withdraw from this campaign." He shrugged.

"I believe that's for you to decide. The New York State primary is upon us. If the people of my state, whom my opponents say I have deceived, reject me as the candidate of this party, I will withdraw my name from any further consideration.

"Because it is your judgment alone, and not the judgment of Mr. Griswold, that matters. God willing, you will have the opportunity to pass judgment on my actions in November.

"Thank you. And good night."

It was only seventeen minutes past the hour in the scheduled thirty-minute broadcast and the control room was frantic.

"What do I do?" the director screamed.

"Go to black," Roe told him.

"Hey, Arthur," someone shouted, "that's six thousand, two hundred dollars a minute. Can't we run the campaign film?"

"Go to black, dammit," he said again, biting out the words.

The bright lights in the study went out quickly. Governor Christman remained at the desk, grinning at the mob that swirled around him. He was quickly surrounded.

"Beautiful, darling," Morganna Christman said, gently kissing his temple.

"Who says I can't turn it on?" the governor whispered to Roe. "The hell I can't."

Joshua Christman grabbed his father's broad bicep and squeezed it hard. He shook the governor. When he finally looked up, his eyes were bright and he suddenly seemed very old.

"You did it, Dad," Joshua Christman said elatedly. "You really did it."

"At least it's nice to think so," Arthur Roe muttered. But no one heard him.

On Friday they were elated by the phone calls, telegrams, and the huge crowds that turned out for Governor Christman in Syracuse, Buffalo, and at a rush hour rally in the late afternoon in Herald Square.

During the next three days, the governor, reading telegrams at every stop he made, spoke and traveled for eighteen hours a day until his voice was little more than a croak and his right hand was blistered with sores.

By Tuesday, they knew it was all over but the counting. And late in the evening, as ten thousand people crowded the sidewalks surrounding the Roosevelt Hotel, the governor sat in an eighteenth-floor suite tapping a spoon on his knee as he watched the returns roll in from every corner of his state. To add icing to the cake, he swept all twenty-eight delegates in the Tennessee primary. As he descended the hotel freight car to appear in the ballroom, Roe handed him a brief victory speech, which he stuffed in his pocket.

To the consternation of network television directors, the packed ballroom refused to stop cheering Governor Alexander Christman. For twenty-three minutes, they yelled his name and chanted, "No third term! No third term!" Volunteers wept with joy, and across the country there was only the picture of sweet and total victory.

He finally stepped before them, arms held high above his head, and for him the audience slowly silenced itself. He looked back at the faces, and they looked at him in expectation as he grinned joyously.

His voice was little more than a whisper, but it only

partially muffled the strength and power for which they loved him.

"Okay," he shouted, cracking his voice, "I have one word for all of you tonight." He paused. They waited, and then he broke through the strain on his vocal cords and croaked back the words they wanted to hear: "On to Miami Beach!"

The deafening noise exploded again as the governor followed Devlin and Roe out of the ballroom, through the kitchen, and back to the freight elevator. It smelled of garbage and they tried to ignore it.

"We've won, Alex. We've won," Roe whispered in his ear.

Christman did not even break stride as his head turned and he looked curiously at Arthur Roe.

"You're really beginning to think so, aren't you, fella," he said.

CHAPTER FOURTEEN

—

THE QUADRENNIAL NATIONAL POLITICAL CONVEN-
tions that nominate candidates for the presidency of the
United States are not very different from the average
buyers' once-yearly bacchanal, escalated to the tenth
power. The national press is watching. But they are not
watching the wooing, the blackmail, the driving, pleading, threatening attack on virtually every delegate, to
which he ultimately responds with his vote. Here there
are rarely deep issues, except who will win, and who
will lose.

The forces supporting Governor Alexander Christman went to Miami Beach with the most complete
and sophisticated data ever assembled in American history on the 1,333 men and women who would nominate
the party's candidate. Financial condition, employment
and investment history, sexual proclivities, and a dozen
other areas of inquiry were carefully examined by
trained investigators as the campaign's political researchers pieced together the political associations,
benefits, alliances, and the flexibility of every man. If
a county leader, elected as a delegate to the convention, had nominated three postmasters for presidential
appointment, Arthur Roe knew it. And he also knew
whether he had asked for five jobs, seven, or a dozen.
Only once did the lawyer test the accuracy of the information crammed into the computer.

Arvid Hamma was a Whitmore delegate from Montana, pledged to the last ballot to Vice-President Whitmore. They met one day in the Algiers Hotel lobby
and Hamma made the mistake of teasing Roe. As they
parted, Roe asked the Bible-thumping rancher from
Butte: "Hey, by the way, how is Mrs. Pardee?"

Hamma turned a brick red, but recovered quickly. "Am I supposed to know who the hell you're talking about?"

It was the best of the laughs he had in the difficult hurly-burly of blintzes, swimming pools, bathing beauties, and backslappers that was Miami Beach. On the surface, Governor Christman's situation was as clear to the vast television audience as it was to the men managing his campaign.

Total Delegate Votes:	1,333	
Votes to Nominate:	667	
Total Votes Contested in Primary:		725
Governor Alexander Christman:		474¾
Vice President George Whitmore:		189
Others:		61¼
Delegates from 31 Nonprimary States:		608

What was clear was that Governor Christman had to pick up 193 nonprimary state delegates to win. Beneath the surface was the shakiness of the governor's existing support after the first ballot. Some elected delegates were pledged for only one ballot. Others maintained that voters in their state had merely shown a nonbinding preference for one of the candidates.

The Whitmore forces understood this clearly, too. Backed by the president and a constant barrage of telephone calls to individual delegates, the vice-president's advisors were slowly convincing themselves and the press they could stop Christman. He was the front runner. But he could not run hard enough to get over the top. After the first ballot, his support would begin to erode. Backing a loser had ended many a delegate's local career in politics.

Christman's pluses a day before the balloting were clear:

ALASKA: 11 of 12 votes; the chairman supporting Whitmore.

CONNECTICUT: 12 of 16 delegates. A neighboring state.

HAWAII: One delegate of 14. A former executive of Christman Airways.

KENTUCKY: 3 delegates of 21.

LOUISIANA: 26 delegates. McCloud had delivered,
  but he could not promise to hold more than half
  beyond the first ballot.

MICHIGAN: 41 of 48 delegates; the labor bloc in
  the delegation.

MINNESOTA: 2 delegates of 26; a homosexual and
  an escaped felon on the New Hampshire State
  Police wanted list since 1931 discovered by the
  Christman investigators.

MISSISSIPPI: 3 delegates of 20; all black.

MISSOURI: 6 delegates of 24.

TEXAS: 4 delegates of 56; the anti-Griswold fac-
  tion.

PUERTO RICO: 5 of 8 delegates; all New Yorkers.

WASHINGTON: 24 delegates; the only Christman
  sweep in nonprimary state.

The top-secret tally sheet in their hands was not
encouraging. Wheedling, blackmailing, and dealing,
they had added 138 delegates to the Christman primary
victories. Total: 612, still 55 delegates short of a first
ballot victory.

The staff filed into his suite early that morning,
copies of the latest delegate computer printout in their
hands. Roe, Kuhn, the speech writers, two statisticians,
the regional coordinators, and Joshua Christman surrounded Christman.

"I'm glad you're here," the governor said to his son,
clapping his arm around him. "It's good to see you."

"Dad," the young man replied, "you think I'd let
you down?"

Roe sat at the head of the semicircle as unofficial
chairman of the meeting. The governor was off to one
side on a purple-and-blue-striped satin sofa. Behind
them, the Miami Beach sun was shimmering on the
water. The campaign's southwestern coordinator,
Sandy Warberg, got up to close the louvered shades.

"Leave it alone," the candidate told him. He sat
down. Roe looked toward him for the signal to begin.

"Let's keep this one short and tight. First, any defections from these figures?"

"We lost two in Michigan," a beefy labor union
lawyer said.

"Okay."

"Any change in Nevada, Sandy?" The state was leaning neither to Christman nor Whitmore, but planned to nominate its senior senator as a favorite son.

"Wilson is the best governor money can buy. Whatever Powell does with the Illinois delegation, Wilson goes with him. Have we got any friends in the mob?" he asked jokingly.

No one laughed.

"Listen," Warberg went on, "I had this middle-aged broad from Missouri halfway into the sack when she got mad at me. We lost one there. Some of the personal information in those dossiers stinks."

Sandy Warberg was young and they were stuck with him. They let it pass.

"Jack?" Roe signaled.

The lean, ascetic research director anxiously had been trying to get the floor.

"We don't need much analysis," he said. "There isn't much that's still shaky. You can pick up Georgia if you're willing to promise another conservative on the Supreme Court. If that happens, it may not even be worth being president, by the way. The Delaware group is all Dupont. Forget it. They would like to shoot you, Governor. Kentucky, no. Oklahoma, nothing. Texas, too tight even for us."

He was rambling and Roe cut him off. They all turned when the governor stood.

"It's Mayor Powell and Illinois, right?"

"That's about it, Governor. The president is laying over these guys like a ton of manure. If you get Powell's fifty-eight delegates, you pick up twelve more in Nevada. That will easily cover late defections."
and leave.

"Right," Alexander Christman said, partly to himself. He was near exhaustion. He lifted his hands, palms upward, shrugged, and they all began to rise

When they were gone, he was left alone with his son and Arthur Roe. The lawyer wished the young man would leave, but he did not. He slowly poured himself a half cup of coffee from the silver carafe. It was lukewarm. Joshua was staring up the beach at a couple running out of the surf. The governor was again seated on the striped sofa, his eyes shut.

"What does he want?" Christman asked, without opening his eyes.

Joshua Christman snapped his attention away from the sunlit scene outside the window.

"Gutstein's pushing Mayor Powell to go with Whitmore."

Christman shook his head. "What does Mayor Powell want for those delegates?"

"The moon."

"Arthur!"

"Powell wants to name your attorney general. That will make the mob happy and protect the Gutstein interest in American Nuclear."

"We are really sure Powell is going to be the ball game for us?" Christman asked.

His son turned from the window to stare at him. Roe nodded.

"Do we have any room for negotiation?" the governor asked slowly.

Joshua Christman was across the room like a sprinter leaving the chocks. He was standing over his father. "You can't do it, Dad. Don't you see that?"

The governor stood and put his arm around his son. The boy turned his face into his father's broad chest.

"Is there another way, Arthur?"

The lawyer sighed and knew he should have worked harder to keep the boy away from his father.

"If there is, we haven't found it, Governor," he said. "You've got to sit down with Powell. You know Griswold is about to appoint a new U. S. attorney in New York."

Christman was grinning. "You mean the only way I can keep the bastards from prosecuting me is by getting elected president of the United States." Roe looked at the governor and almost believed the notion amused him. "That's a helluva state of affairs," Alexander Christman said.

The governor turned away, but the decision came quickly. "Okay, fella," he said, "but don't push him too hard. I'm afraid we are going to have to live with that son of a bitch."

That evening, in the vast Miami Civic Auditorium, the name of Governor Alexander Christman of New York was placed in nomination for the presidency of the United States. The demonstration, limited to twenty minutes by the streamlined rules of the convention, was carefully programmed, using five brass bands, 105 hired Christman girls and 6,000 balloons suspended in a huge net under the domed auditorium. The Christman forces roaming the floor were each equipped with miniaturized two-way radio transmitters that permitted the candidate or his campaign manager to talk directly at any time with any delegate. The same two-way radio, hooked to the Arizona computer circuit, provided instant information to every one of the men on the floor. Later that evening, despite the overwhelming enthusiasm for Christman on the floor of the convention, his staff would find they showed a net loss of six delegates.

"It's up to the governor now," Roe told them, when they caucused in his suite.

"Well, push him, for chrissake," Sandy Warberg complained. "We've got this goddamn thing won. We've got it won."

"I can't believe this convention can deny the nomination to a clear-cut winner in the primaries. That's suicide."

"If we keep standing around," Roe told them, "that's exactly what we are going to watch them do."

It was the eve of balloting at the convention, and Governor Christman had had enough of staff meetings, strategy sessions, tête-à-têtes with delegates, and the effusive mirage of the convention that masked this battle for power. His hand was sore, his spirit ached, and he was sufficiently tired to feel his body was no longer his own. Despite his pleading she stay away from Miami Beach, Athena Courtland had her own suite at the Kenilworth. He had not seen her. But now he knew that regardless of the danger, her very pres-

ence in the same city was a demand for attention he
could no longer ignore.

Devlin had planned a cautious route. They took
the bellman's elevator to the subbasement beneath the
swimming pool, walked up a staircase to the darkened
lanai area smelling of jasmine, and out past the motel-
like rooms to a car parked at the edge of the hotel.
It was a short ride to the Kenilworth, and he sensed
Devlin watching him out of the corner of his eye.
When they stopped for a traffic light, the detective
asked casually, "How is it really going, Governor?"

He took the question very seriously. "I keep asking
myself what the hell am I doing here." And then he
knew that was precisely how he felt. He had talked to
Roe twice since their meeting that morning, but found
he still could not bring himself to see Mayor Powell.

"Absolutely not. That's final," he had told the
lawyer. "And what's more, I don't even want to talk
to the son of a bitch. You tell him that if he supports
us, he has my promise of absolute immunity from personal prosecution."

"I can't tell him that."

"Give it to him straight," Christman said, and then
he laughed for the first time in weeks. "Who knows, it
might just work."

He knew that he was right. Walter C. Powell had
wholly controlled every aspect of Chicago life, from its
banks to its barber shops, for twenty-eight years. He
could brag of the lowest crime rate in the nation. He
had not held that power because he ever submitted to
blackmail, least of all from presidential candidates.

The path Devlin had charted through the Kenilworth was worthy of a second-story man. Though it
was not being used as a conventioneers' hotel, it was
still filled to capacity. They were seen by no one. He
knocked on Athena Courtland's door.

She was wearing a shimmering white satin peignoir
that exposed the tops of her suntanned breasts.

"I was worried about you," he said, knowing that
he meant it.

She was startled, and the governor gently pushed
the paneled door. He wanted to get out of the hallway.

When it was closed behind him, he stood looking down into her face, his arms holding her soft arms very gently.

"Why, Alex?" she asked warily.

"I can't do anything halfway. It isn't fair to anybody."

She looked as if she had died, and without wanting to do anything but lighten her pain if he could, he said, "Maybe after the campaign is over."

He thought she was as angry as he had ever seen her.

"No," she told him. "It won't be the same."

She pulled away from him. He followed her clicking heels into the sitting room of the suite. He wanted to touch her, comfort her, but she lit a cigarette and then sat straight up on the edge of the couch, the peignoir pulled tightly over her legs. She looked older than he remembered her, and he sat down opposite her, taking one of her carefully manicured hands in his huge hand.

She pulled away. "Alex, you really don't need me anymore."

He smiled to mask his own discomfort and said gently, "I haven't even got me anymore."

He watched her smoking the cigarette, tapping the ash before there was an ash. The governor said nothing, wishing only that he might bring back the woman inside this person that he had known so well. He wanted to tell her what had happened, but he did not know how to end it without causing her pain.

"This is not exactly what I had in mind," he said cheerfully, as if he had started on his way to a magnificent dinner to find that only the corner diner was open.

She acknowledged neither the words nor his presence. Because he did not know what else he might do, he moved slowly to the couch beside her, turning her body gently with his hands, and kissed her on the lips. The cigarette stub was still between her fingers.

"Are you going back to Roger?"

He saw the tension in the corners of her mouth. "I can't do that," she told him, as if it were a statement of her purity, an example of her inflexibility in a world where people for whom she had no respect did the best they could with what they had. For a second, she reminded him of his wife. But he drove the thought from his mind.

The governor kissed her again, still believing as he always had that it was within his power to heal pain, obliterate the hurt, and by the very act of his presence, make things right again. He had come tonight to give of that to her, the fact of his attendance, and she no more accepted it in the currency of her emotions. She had banished herself to a country foreign to him, where there was no feeling other than anger.

"Our last fuck, Alexander? Is that why you're here?"

She had meant to hurt him, to denigrate him, to repay him for her pain, but now she realized she had only been vulgar, and so she stood in front of him and reached out until he touched her fingertips and rose with her. Her arms moved behind his head and she stretched her long body to reach his lips.

In his mind's eye, he saw himself gently kissing her neck and quietly saying goodbye. But when she released his head, his hand reached for the satiny material covering her breast, and he squeezed her gently. His right hand caressed her buttocks through the tantalizing satin, but she did not press her body against him. When he released her, they looked at each other for a moment.

He took a half step away from her and looked at her face as if he were trying to tell her that he would not find what she had given him anywhere else on earth. But he did not want to force upon her the painful withdrawal of another separation, and he did not wish to hurt her or give her up.

"I have to win whether I want to or not," he said slowly, taking another step away. "I'm sorry."

She stared at him like a frightened animal who has lost the ability to anticipate danger. It had been right to come, Alexander Christman told himself, as he turned quickly and left her room. At the door he said goodbye. He knew that she had meant more to him when he was with her than he had realized, and he wondered how much he might need her again.

Buddha-like he sat there, his stomach protruding over his thighs, the sweat from the dry heat in the sauna dripping slowly over the half-open eyes that carefully studied the face of Governor Alexander Christman's campaign manager, Arthur Roe. To the right of Mayor Walter C. Powell of Chicago, Illinois, Julius Gutstein, the man who had backed his candidacy for twenty-eight years, nervously sipped a glass of White Rock soda.

Powell's gray cat's eyes were wide open and he looked at Roe.

"Do you know," he said, "in this whole fucking city there isn't a Roman Catholic church with a good Irish priest?"

The mayor's twice-daily trips to confession were well publicized in Chicago. It was generally believed they were necessary.

"What is he doing here?" Roe asked the mayor.

Powell poured a glass of cold water on his hairy chest and wiped it across his stomach. "This one," he said, flicking his thumb toward the thin, ascetic banker, "is my advisor." He dipped his hand in the cold water and rubbed it across his face. Then he reached down again, and doused his armpits. "I am assuming you are here because my proposal is acceptable."

"Within reason," Roe told him mildly.

Powell's eyes narrowed, measuring Roe. "You want an attorney general who can clean up crime," he said evenly. "So do my friends. And believe me, they can be of real help to the man I pick for the governor to put in that job."

The lawyer had no leverage as he did with other delegations, and he knew it. If Powell did not know the existing Christman delegate count, Vice-President Whitmore's campaign manager would be glad to tell him.

"The governor," he said slowly, "has authorized that I convey his approval."

Powell looked at Gutstein. "I also think I'm entitled to veto power over the rest of the cabinet, except for chicken shit things like Agriculture, the Postal Service, the Army, and crap like that. What I'm telling you is that I have a right to keep out guys that are hostile to me. Right?"

He had come far enough to convince himself that it was winning the nomination that mattered first, and he knew there was no room for bargaining now. But he also knew Mayor Powell was testing him, as an alien power might test the tenacity of a new American president.

"No," Roe told him. "You've got enough."

The lawyer saw Mayor Powell's jaw go tight. It was always difficult to restrain himself in the face of anyone who showed defiance. But the corners of his mouth turned softly. Roe thought he was about to smile. Instead, Powell merely shrugged to indicate he accepted the lawyer's contract.

"You ever think of coming to work in Chicago?" he asked.

Roe sat down, but he did not reply.

The mayor's eyes were wide open, like a poker player wary that someone is going to steal a pot he has won.

"You've got a deal," he told Roe. "There's only one thing. I want to hear it personally from himself." Gutstein put his large hand on the mayor's thick wrist and said, "One knows that Mr. Roe does not speak unless it is for Alexander Christman."

"I want to hear it from him," Powell said, the words like bites from an apple, spat out of his mouth one at a time.

Roe stood and waited for a sign from the Buddha. The dry heat made his body uncomfortable, and the sight of them offended him. He had never felt so much in jeopardy. Christman had changed his mind before.

Powell did not move, the heavy lids of his eyes slowly half closing again. Gutstein stood over Roe and reached down to take his right hand. He shook it slowly and told him, "One is certain it will be all right. We will win, my friend. I always told you that. Mayor Powell has never been an unreasonable man."

Whatever Governor Alexander Christman might be feeling, it was not visible on his face. The big glasses perched on his nose as if they had been absently set on a clay-sculpted bust. Key staff members, a few friends, and less than a half-dozen members of the friendly press flowed to the bar in the six-room suite, through the bedroom and living room and back into the small library. The governor sat watching preparations for the convention's Roll Call of the States on a bank of three color television sets.

Arthur Roe hovered within a few feet of the governor, prepared to anticipate any wish or carry out any order.

"What happened?" Christman asked.

"We are going to win on the first ballot," Roe whispered in his ear.

The governor was slowly shaking his head. "Fella," he said, "what makes you so sure he hasn't made an even better deal with Whitmore?"

The lawyer walked quickly to his desk. Near his fingertips was the multiline telephone console that, with the flick of a button, connected him with each of the 107 Christman campaign workers strategically placed on the floor. But it was late for that now, unless there was an unforeseen problem on the floor of the convention. He could not yet bring himself to judge the effect on the governor of the commitment they had given to Mayor Powell, and it had become his hope that in the flush of victory, it would be forgotten. If there is a victory, he thought. All the machines, the statistics, the computers, and the formulas are fine. Until you count the votes.

Governor Christman raised his second finger, his eyes never leaving the console. Roe moved quickly to the side of his chair and leaned over to allow him to whisper.

"Where is Joshua?" Christman said, the voice sounding almost weary of words, as if he might regain his strength by using them with the greatest economy.

"I don't know," he replied, knowing he did not want the boy anywhere near the governor now. He saw the ballot sheet in the governor's open black folder next to the last computer printout of the Christman tally. It was a bad time for words.

"Find him," Alexander Christman commanded. "And get me a glass of water."

When Roe returned, Selig Brown, historian of the last four presidential election compaigns, was seated on the ottoman beside the governor's chair. A good sign. If Brown wanted to watch Alexander Christman watch the balloting, he had picked him as a winner. The lawyer saw the open, playful grin on Christman's tired face and was glad to know he still had something left. Brown had buck teeth, but he was tall, with a touch of gray at his temples.

"What do you make of Mayor Powell cancelling his press conference this morning after the state caucus?" Brown asked, as confidentially as if he were a member of the staff.

"He's always been an exhibitionist," Christman told him wryly.

"What do you really think, Governor?"

Christman smiled. "I think he'd like to put somebody over the top. I think he'd like to put anyone over the top."

"You don't have a deal with him to put you over?"

"No, Selig, I don't." He looked at the journalist's face, wondering if the reporter sensed he was lying. It was an unfamiliar role for him, so he added: "I really don't."

Brown seemed perplexed, and Roe stepped in to hand the governor the glass of water, wishing he could ease him away from the reporter.

Brown held up his hand to fend off Roe for one final question.

"How do you feel right this moment, Governor?" he asked. "I mean, how do you really feel?" There was compassion in the question. Brown was one of the few political reporters who had any feeling for the incredible demands on a man in this kind of campaign. His eyes were trying to judge the extent of the toll it had taken of Alexander Christman.

"Selig," the governor said, almost appreciating the

question, "this is the moment of truth when you find out whether you've been the bull or the bullfighter."

"Thank you, Governor," Brown said, pushing himself up. "And good luck. It should be a great campaign."

Roe took the low seat and looked at Christman. The muscles in his face had sagged, and he was tapping the palm of his hand with the spoon impatiently, his eyes not leaving the three screens.

"That's a nice fella," he told Roe, "a real nice fella."

On the screens it was clear the 1,333 delegates to the convention had settled in their seats, and the camera slowly picked up a dozen familiar faces. One anchorman was explaining they still had no word from Mayor Powell's Illinois delegation, and apparently there would not be any word until the actual roll call. "It may well be," he concluded, "that the state of Illinois will determine the outcome of this convention. Our own polls show that despite the influence of the White House and despite considerable politicking in the last three days, Governor Alexander Christman of New York remains some thirty votes shy of the nomination. What effect a failure of the New York governor to gain a first ballot victory will be is anybody's guess."

There were twenty people in the small study. Each of them watched both the screen and Alexander Christman's reaction to it as Mrs. Gwen Gary, secretary of the national party, stepped to the rostrum, a long sheet of paper containing the Roll Call of the States in her hand. She stepped aside briefly as a Roman Catholic clergyman delivered the Invocation. Then the convention's diminutive permanent chairman banged the oaken gavel that seemed three sizes too large for him. The balloting had begun.

"Alabama," Mrs. Gary intoned, "twenty-six votes."

The cameras focussed on the chairman of the delegation, a handsome young man in a white seersucker suit, wearing a red papier maché carnation. "The sovereign state of Alabama is proud to cast the first twenty-six votes for the next president of the United

States, that guardian of liberty, that great American, Vice-President George Whitmore."

A primary state. Not a flicker of recognition on the governor's face as the legend was superimposed on the screen:

CHRISTMAN: 0   WHITMORE: 26
NEEDED TO NOMINATE: 667

There were no surprises in the early balloting. Arkansas passed to Illinois in the hope that their eighteen delegates might know in advance which bandwagon to join, and the camera quickly switched to the front row section where the Illinois delegation was seated. Two delegates were reading newspapers, and the UBS camera focussed on the empty seat that should have been occupied by Mayor Powell.

"Switch up the sound on UBS," Roe called, as he pressed a button to reach the floor man assigned to the Illinois delegation. Where the hell was Powell?

The break in the cheering and the jeering as the call rolled through the states came with a cry for the individual poll of Idaho's fourteen delegates. The numbers held on the screen.

CHRISTMAN: 154   WHITMORE: 143
NEEDED TO NOMINATE: 667

Still no surprises. The Christman total already included the 86 votes he had won in California. Roe knew they had lost two in Connecticut and picked up a delegate-at-large elected in Florida who was building a new airport in Orlando. Idaho finally was polled and it split as originally announced: two for Christman, twelve for Whitmore. If Roe's computer tally held, without votes in Illinois or Nevada, the governor would tally 617¼ votes on the first ballot. He did not like the empty chair in the Illinois delegation.

"Illinois," Mrs. Gary called.

A pug-nosed man in a checkered suit stood and pulled the microphone toward himself.

"Missus Chairman," he called, as the delegates

laughed, "the state representing the great land of Lincoln and the city of Chicago is going to throw in a temporary pass."

"Is the Illinois delegation caucusing?" the chairwoman asked.

"You might say so. Mayor Powell ain't here."

The convention hall roared affectionately as the UBS commentator explained, "There you see, I think, the kind of control Mayor Powell has over the politics of his state. The mayor won all fifty-eight delegates as a favorite son in his state's primary election. The fact that the delegation did not automatically cast its votes for the mayor is an indication that Mr. Powell may personally try to swing this convention to either Governor Christman or Vice-President Whitmore on this, the first ballot."

Christman turned his head and looked at Roe. None of the floor men had found Mayor Powell.

The roll call was picked up again. Governor Christman held all thirty-four Massachusetts delegates won for him by Governor Clawson in his state's primary. At Minnesota, with the balloting almost half over, the tally flashed on the screen.

CHRISTMAN: 276   WHITMORE: 303
NEEDED TO NOMINATE: 667

"Minnesota."

"The land of lakes, the land of fishermen, and the World Champion Minnesota Vikings, is proud to cast its votes." The chairman covered the microphone and obviously leaned over to ask an aide the tally. The roar finally subsided. "Governor Alexander Christman, two votes. Vice-President George Whitmore, twenty-four votes," he shouted.

Across the study, the outside telephone line rang. Sandy Warberg picked it up. He was startled. "Arthur! Arthur!" he whispered feverishly, gesticulating at the phone as he tried to avoid drawing Governor Christman's attention. "It's Powell!"

Roe took the phone like a man about to be told he will be executed twice for the same crime.

"Good evening, Mr. Mayor," he said softly, his eyes on Governor Christman.

"Mr. Roe," the voice that sounded like a fingernail scraping a blackboard rasped, "I want to hear it from him personally."

"We have no difficulty, Mr. Mayor." He was sweating.

"I want to hear it from him."

Roe covered the phone and motioned to Warberg. He tapped the governor on the shoulder.

"Powell," the lawyer mouthed.

Christman waved his hand and turned back to the bank of television screens.

Warberg tapped the governor's shoulder again.

"Talk to him, Alex," Roe pleaded, as he never had before.

The governor pushed himself to his feet and snatched the phone from Arthur Roe. "Mr. Powell," he said, his throat straining with anger, "we understand each other. Why bother to call me?"

He pushed the phone back at the startled lawyer, who turned around and spoke softly to the mayor. Slowly he calmed him, knowing the governor would keep his commitment whether he liked Powell or not. But the mayor of Chicago would get nothing more than what he had been promised by the governor.

"What's he so high and mighty about?" Powell demanded.

"He is under a lot of tension, Mr. Mayor."

Powell did not hesitate. "Things between him and me are going to be different when he gets to the White House."

"You're absolutely right, Mr. Mayor," Arthur Roe told him, straining his ear for the grunt of approval he knew he must have from Powell.

By the time Nebraska cast its sixteen votes, the running tally on the screen showed:

CHRISTMAN: 285   WHITMORE: 368
NEEDED TO NOMINATE: 667

"Did you find Joshua?" Christman asked over his shoulder.

Arthur Roe said he had not.

"Nevada," Mrs. Gary called.

As if he had but been waiting in the wings, the doors at the rear of the auditorium opened, and Mayor Walter C. Powell, flanked by two bodyguards, walked down the aisle toward his delegation. He waved to the gallery, counting the boos and the applause, as each of the networks picked up his entrance. The chairman of the Nevada delegation stepped into the aisle to shake his hand, and the mayor whispered a word in his ear. When he reached the empty seat that had become famous across America, the newspapers in the delegation disappeared, but no one spoke to the mayor.

No one could miss the tension in the auditorium. The chairman of the Nevada delegation finally pulled the microphone toward him.

"Madam Secretary," he said, "the Nevada delegation, representatives of the playground of the nation, pass to the great state of Illinois."

There were shouts of "No, no, no," throughout the auditorium. Mrs. Gary turned to the permanent chairman who motioned to the convention parliamentarian, who was clearly aware that a state could not pass to a state previously called until the roll call had been completed. The permanent chairman looked down at Mayor Powell, sitting with his arms crossed in front of him in the first row, and knew this was not the man he wanted as an enemy.

Mrs. Gary returned to the microphone. "The Chair has ruled that the convention recognizes the great state of Illinois."

There were boos again that were quickly hushed as Mayor Powell tapped the huge wrestler on the knee and whispered in his ear. The delegate who had passed a half hour earlier stood and, in a flat monotone, turned the convention into bedlam.

"Illinois," he announced, "casts fifty-eight votes for Governor Christman of New York."

If the networks were not sure of their head count before, they were now, as the jubilant Christman supporters tore apart the convention. In the governor's suite, the whoop that went up sounded like a U. S. cavalry charge into an Indian war party.

The governor's press secretary, Harvey Kuhn, waddled across the room with tears in his eyes. "We did it!" he blubbered joyously to the governor.

Christman grabbed him by the fat on the back of his neck. "You did it," he shouted back at him. Kuhn shook his head back and forth, but the governor would not let him go. "You did it, and you know it, you fat son of a bitch," Christman yelled over the din.

On the floor of the convention, the Whitmore forces worked feverishly in the delegations not yet polled to hold the line for one ballot. Roe was back on the phones, pushing the two-way radio buttons to all the Christman liaison men on the floor. The message was simply, "Go! Go! Go! Go! Go! We are over the top!"

And over the top they were. Nevada went with Illinois. By the time the roll call reached New York, Christman's 86½ votes in his home state brought his total to 505½. Tennessee brought the total to 653. The Texas delegation, which had been counted as 52 votes for Whitmore and only 4 for Christman, caucused quickly on the floor. Like the commentators, the delegates, and the rest of the nation, they knew Christman had 43 committed votes not recorded on the roll call from primaries in West Virginia, Wisconsin, and the District of Columbia.

"Madam Secretary," the chairman of the Texas delegation said, "he is not our favorite son, but Texas loves him no less for it. The greatest state in the union is proud to cast all fifty-six of its votes for the next president of our great nation, Governor Alexander Christman of New York. And we hereby move that his selection be acclaimed unanimous!"

The delirious New York delegation seconded the motion and its delegates stood limp as state after state from the Whitmore column switched to Governor Christman.

There was pandemonium, too, surrounding the governor as he sat in the wing chair facing the bank of monitors, speaking to no one. The staff and the reporters were saddened by his mood, but they respected his silence and slowly, as the party stretched out into the hallway and the ballrooms of the Americana, they left him alone with his thoughts.

Roe sat silently watching him, knowing how old the governor had become.

"Did you find Joshua?" he asked.

"No."

"There is an awful lot to do, Alex," the lawyer said very gently.

"Do it," he replied. "Tell them I'm writing an acceptance speech. They don't own me yet."

"You really want to quit, don't you?" Roe asked.

Christman smiled grimly. "I thought the only way to turn this country around was outside the system. Away from the power that was always dependent on someone else. Turn it around by doing what you can when you are only answerable to yourself. I tried. God, I tried like hell. This is the only way left. And maybe, just maybe if you push hard enough and know clearly enough where you're going, it might work this way."

His voice trailed off. Roe saw in the governor's eyes the pain that came from the conditions he had been forced to accept. The lawyer knew that this man, whom he had come to love deeply, had renounced the dream he once had of totally independent power. But he had not quit. He had allowed himself to accept fully the grotesque anguish with which he saw the presidency: power shared with the Powells, the Whitmores, the labor unions, the bankers, and the thousands of other pressure groups that would have to be cajoled, catered to, and satisfied.

"I can win," Christman said hoarsely as if he were convincing himself. "I have to. And maybe by the time I'm through I can change it enough so that this country is on its way to being all of the things we keep saying about it."

Roe wanted to stop him, to save him from the raging anger of his broken dream. But he found no words, knowing only that he would not return to Whitman, Gelman or the practice of law. His commitment was wholly to the dream of another man, and for the first time since he had known Alexander Christman it did not bother him at all.

The lawyer sat opposite the governor for another forty minutes, but they did not exchange a word. At midnight, the governor was sitting in the wing chair in the darkened room, still alone with his thoughts. He moved to the desk, found the lamp switch and sat for a time, making notations on a long, yellow legal pad. When he was finished, he switched off the light and opened the door to the guarded hallway, walking the few paces across the russet carpet to his son's room.

The boy was lying in bed, his eyes open, staring at the ceiling. The moonlight played across his face and the governor brushed the hair back from his son's eyes. He sat down on the edge of the bed.

"I had to do it," the governor said. "Can you understand that?"

The boy nodded. "Mayor Powell," he replied. "Jesus."

Christman winced. "He was the guy that controlled the votes, fella. It's as simple as that."

The governor sat there for what he thought was a few moments, watching the moonlight play across the room. After a time, he saw brighter light playing across the line of the horizon, and he knew it was later than he thought. He rose slowly, rubbed his eyes, and saw that the boy had finally fallen asleep. Quietly, he let himself out of the room, walked across the hall, undressed, and went to bed.

Two days later, he had in his pocket what historians would eventually acknowledge as the most carefully written acceptance speech in American history. It touched all the bases. It was the nucleus of a well-planned campaign. It omitted nothing of importance. And it could be repeated over and over again right up to election day, its very repetition continually demonstrating the consistency of the candidate.

He had read and reread the formal speech, reworked it with Roe and the staff, and he patted the right-hand pocket to assure himself it was there.

Blocks before the limousine reached the convention hall, Collins Avenue was lined three deep with tourists, visitors in sport shirts, here and there a ten-gallon hat, and they waved and cheered as Sergeant Devlin drove slowly past. The Miami Beach air was humid, and pimples of sweat began to form on Christman's skin under the television makeup as he waved again to the crowd. He reached for a handkerchief as his right hand touched the outstretched fingers along the barricade.

"Don't rub it, Governor," one of the Secret Service men whispered. "They'll blot it off when you get inside."

He turned and smiled quickly, murmured, "Thanks," to the bodyguard, and then plunged back to the crowd, diving into their outstretched hands as if he had no real desire to face the delegates, the press, or his party leaders inside. But slowly, the guards and the entourage pushed him along until finally he was inside the building. The air conditioning quickly cooled him and the sweated shirt coldly clung to his back, his armpits, and the upper part of his stomach. A lady in a bright green smock carrying a starched blue shirt on a wire hanger pushed her way toward him, but he waved her aside.

"I'm a rumpled kind of fella," he told her with a grin.

There were fifty men he knew, and as they were able, they pushed their way onto the huge freight elevator that lifted them to the hallway in back of the podium. As if they were a vast audience at a World Heavyweight Championship Fight, the packed audience began chanting his name as he waited for the signal to enter. The sound rolled back across the podium and through the vast auditorium as six thousand excited voices shouted, "Christman! Christman! Christman! Christman!" the sound reverberating and reechoing.

He raised both his arms to contain them, but they shouted his name back again and again. The voices became a chant taunting him, begging from him the Christman smile. The governor stared solemnly back at them as their voices bathed him in sound. Through the lights there were faces he could see: Morganna,

Mayor Powell, Sandy Warberg shouting in the front row, his fist high in a victory salute, Arthur Roe, and a hundred others he knew well.

His arms went up again and slowly the noise began to lessen, as if a hand on a control room panel had simply reduced the volume. Governor Christman saw the teleprompter, that projected words on the two vertical panels on either side of the podium, light up. He motioned to the permanent chairman, spoke to him for a moment, and then stepped back to the rostrum and waited for his audience to silence itself. It would not.

Roe stood at his side for a moment, as the ovation roared back from the floor of the convention hall. The governor waved to his wife and son in the presidential box, where the boy was jumping up and down with excitement. With relief, he winked at the boy and hoped he could see the gesture. He was still waving at the audience when the lawyer leaned over and whispered:

"The real fight has just begun."

Roe was watching the governor's face. The fixed grin for an instant gave way to anger so violent it frightened Roe.

"I told you we're going to win," Christman rasped. "We've got to."

The familiar grin returned to Governor Christman's face as he turned back to the vast audience, lifted his arms to silence their cheering voices, and began his speech accepting their nomination for the office of President of the United States.

ABOUT THE AUTHOR

PAUL WEISSMAN served as a political and investigative reporter for the New York HERALD TRIBUNE, NEWSWEEK and CBS. He has observed several governors and presidential candidates at close range.

RELAX!

SIT DOWN

and Catch Up On Your Reading!

- ☐ THE HARRAD EXPERIMENT by Robert Rimmer   (4690—$1.25)
- ☐ THE FRENCH CONNECTION by Robin Moore   (5369— 95¢)
- ☐ HER by Anonymous   (6669—$1.50)
- ☐ THE PATRIOT by Charles Durbin   (6947—$1.50)
- ☐ THE BELL JAR by Sylvia Plat   (7178—$1.50)
- ☐ THE EXORCIST by William Peter Blatty   (7200—$1.75)
- ☐ WHEELS by Arthur Hailey   (7244—$1.75)
- ☐ RAGA SIX by Frank Lauria   (7249—$1.25)
- ☐ HIM by Anonymous   (7369—$1.50)
- ☐ THE DAY OF THE JACKAL by Frederick Forsyth   (7377—$1.75)
- ☐ THE FRIENDS OF EDDIE COYLE by George Higgins   (7504—$1.50)
- ☐ THE TERMINAL MAN by Michael Crichton   (7545—$1.75)
- ☐ MEMOIRS OF AN EX-PROM QUEEN by Alix Shulman   (7565—$1.75)
- ☐ THE LEVANTER by Eric Ambler   (7603—$1.50)
- ☐ SHEILA LEVINE IS DEAD AND LIVING IN NEW YORK by Gail Parent   (7633—$1.50)

Buy them at your local bookstore or use this handy coupon for ordering: